"Elkin[...]
—The D[...]

UN
RELATIONS

AARON
ELKINS

Edgar® Award–Winning Author of *Little Tiny Teeth*

BERKLEY
PRIME
CRIME

$7.99 U.S.
$9.99 CAN

ISBN 978-0-425-22908-8

9 780425 229088

5 0 7 9 9>

S > EAN

continued . . .

UNNATURAL SELECTION

"Engaging . . . Elkins excels in making his hero's skills plausible and accessible." —*Publishers Weekly*

"The forensic accuracy is admirable, and the plotting compelling." —*Booklist*

"Elkins's plotting is devious, and the forensics information is thoroughly terrific." —*The Olympia (WA) Olympian*

Praise for the other Gideon Oliver novels

"Great stuff." —*The New York Times Book Review*

"First rate! Elegant, ingenious, and beautifully crafted." —Sue Grafton

"A likable, down-to-earth, cerebral sleuth." —*Chicago Tribune*

"Aaron Elkins always tells a story that keeps the reader turning pages." —*The Denver Post*

"[An] intriguing mixture of forensic anthropology and real skull-duggery." —*Los Angeles Daily News*

"One of the best in the business and getting better all the time." —Elizabeth Peters

"Witty and oh so clever." —*New York Daily News*

UNEASY
RELATIONS

AARON ELKINS

BERKLEY PRIME CRIME, NEW YORK

THE BERKLEY PUBLISHING GROUP
Published by the Penguin Group
Penguin Group (USA) Inc.
375 Hudson Street, New York, New York 10014, USA
Penguin Group (Canada), 90 Eglinton Avenue East, Suite 700, Toronto, Ontario M4P 2Y3, Canada
(a division of Pearson Penguin Canada Inc.)
Penguin Books Ltd., 80 Strand, London WC2R 0RL, England
Penguin Group Ireland, 25 St. Stephen's Green, Dublin 2, Ireland (a division of Penguin Books Ltd.)
Penguin Group (Australia), 250 Camberwell Road, Camberwell, Victoria 3124, Australia
(a division of Pearson Australia Group Pty. Ltd.)
Penguin Books India Pvt. Ltd., 11 Community Centre, Panchsheel Park, New Delhi—110 017, India
Penguin Group (NZ), 67 Apollo Drive, Rosedale, North Shore 0632, New Zealand
(a division of Pearson New Zealand Ltd.)
Penguin Books (South Africa) (Pty.) Ltd., 24 Sturdee Avenue, Rosebank, Johannesburg 2196,
South Africa

Penguin Books Ltd., Registered Offices: 80 Strand, London WC2R 0RL, England

This is a work of fiction. Names, characters, places, and incidents either are the product of the author's imagination or are used fictitiously, and any resemblance to actual persons, living or dead, business establishments, events, or locales is entirely coincidental. The publisher does not have any control over and does not assume any responsibility for author or third-party websites or their content.

UNEASY RELATIONS

A Berkley Prime Crime Book / published by arrangement with the author

PRINTING HISTORY
Berkley Prime Crime hardcover edition / July 2008
Berkley Prime Crime mass-market edition / August 2009

Copyright © 2008 by Aaron Elkins.
The Edgar® name is a registered service mark of the Mystery Writers of America, Inc.
Cover illustration by Dan Craig.
Cover design by Steve Ferlauto.
Interior text design by Kristin del Rosario.

ISBN: 978-0-425-22908-8

BERKLEY® PRIME CRIME
Berkley Prime Crime Books are published by The Berkley Publishing Group,
a division of Penguin Group (USA) Inc.,
375 Hudson Street, New York, New York 10014.
BERKLEY® PRIME CRIME and the PRIME CRIME logo are trademarks of Penguin Group (USA)
Inc.

PRINTED IN THE UNITED STATES OF AMERICA

10 9 8 7 6 5 4 3 2 1

Acknowledgments

As usual, I relied on a lot of expert counsel. In Gibraltar, Professor Clive Finlayson of the Gibraltar Museum patiently shared his vast knowledge of Iberian Neanderthal prehistory, and Detective Chief Inspector Emilio Acris of the Royal Gibraltar Police answered all my questions on the way they do things there. In addition, Stephen Davenport, general manager of the wonderful Rock Hotel, provided information and many courtesies.

"Identification of Traumatic Injury in Burned Cranial Bone: An Experimental Approach," by Elayne J. Pope and O'Brian C. Smith, *Journal of Forensic Sciences*, v.49, no.3, May 2004, was the impetus for an important part of *Uneasy Relations*. Dr. Pope was also extremely helpful in responding to further questions and in reviewing parts of the manuscript.

Forensic chemist Martin McDermot of the Washington State Patrol's Seattle Crime Lab educated me on explosives and also reviewed a part of the manuscript.

Stanley J. Rhine, Professor Emeritus, University of New Mexico, straightened me out on a few forensic matters with his usual enthusiasm and good humor.

My friends John Matthews and David Bailie, orthopedic surgeons both, provided very helpful information from their specialties and reviewed a section of the manuscript as well.

Thank you all most sincerely.

ONE

**PROMINENT SCIENTIST TO REVEAL
"STUNNING" SCIENTIFIC FRAUD IN GIBRALTAR
By Mike Fender
Affiliated Press**

The annual conference of the International Paleoanthropological Society isn't usually associated with pulse-
pounding levels of excitement, other than in some of the
more remote halls of academe, but next month's meeting in Gibraltar promises something different.

Gideon Oliver, a well-regarded professor of physical
anthropology at the University of Washington's Port Angeles campus, and the author of *Bones to Pick*, an examination of hoaxes, dead ends, and frauds in archaeology
and anthropology, is set to reveal his most stunning exposé yet. The occasion will be a public lecture during
the twenty-third annual conference of the august group,
which is meeting in Gibraltar this year to celebrate the

fifth anniversary of the discovery there of the celebrated prehistoric double burial known as the First Family, consisting of a mother and young son (Gibraltar Woman and Gibraltar Boy) in a close embrace.

Oliver's publisher, Lester Rizzo (Javelin Press), describes Oliver's bombshell as "the most sensational exposé of a scientific scam in history." Oliver himself, known in forensic circles as the Skeleton Detective, is slightly more circumspect. "Oh, I wouldn't say it's the most sensational one in history," he said during a recent telephone interview, "but it's right up there."

"More sensational than Piltdown Man?" he was asked by this reporter.

"Oh, no comparison. It'll leave Piltdown in the dust," he promptly replied. "Piltdown was nothing compared to this."

When asked for a hint, the scientist declined. "Nosirreebob, I'm not letting the cat out of the bag ahead of time on this one. It's too big. There's too much at stake. My publisher doesn't know what it is, my colleagues don't know what it is, even my wife doesn't know what it is."

Rizzo admits that, indeed, he hasn't been let in on the details. "But I know Dr. Oliver and I can promise you this," he says with relish. "It's going to stand the scientific world on its ear."

"Oh, jeez," Gideon said, slapping his copy of the *Peninsula Daily News* down suddenly enough to make a fellow diner, dozing over his English muffin and coffee two tables away, sit up with a jerk. "Look at this, will you, Julie?" He tapped the headline with his finger. "Sheesh."

His wife, dressed in the trim, gray-and-green park ranger uniform in which she would be reporting to work in twenty minutes, paused in buttering a cinnamon-raisin bagel to read the article. Then she read it again.

"Nice going, prof," she said, only barely managing to keep a straight face. "Did you really say that? 'It'll leave Piltdown in the dust'? Talk about over the top."

The Piltdown hoax was the most celebrated deception in the history of anthropology, the sham discovery of the "missing link," decisively proven only after forty years of widespread acceptance to be a combination of fossil human skull bones and the jaw of an orangutan. Even now, anthropologists found it painful to joke about, Gideon among them.

"No, of course I didn't say that," he said petulantly, "and this isn't funny. Well, okay, maybe I did say it, but I was kidding. I mean, this reporter calls—Lester told me to expect it; he set it up—and the first thing out of his mouth, the reporter's mouth, is: "Dr. Oliver, would you agree that this is really going to be the most sensational scientific exposé in history?" I thought *he* was kidding. So I said . . . whatever the heck it says I said. It was a joke. Am I the kind of person who would go around saying things like 'nosirree-bob' under conditions of anything but extreme stress or ill-considered jocularity?"

"Uh-huh," Julie said. "And how was he supposed to know it was a joke? From the twinkle in your eye? It was a phone conversation."

"From my tone. From my manner. It should have been obvious. It *was* obvious. Besides, that was just the start. We talked for another ten minutes. I told him in all seriousness that Lester had a tendency to exaggerate, and that it was true that while I was down there at the conference I might or might not do a little research on the Atlantis myth for the next edition of *Bones to Pick*, but that I had no earth-shattering exposé in mind, and the lecture I'd be giving was actually about something else altogether."

Julie scanned the article again. "He seems to have left that part out."

"He left it out, all right. I was sandbagged. This is Lester's doing, Julie. As far as he's concerned, any publicity is good publicity. He thinks it'll sell a few more copies of the new edition, even though it won't be out for eight months. I haven't even finished the damn thing."

Julie put down her muffin and the knife. "Gideon, sweetheart, don't take this as a criticism, but maybe you ought to think twice about joking with reporters? Remember that story that showed up everywhere that had you predicting that in ten thousand years human beings would be four feet tall? Or was it three feet?"

"It was four feet," he grumbled, "and ten *million* years, but you know that wasn't what I really said. I said we *could* be four feet tall—or seven feet tall, or extinct, for that matter. I was just making the point that you can't take a teleological approach to evolution, that just because we've been getting taller, that doesn't mean we're going to continue to get taller. Selective forces in the environment change, and we, or any other organisms, respond to those forces, not to some long-range design or some supposed future condition. If we—oh, heck, you know all that. Anyway, the woman I talked to had no sense of humor at all." He shook his head in frustration. "Everything I say, these people take literally."

"Which is my point."

Gideon shrugged and nodded. "You're right," he said, returning with only slightly diminished appetite to his cream cheese–chives-and-egg bagel, a specialty of the Port Angeles Olympic Bagel Company, where they breakfasted once or twice a week. "But *this* guy was an Associated Press reporter!" he suddenly blurted. "You'd think I could trust him!"

"Look again," Julie said, turning the paper around so he could read the byline.

" 'Mike Fender,' " Gideon read aloud. " 'Affiliated Press.' "
He looked up. "What the heck is *Affiliated* Press?"

"I'm not sure," Julie said, "but on a guess, I'd say it's the
agency that supplies the checkout magazines with all those
snazzy news items: 'Monkey Woman Gives Birth to Twin
Lobsters', 'Talking Gorilla With I.Q. of 250 Seeks "Significant Relationship" with "Large" Woman'. . . ."

" 'Noted Anthropologist Stands Scientific World on Its
Head,' " Gideon said, smiling at last. "Oh, boy, I'm going
to take a lot of flak about this. I guess I'd just better resign
myself."

"I'm afraid so. So this talk you'll be giving in
Gibraltar—it's open to the public? Not part of the society
meetings?"

"Right. I'm not giving a paper at the meetings. But apparently there's a very active cultural association down
there, and they hold these monthly noontime Heritage Lectures on everything under the sun. So they've asked me if
I'd be willing to do the June one; something that would be
interesting to the general public."

"Why you, do you think?"

"Probably because I'm the only one they've ever heard
of. The Skeleton Detective, you know? But it's fine, I'm
glad to do it. It sounds like fun, actually. They hold them in
someplace called St. Michael's Cave, which I gather has a
natural underground amphitheater they use for this kind of
thing, and for concerts and such."

His cell phone, lying on the table, tinkled out the melancholy opening bars of the overture to *La Traviata* just as
he chomped down on bagel and egg, and Julie answered it
for him.

"Why, hello, Lester!" she said brightly. "We were just
talking about you. Yes, we did see the article. Yes, it certainly is that."

"I'm not here!" Gideon cried around a mouthful of food. "You don't know where I am. You haven't seen me since last Friday. You don't know when I'll be back, if ever."

"Why, yes, of course he's here," Julie said pleasantly. "Gideon, guess what?" she burbled, batting her eyes. "It's Lester Rizzo. Your publisher." She held out the phone.

Scowling, Gideon took it. Lester was already babbling away. "You read it, Gid? Is that good copy, or what? You did great, buddy. Fender tells me it's been picked up by over a hundred papers."

"Oh, wonderful, Lester. But the fact is—as you damn well know—I don't have any sensational exposés to pull out of my hat. I don't have *any* exposés to pull out of my hat. And my public lecture in Gibraltar is about the evolutionary concomitants of erect posture, not—"

"Yeah, yeah, I know, I know, but who cares about that stuff? With all due respect, nobody. Look, by the time *Bones* comes out, this'll all be ancient history. You think Fender or anybody else is gonna go to Gibraltar to check up on you? Don't worry, they won't. Trust me. But *your* name's gonna be a little more familiar to people, you see? They won't know why they know it, they'll just know they know it when they see it at the bookstore. And they'll be more likely to reach for it. 'Oh, yeah, here's one by that guy, Gideon Oliver. I think I've heard of him.' And if they reach for it, maybe with a little luck they'll buy it."

"Maybe, but—"

"*Definitely.* Market research proves it, pal." His voice deepened with veneration at the magical words. "That's what it's all about: Market research."

"Fine, but what about the people who buy it expecting something fabulous? What about them? And what about me, how does that make me look?"

"Ah, yeah, that's the beauty part, see? Eight months is perfect. Any more than that and they forget they ever heard of you. Any less than that, and they still remember what you said. Market research, buddy."

With a sigh, Gideon dropped whatever it was he was going to retort. He and Lester went back a few years now, and Gideon knew there wasn't much point in arguing. Lester Rizzo, the associate publisher of Javelin Press and the improbable executive editor of their Frontiers of Science imprint, had approached Gideon after an open lecture he'd given on scientific fraud at the university and asked if he'd be interested in expanding it into a book-length manuscript for the Frontiers series.

Gideon had accepted, partly because the manuscript wouldn't be due for almost a year and anything that far away was always doable, and partly because he was flattered at the thought of joining the august roster of contributors to the series. The $15,000 advance, a delightfully unusual prospect to anyone accustomed to dealing with the academic presses, hadn't hurt either. Besides, as opposed to the necessarily arcane monographs he turned out for the scientific journals (his contribution to the current *American Journal of Physical Anthropology* was "Sexual Dimorphism in Tibial Diaphysis Robusticity among Eastern European Upper Paleolithic Populations"), the idea of writing something for popular consumption seemed like fun.

And it had been. To Gideon's surprise—but not, apparently, to Lester's—the book had done well, and Gideon was now finishing up an expanded section on mythology and science (thus, his interest in Atlantis) for a new edition. But from the very beginning, there had been differences, and a long string of compromises, between his editor and himself. The title had been one such. When Gideon had proposed *Error, Gullibility, and Self-Deception in the Social Sciences*, Lester had looked at him as if he were crazy. "You're writing for the masses here," he'd pointed out. "What do you say we dumb down the title a little?" But

Lester's idea (*Bungles, Blunders, and Bloopers*) had left Gideon equally dismayed. They had settled, each with his own reservations, on *Bones to Pick: Wrong Turns, Dead Ends, and Popular Misconceptions in the Study of Humankind.*

More often than not, however, he had been outfoxed by Lester one way or another, and obviously it had just happened again. Well, Lester was probably right; it might sell a few more copies. But it wasn't going to be easy to live with.

"Okay, Lester," he said, "what's done is done."

"Hey, don't say it like that, buddy; it hurts my feelings," he said cheerfully. So, you going to be down here in L.A. any time soon?"

"Not if I can help it."

"Okay, then, see you in Gibraltar."

"Right, see you—*what*? You're coming to Gibraltar?"

"You better believe it. We're going to do a book launch at that conference you're going to that'll knock 'em dead. Drinks on the house, speeches—"

"Lester," Gideon said, appalled, "give me a break. Why do we want to do a book launch *there*? These are my colleagues, they'll—"

"Hey, get off your high horse. This's got nothing to do with you. You're not my only author, you know. You know a guy named Rowley Boyd?"

"Uh-huh, I've met him a few times." Rowley, Gideon remembered, was the pleasant, unpretentious, somewhat bookish director of the archaeological museum in Gibraltar.

"Well, he's been piddling around with a book about Gibraltar Boy for almost three years, and we finally squeezed it out of him—pub date early October. You have any objections to my giving a book party for him?"

"None whatever. If it's okay with him, it's okay with me."

"It's more than okay with him. He's overjoyed. He's

thrilled. *Some* people appreciate the efforts made on their behalf."

"Well, I'm glad for him, Lester, and for you. I hope the book's a big success."

He said good-bye and hung up with another sigh. "According to Lester, a hundred newspapers have picked the article up. It's going to be all over the place. LeMoyne and the others are going to have a ball with this, Julie. So are my students. Life is going to be hell for me for a while." All the same, he couldn't help chuckling. "Still, I guess it's pretty funny, in a way."

"It is, really. 'It'll leave Piltdown in the dust,'" she said, shaking her head. "Quite a statement."

He grimaced. "I really wish you wouldn't keep repeating that."

She glanced at her watch. "Gotta go. Well, you know what I think? I think you should think about what Abe might have said at a time like this."

"That's a good idea." Abe was Abraham Goldstein, the impoverished, persecuted, Jewish immigrant from Russia who had made an improbable place for himself in America as an eminent professor of anthropology. At an advanced age, as Gideon's major professor at the University of Wisconsin, he had been Gideon's mentor in life as in anthropology, and his presence was still very much missed.

Gideon smiled. "So what would Abe have said?"

"'Oy,'" said Julie, draining her coffee as she stood up.

He responded with a full-throated laugh and lifted his cup. "I'll drink to that."

TWO

IT wasn't as bad as he'd feared. Inasmuch as he didn't have a teaching load during the summer session, there were few students to contend with, and the faculty that he ran into on his visits to campus tended to be sparse. Oh, Rupert Armstrong LeMoyne couldn't resist his little jab ("Don't tell me . . . please don't tell me . . . that you're going to . . . gasp . . . tell us that there is no . . . gasp . . . Bigfoot!") and one of his better graduate students, depressingly, swallowed the article hook, line, and sinker, and asked if he could possibly be let in on the secret. He would tell no one, he promised.

All in all, however, Gideon thought he'd gotten away cheaply. And so, a few days later, he was in a characteristically upbeat mood when he picked up Julie at park headquarters to head out for an Italian dinner in town. "Julie, could you get away a day early on the Gibraltar trip?" he asked once she'd slid into the car and he'd gotten his warm, wifely peck on the cheek. "The foundation will pick up any costs for changing flights, and also put us up for an extra night at the hotel."

"Sure, I could do that," she said, obviously liking the idea of another day in exotic Gibraltar, to which neither of them had been, and another night at the Rock Hotel, reputedly its most luxurious lodgings. "But what's up? Is the conference starting earlier?"

"No, it's not that," he said, pulling the Camry out of the lot and turning right onto East Park Avenue, "but there's going to be a small dinner symposium in honor of Ivan Gunderson the evening before it officially opens. Very informal, just five speakers. Everybody who had any association with Gibraltar Boy or the First Family—well, not the hired locals and student workers on the dig, but all the professionals. You know some of the others—Audrey Godwin-Pope, Pru McGinnis—and I've been asked to be part of the program."

"Oh, that's great. Congratulations."

"Oh, well, it's nothing special. It's a testimonial dinner, really; nothing scholarly."

"Explain something to me, Gideon. You've always said that Gunderson was a better TV personality than he was an archaeologist."

"True. He's intelligent, he's articulate—eloquent, in fact—and he has a quick mind, but he's just not a well-trained scientist, although he obviously thinks he is. He's very good at explaining archaeology to a lay audience, but nobody in the field takes his work as an archaeologist very seriously anymore. Never did, really."

"Okay, that's my question. If nobody takes his work seriously, why are you holding a symposium in his honor?"

"Well, first of all, because he's a genuinely nice guy, a real, old-fashioned gentleman—kind, helpful, not full of himself like some TV celebrities—and you can't help liking him as a person—you'll see—but mainly because of his very real contributions to archaeology. See, it's the Horizon Foundation that's putting it on, and putting the five of us up—"

"And spouses, let's not forget about spouses."

"And spouses, and they're doing it largely to show their thanks for all he's done for the field, and especially for the foundation itself. Ivan's getting to the end of the road now—he's over ninety. And this is a perfect opportunity. It's the fifth anniversary of the finding of Gibraltar Boy and Gibraltar Woman, and in a very real way he's responsible for that. And the odds are he won't be around for the tenth anniversary."

"That's one of the things I'm confused about. I thought it was, what's his name, Adrian sŏmething, that found them."

"Yes, sure, Adrian Vanderwater was actually running the dig, but—" He glanced over at Julie. "Didn't I already explain this once?"

"I think possibly you did," Julie said casually.

"Or twice?"

"Could be. Would you mind going through it again?"

"Will you promise to pay attention this time?"

"I *was* paying attention. I just fell asleep, that's all. You can hardly blame that on me."

She laughed; that sudden, two-note chirp of giggle that made her nose crinkle, something he found unbearably coy in other women, but in Julie, he thought it was absolutely adorable. (He knew no men whose noses crinkled; now why was that? Was there a sex-linked gene involved? Perhaps a master's thesis for one of his students?)

As always, it made him smile. He put a forefinger on the tip of her nose. "You're just lucky you've got that twitchy little *quadratus labii superioris*," he said. "Otherwise you wouldn't get away—"

"If you think you can distract me by talking dirty, forget it. Now tell me about Ivan Gunderson."

"Okay, one more time . . ."

Ivan Samuel Gunderson was a throwback and very probably the last of his kind. In the late nineteenth century they had been common, these men of wealth, amateur archaeologists who dug the ancient sites of Egypt or Europe or Mesopotamia. But since the 1930s, the field had become institutionalized. Excavations were funded by universities or foundations and conducted by formally trained PhDs with ever narrower specialties. Amateur, self-taught archaeologists were no longer welcome. More than that, they were kept at a distance.

Except for Ivan S. Gunderson. Without even a bachelor's degree in archaeology, he had been a well-known figure in European and Middle Eastern prehistory for four decades. A self-made multimillionaire—as a young man he had speculated with fabulous success in South American tin mining—he was unique in being able to purchase the land on which promising archaeological sites lay, rather than having to wangle permission from reluctant landowners to excavate on their property. This he did, freely and often, so that it wasn't uncommon for him to be working two or three sites at a time, using local people as workers and overseers. Where permission from government officials was necessary, particularly in the Middle East, his freehandedness with money came in particularly helpful.

His slapdash, untrained approach to excavating naturally enough made the professionals nervous, but since he was working on his own land, there was nothing they could do. Besides, he was extremely popular with them, having endeared himself to them with a practice that outdid anything the nineteenth-century amateurs ever did. Quick to lose interest if a site failed to spark his restless imagination, he would often donate the land to a university or professional organization for them to pursue the dig on their own. A great deal of useful data and many Stone Age materials that now resided in museums had come from his generosity. One of his main beneficiaries through the years had been the Chicago-based Horizon Foundation for Anthropological Research, the highly respected organization with which Gideon had had a long informal association. It was this foundation that was sponsoring the dinner in his honor.

Gunderson's unsophisticated theoretical spoutings, while always politely received by his fellow archaeologists (everyone wanted to stay on his good side; you never knew when the next donated site was coming), were privately regarded as naïve, erratic, and generally half baked. His specialty was the Neanderthals, who had always been a focal point for dispute among paleoanthropologists. Until the 1990s the fight had been over whether or not we humans were directly descended from them. Gunderson had been at the forefront of those who believed we were.

But in the 1990s the DNA scientists, having found a way to extract mitochondrial DNA from prehistoric skeletons, had pretty well resolved the matter.

We weren't.

The ground shifted. Now the question became whether humans—*Homo sapiens*—and Neanderthals—*Homo neanderthalensis*—had interbred at all, or were distinctly separate species that did not—could not—interbreed. Gunderson put down one cudgel and picked up another. Handsome, silver haired, and articulate ("a combination of Alistair Cooke and Walter Cronkite," as one TV magazine put it) he became one of the most publicly visible proponents of "admixture theory"—that is, the theory that Neanderthals and humans had intermittently interbred during the four or five thousand years that they coexisted in Europe before the Neanderthals died out altogether about 24,000 years ago. Ivan Gunderson's support notwithstanding, this was a perfectly respectable theory held by many reputable scientists. As was the opposing one; that is, that they were separate species who never interbred. Whether they had or hadn't was of course of no importance at all, and even less interest, to 99.9999 percent of the civilized world, but it was an issue that had sharply split the scholars of the Paleolithic era— the Stone Age. Invectives had been hurled and, on one notable occasion, fists had flown, as gray-bearded academics fought it out at their conventions.

Then, five years ago, the matter was settled, at least in the popular mind; through Gunderson's doing, no less. He had been excavating several Neanderthal and *Homo sapiens* sites in Spain and Gibraltar at the time, commuting between them as needed. The Gibraltar site, a coastal rock shelter known as the Europa Point Cave, had come to his attention when the owner of the land, bulldozing the area in a crazy scheme to turn it into a mushroom farm, had uncovered some Stone Age tools, soon determined to be Neanderthal. When Gunderson had offered to buy this promising land from him, the man had jumped at the chance to rid himself of it, and Gunderson and his crew of local workmen had started digging.

Two months' work turned up a few more stone tools, some butchered ibex bones, and a handful of charcoal dated at 26,000 years before the present. No human remains. Mildly interesting, but not exciting enough for Gunderson; just one more meager Neanderthal encampment, little different from the many others that had been found. He offered it to Horizon, which jumped at the chance to excavate at Europa Point, and the dig thereupon proceeded in orderly, highly professional fashion for some months under their oversight, with the eminent Adrian Vanderwater of the University of California in charge of work in the field. Their efforts were generally rewarding. Two more Neanderthal burials were found, along with more tools and butchered bones, and an unusual pendant (if that's what it was) carved from a wolf's tooth.

Highly satisfactory results. But then a truly remarkable find was made. In a sediment-filled hanging crevice along one wall of the shelter, the ceremonial burial of a female and a young child was unearthed, somewhat scattered and with fewer than half the bones still present, but with the remains of the female's skeletal arms tenderly cradling the remains of the child to her skeletal breast. The conclusion was inescapable: they were mother and child. Nothing like this had ever been seen before in a Stone Age burial. The poignant photographs, retouched for emphasis but essentially accurate, that were shown on TV news programs from pole to pole, soon established them as Gibraltar Woman and Gibraltar Boy: the First Family.

That would have been extraordinary enough, but when the bones were sent to the Horizon Foundation's anthropology laboratory for detailed study by an interdisciplinary team, the results were even more amazing. The three-person team, of which Gideon was the lead scientist, issued a thorough, meticulous report indicating that the female, who was in her mid-twenties (an old woman in Paleolithic terms), was not Neanderthal at all, but human. This sent a shock wave through the world of prehistoric archaeology: it had now been irrefutably shown for the first time that humans and Neanderthals could and did live together, at least in this one case, and that the human—an outsider, an alien female—had been ceremonially buried with the love and respect due a member of the clan. (The ceremonial nature of the burial was established by red stains on the bones, indicating that the bodies had been wrapped in an ocher-stained skin, the pigment of which had been absorbed by the skeletons as the shroud decayed.)

As spectacular as that was, it was the examination of Gibraltar Boy that opened up even more stunning avenues of conjecture and dispute. The child, it seemed, could arguably be described as combining characteristics of both Neanderthals and humans. Despite the intriguing possibilities that this raised, Gideon was determined that the team's report would not be a source of controversy—and especially of controversy based on insufficient data. Just the facts, ma'am. No theoretical stands were taken, no sweeping conclusions were drawn.

Of course, others did draw them. To the proponents of human-Neanderthal interbreeding, here was concrete evidence that mating had occurred. A few—a very few—other skeletons had been found that seemed to exhibit similar blends of human and Neanderthal traits, but the noninterbreeding proponents had argued them away as mere variations of either Neanderthals or humans, well within the range of variation to be found in any species.

But never had a find like this been made in such affecting circumstances. That the two skeletons were mother and son, few who had seen the photographs doubted. And what could the boy's human-Neanderthal mixture of traits (if such it was) mean other than that he was a hybrid, that he had mixed parentage? His mother was indisputably human. His father had to have been Neanderthal. A human woman had mated with a Neanderthal male many thousands of years ago, and they had produced a child, quickly dubbed Gibraltar Boy in both the popular and scientific press. In actuality, it was a misnomer; one that had always bothered Gideon. The child was only about four years old, too young to determine the sex from the available bones, and he had clearly indicated as much in the report. Nevertheless, some reporter's appellation of "Gibraltar Boy" had caught the popular imagination, and it had stuck. Gibraltar Boy he was, and Gibraltar Boy he would always be, and the objections of a few stuffy pedants like Gideon Oliver weren't going to change matters.

In any case, as far as the human-Neanderthal-admixture-theory people were concerned, the argument was settled. When you were talking about things that had happened more than twenty millennia ago, how could you ask for more solid proof than this? In the popular mind as well, the theory was now a fact, but scientists were still divided. The no-mixing contingent suffered quite a few defectors, but many refused to throw in the towel. The embattled true believers fought on, claiming that the measurements were inconclusive and fragmentary (which they were); the so-called human traits were ambiguous, mere within-species variations. Not all Neanderthals looked alike, not all chimpanzees looked alike, and not all human beings looked alike. The boy was, like his mother, a Neanderthal, pure and simple. A little less chunky than most, maybe, but Neanderthal all the same.

So what was a human woman doing buried in a Neanderthal rock shelter with a Neanderthal child in her arms? Who knew? Maybe she was the original nanny. Captured as a slave, perhaps. Or maybe she was an outcast from her own group who had been accepted into the Neanderthal fold. But then why was she buried with the child? Who could say? But to build from this scanty, questionable evidence, the conclusion that they were human mother and human-Neanderthal offspring? No, they would need a lot more evidence before they accepted that.

In the larger world, however, there was no longer any debate, especially after *Who We Are: The Legacy of the First Family*, The Learning Channel's highest-rated series ever, was shown, hosted by Gunderson himself at his urbane, avuncular best. In the popular mind, intergroup mixing between humans and Neanderthals was now a fact. (You couldn't say "interspecies mixing" anymore, as Gunderson lucidly, if a bit simplistically, explained, because the biological definition of species turned on the idea that only members of the same species could interbreed.) The fight was over.

The reverberations were felt not only in the world of prehistoric anthropology, but throughout the social sciences. For one thing, the theory that the Neanderthals had become extinct because their rivals, the more advanced *Homo sapiens*, had wiped them off the face of the earth by either ruthless, outright aggression or by outcompeting them for scarce resources took a major hit. Proponents of this theory, while unconvinced by the find, were forced to retreat to their ivory towers, muttering and licking their wounds. More broadly, the study of the relationships between more and less advanced societies was given new life. And champions of multiculturalism had a new and appealing poster child. (If Neanderthals and early humans could get along well enough to produce a child, and if the human mother of that child was lovingly taken in by the child's extended Neanderthal family, then surely we humans of merely different skin colors—genetically so much closer to each other—could hope to get along too . . . could we not?)

Gideon's story took them through their main course— they both had had the smoked salmon fettuccine—at the Bella Italia on Front Street, and Julie nodded as he finished.

"Okay, thanks. I think I get the picture now."

"You managed to stay awake the whole time?"

"Oh, there may have been a teeny-weeny lapse or two, right around the mitochondrial DNA part, but I managed to get most of it."

Their waiter, Bruce, finished clearing away their dinner plates and offered them a dessert menu.

"Just a latte for me," Julie said, fending it off.

"And I'll have an espresso," said Gideon.

Bruce feigned shock. "No *postre*? But our *chef della*

pasticceria will be grossly offended. I fear to tell him."
Bruce had served them many a fine meal and had earned
the right to talk with them like this.

"Oh, in that case . . . ," said Julie, snatching back the
menu and poring over it. "Gideon, will we be able to get
zabaglione in Gibraltar?"

"I doubt it. It's pretty British there, from what I hear.
Pasties, gateaux, trifle, yes. Probably Spanish and Moroccan food too, I'd guess. *Zabaglione?* Don't count on it."

"Well, then, you'd better have it here," Bruce said reasonably.

Gideon handed back the dessert menu. "Makes sense
to me."

THREE

"IT'S so tiny," Julie said disappointedly, her face pressed to the window of seat 17A.

As indeed it was. They were nearing the end of their three-hour flight from London, and from the air Gibraltar was a bit of a letdown, an insignificant little worm of a peninsula—shaped remarkably like a human vermiform appendix, Gideon thought—sticking improbably out into the Mediterranean from the vast, flat mainland of Andalusian Spain. They could easily see the whole of it from their seats over the wing as the Boeing 747 banked out over the Strait: the humped mass of the famed Rock itself, surrounded by its skirt of flat, coastal plain, with almost all of its population of thirty thousand crowded into the narrow, dense warren of streets at the base of its western flank.

"It is, isn't it?" Gideon agreed. "I imagine it'll look more impressive when we're down there looking up at it."

"Oh, it will, it will, I can assure you of that." The affable, self-possessed voice, borne on a faint waft of Irish whiskey, came from 18B in the row behind them. "And more impressive still when you're standing on top of the Rock looking down over the edge."

The voice was that of Professor Emeritus Adrian Vanderwater, who had leaned forward to make himself heard, unconcerned with not having been invited, and un-apologetic for having been eavesdropping. Vanderwater, the renowned archaeologist who had directed the Europa Point dig five years earlier, was of the opinion that such niceties were neither here nor there, at least inasmuch as they applied to him. He was, after all, Adrian Vanderwa-ter. Who could be other than pleased to have him partici-pate in a conversation?

As a brilliant young graduate student at the University of Michigan forty years before, he had been anointed the next generation's great paleoarchaeologist, and many schol-ars in the field—like anyone else, he had his detractors— would have agreed that the prediction had come to pass. For the last several decades he had been one of the two or three most eminent men in the discipline, an admirably exacting field-worker, and teacher of half the current crop of European Neolithic archaeologists.

The whiskey breath that hung about him—and it was still well before noon—came as no surprise. It was as in-extricably attached to him as his voice. In a leather-clad, stainless steel flask in his attaché case, Gideon knew, was a pint of Tullamore Dew Irish whiskey, the day's (but not the evening's) supply. Gideon had never seen him drunk, nor heard tales of binges from others (and academics are eager tale-tellers), but he'd never seen him wholly sober either. He drank from the time he got up—Gideon had been at a seven A.M. conference breakfast with him once, and the flask was already in use, spicing up his coffee— until he went to bed. But he did it only a very little at a time, just a few drops, so that there was always alcohol in his system, but never enough to make him even close to tipsy. Whether his typical good humor was whiskey-induced there was no way of knowing, since he was never without the flask.

Round, soft, and rosy, he was built more like an infant than a man of seventy. His head was large for his body, his arms and legs stubby, and his hands small and fat, with puffy, dimpled wrists. A belly like an overinflated beach ball; a globular forehead; pink, smooth, bulgy cheeks; a gurgling, throaty sort of chuckle always at the ready. One of Gideon's associates (not a fan of Vanderwater's) referred to him as Big Baby. "Did you know Big Baby's getting the Childe award this year?" "Did you hear Big Baby's coming out with *another* damn book?"

"But you're correct," Big Baby went on cheerfully enough. "It is astonishingly small, considering its history. A mere two and a half square miles, but *what* a two and a half square miles! In classical times, you know, the Rock was one of the Twin Pillars of Hercules. The Phoenicians knew it as *Calpe*. The Carthaginians came here, and the Romans. The Vandals swept ruthlessly into it on their southward rampage through the Roman Empire, and then the Visigoths."

Gideon couldn't help smiling. Retired for two years from his position at the University of California, Vanderwater couldn't stop being a professor. He could—and did—slip into a full-scale, seemingly well-prepared lecture at the drop of a hat. For a man recognized as one of the great figures of archaeology, recipient of almost every award and honor the field had to give, he had an inextinguishable need to demonstrate that he knew more about anything than anyone else, *whatever* the subject might happen to be. He did it engagingly enough, and with genuine erudition, but after a while it could get on one's nerves, not least because he was just about always right.

"From the other direction," Vanderwater continued, "it was at the southernmost tip of Gibraltar—right down there, Europa Point, in fact—can you see where that lighthouse is?—that Tarik ibn Zeyad set foot in 711 to begin the long Moorish domination of Iberia. Yes, right there."

He was close to purring as his plummy voice caressed the words *Europa Point*, and with good reason. His appointment five years earlier as director of the Europa Point dig, and the subsequent discovery, under his supervision, of the First Family, had provided the brightest jewel in the crown of his reputation. Late in his career, on the verge of retirement and an inevitable drift into relative inconsequence, he had suddenly become, in the eyes of his peers, the acknowledged authority on the most sensational find of the decade. (Outside the narrow, arcane circle of academe, of course, in the less demanding world of popular culture, it was Ivan Gunderson who enjoyed that position.) Since the find, Vanderwater had been the sole or senior author of a dozen monographs and two well-received scholarly books, all dealing with the social and cultural implications of the First Family and Gibraltar Boy, and their many ramifications. Even now, he was rumored to be working on a third.

"The name *Gibraltar*, as you may know, is a corruption of the Arabic *Jebel Tarik*, or 'Tarik's Mountain.' And Tarik's Mountain it remained until 1462, when the Arabs were driven out by Spain, which held the land for more than two centuries, until Britain took it in 1704."

"Yes," Gideon said. "They—"

"This they accomplished, during the War of Spanish Succession, by means of an Anglo-Dutch fleet under the command of Admiral George Rooke, and the British have held it ever since, the much-fortified Rock proving an impregnable military outpost of Empire—'safe as the Rock of Gibraltar' has been a catch phrase since the nineteenth century, you know—through the long years of the Great Siege, the Napoleonic Wars, and the terrible world conflicts of the twentieth century."

Julie, who had been listening courteously until now, her head cocked, glanced at Gideon with her eyebrows raised, her forehead creased. "Is he reading, or what?" she whispered.

Gideon suppressed his laugh. "I've never been able to figure out how he does that."

Still, it was, as always, an impressive performance. Not an *uh*, not an *um*, not a pause. Not for the first time he wondered if Vanderwater didn't prepare these sermons ahead of time, knowing he'd have the chance to use them at some point.

The older man had leaned back in his seat now, and was orating, rather than merely lecturing, supremely confident that his seatmate, and anyone else within earshot, would be appreciative of the edification provided.

"But as the technology of warfare changed, you see, and this great rock that had stood guard over the entrance to the Mediterranean for so many centuries lost its value and sank into obscurity, a staunchly British outpost improbably tacked onto the southern extremity of Spain and notable, if it was notable at all, for the never-ending squabbles between Spain and Great Britain over access, duties, governance—"

"Folks," said the pilot's voice, "you're not going to believe this, but a furniture lorry has broken down on the runway, so we're going to be circling for a while to permit them to clean up and get it out of there. Shouldn't be long."

Frowning, Julie turned to Gideon. "What is a furniture van doing in the middle of the runway?"

"That's a curious aspect of the Gibraltar airport," Vanderwater answered for him. "You see—"

But the pilot, with a superior audio system, overrode him. "Now, folks, I know what you're thinking: 'What is a furniture lorry doing in the middle of an airport runway in the first place?' Well, among the many unique aspects of Gib is the fact that it has the only international airport you're likely to see whose runway is crossed by the main road into town. The only road into town, actually. As you'll see as we circle past it, the runway extends crosswise across the entire isthmus and then some way out into the bay, so there's no way for vehicles to get around it. They all have to drive over it. Sorry about the delay, but just settle back for a little longer and enjoy your VIP aerial tour of Gibraltar, courtesy of British Airways."

"It's hardly the only thing about the Gibraltar airport that's unique," came from 18B. "It's closer to the city it serves than any other international airport in the world. A lot of people just walk into town from it . . ."

"Really," said Julie, who was perhaps becoming just a little lectured-out. "That's—"

"A five-hundred-yard stroll, and you're at Casemates Square in the town center. An extremely interesting history there, by the way . . ."

Julie quietly sighed, closed her eyes, and settled back.

For the next half hour they circled, Vanderwater eventually running out of things on which to elucidate (not something that happened every day) and Julie running out of attention span, not in that order.

"Gideon," she said quietly, when there had been a welcome silence from behind them for a few minutes, followed by what sounded suspiciously like a soft, tranquil snore, "I wanted to ask you something about this whole mixing-theory thing."

"Ha. I knew you weren't really awake at the Bella Italia. You were faking it."

"No, I was paying strict attention. This is something

you didn't talk about. I get the impression that you don't really buy into the admixture-theory idea."

"Oh, it's not that I don't buy into it. Humans and Neanderthals coexisted in the same area for several thousand years, after all, so I wouldn't be surprised if the occasional particularly cute human babe caught the eye of some horny Neanderthal caveman, or vice versa. Genetically, there really doesn't seem to be that much difference between us. But I'm not about to jump on the bandwagon and declare it to one and all as Revealed Truth. I mean, there's not that much difference between us and chimps either, but I haven't heard of any hot romances lately, have you? Not that I'm definitively on the other side either. There are still plenty of uncertainties."

"But you're the one who did that analysis on the skeletons."

"Well, one of the team, yes. Don't forget, there were Lyle and Harvey too."

"Don't be modest. You were the senior author of the paper. And if the child is a hybrid between the humans and—"

"That's the issue, Julie. We never used the term *hybrid*. We just described what we found."

"You weaseled, in other words."

"Precisely." He laughed. "Well, no, not that I haven't been known to weasel when the situation demanded it, but in this case the data just didn't warrant anything more conclusive See, most of the differences between Neanderthal and human skeletons are really quantitative, not qualitative. Oh, there are some specific, pretty minor distinctions— Neanderthal jawbones have this space behind their molars, the retromolar gap, that we don't have, and there's a difference in the shape of the mandibular foramen—but essentially, we're talking about matters of scale."

"The Neanderthals were bigger? More rugged?"

"Not bigger overall, no. They did have thicker bones, bigger brow ridges, bigger occipital buns; but we have bigger chins, bigger foreheads. And there are differences in the relative proportions of long-bone lengths. It's that kind of thing. So, sure, we all can agree that such and such an adult skeleton is Neanderthal, and another one is human, but when it comes to somebody like the First Kid, Gibraltar Boy, he's still a child; you're dealing with traits that haven't yet reached their adult form. He looks a little like both. So, yes, he might be a hybrid, or maybe you're simply looking at a Neanderthal that just happened to have a smaller brow ridge than his friends. Or maybe you're looking at a human child who had a receding chin."

"Well, what do *you* think? I mean, you personally, not professionally?"

"I honestly don't know. I certainly wouldn't be bowled over if he *is* a hybrid. I also wouldn't be bowled over if he isn't. Could be human. Could also be Neanderthal."

"Oh, that's helpful."

"Sorry, it's the best I can do. The thing is, it's not as if we have thousands of Neanderthal remains to look at and compare. At most there are only a few hundred in the entire world, and most of those are just fragments, and very few are children, so we're still learning what their traits were. Anyway, the truth is, I was more excited about the pathology on the female's skeleton. That was something you could hang your hat on. The earliest known case of ankylosing spondylitis in a human being. Until Gibraltar Woman, the first case we knew about was from the Egyptian Neolithic, a good fifteen thousand years later!"

"I remember how excited about that you were." She smiled. "I can see how excited you are about it *now*. And wasn't there some graduate student somewhere who was going to do her dissertation on it?"

"Yes, from Cal, I think. She contacted me a year or so

after Europa Point. She was pretty sure she'd run across another case of it from about the same time period, at some little site in Portugal, or was it Spain? Spain, I think. She thought there might be a dissertation topic there, on genetic anomalies among early modern humans."

"And was there?"

"I don't know. She e-mailed me a couple of times with questions and then I never heard from her again. Which probably means there wasn't. Maybe the case she'd come across wasn't ankylosing spondylitis after all; maybe it was just advanced arthritis and she hadn't been able to tell the difference on her own. She probably found something else to work on."

"Well, the runway's clear, folks," the captain announced. "We're on our way in."

There was scattered applause, and then, after a thoughtful pause, Julie said, "Gideon, back to the hybrid issue, what about those specific traits you mentioned? That space behind the molars, that mandibular foramen thing? Did Gibraltar Boy have them or didn't he?"

"Moot point. The jawbone's missing. They're both partial skeletons, remember, and pretty banged up at that."

"Okay, what about DNA? Wouldn't that tell if he was human, or Neanderthal, or a mix?"

"No DNA. It's always pretty iffy with things that old. In this case the bones have lost too much collagen for a reliable test."

"So I guess we'll never know for sure."

"I guess we won't." He smiled. "I can live with it. There are more important things to worry about."

FOUR

"THE Rock itself," said the donnish-looking, donnish-sounding gentleman to his huddled audience of four men and three women, "on the very crest of which we now stand, is, as most of you already know, not really a 'rock' in the sense of a single giant monolith, but a narrow, limestone spine running north-south for approximately, ah, mmm, three miles. The famous massive, perpendicular aspect that we know from photographs is simply its northern terminus. Now, to the west, behind us, it slopes less precipitously down to Gibraltar town, which you can see spread out approximately thirteen hundred feet below us—or rather four hundred *meters*, as the lords of Brussels now decree that I must say, ah-ha-ha."

Donnish he might be, but in fact he was the only member of the group, other than Julie Oliver, who was not a teacher. Rowley G. Boyd, MA (Oxon), Gideon's soon-to-be fellow author in Javelin's Frontiers of Science series, was the director of the Gibraltar Museum of Archaeology and

Geology. It was the museum that had arranged this visit to the Rock (including a complimentary three-course lunch) for this group of five scholars and two spouses who had arrived a day early for the Paleoanthropological Society conference, so as to be able to participate in this evening's symposium for Ivan Gunderson. Rowley had thought that the distinguished assemblage would appreciate a recreational outing to the top of Gibraltar's celebrated monolith, even though several had been there before. Part of the treat was to have been the breathtaking ride up by cable car, but they'd had to drive up in a stuffy, uncomfortable taxi van instead because the cable was shut down today on account of the strong winds at the top.

Which was also the reason that Rowley's audience was huddled so tightly.

"Now then, to the south," he continued, "across the straits, the dun-colored mountains are the, ah, er, Atlas Mountains of Morocco. To the west, across Gibraltar Bay, we have Algeciras, Spain, about which, heh-heh, there is an amusing saying . . ."

But they were not to learn what the amusing saying about Algeciras was, at least not yet. Rowley was somewhat of a mumbler—a hem-and-hawer—at the best of times (an impediment not helped by the small, ceramic-bit pipe that was forever clenched between his teeth, usually unlit), and this morning's wind gusts sporadically plucked the words out of his mouth and whirled them, unheard, out over the strait.

"Can't hear a damn thing, Rowley," said Audrey Godwin-Pope, the Horizon Foundation's director of Field Archaeology, whose metallic, incisive voice would have had no difficulty being heard above buffeting that was far stronger than this. "Too windy. And please make an effort not to swallow your words."

Rowley, taking no offense (Audrey was Audrey; what

could one do?), expanded his chest and attempted to raise his volume a tad, though he didn't go so far as to take the pipe from his mouth. "Yes, this wind is a curious meteorological phenomenon, you know, and unique to the Straits of Gibraltar. The Spaniards refer to it the *poniente*, and it—"

"Far be it from me to correct a native, Rowley, especially you, but I'm afraid you're in error there," said Adrian Vanderwater. "The *poniente* is the westerly wind that comes in from the Atlantic. This one, coming from the east, out of the Mediterranean, would be the *levanter* . . ."

"The *levanter*?" echoed Rowley, removing the pipe and tapping it against his teeth. "Are you sure? You know, I always remember the difference by—"

". . . which, might I add, would mean that the rain and fog are not likely to be very far behind."

"Well, whatever the hell you call it, it's getting pretty bad out here," Audrey grumped, drawing her coat around her lean, spiky frame. "The fog's starting to come in, all right, and I just got a spatter of rain on my glasses. And it's getting cold."

"Oh, now, Aud," said her burly husband, Buck, standing beside her, "it's not as bad as all that." As he spoke, he swept off his jacket—he wore only a polo shirt underneath—and offered it to her.

Gideon, knowing Audrey (but not Buck), expected her to swat it irritably aside. Instead, he watched in amazement as she practically melted, allowing Buck to place it tenderly around her shoulders, from which it hung down to her knees. And all the while she looked up at him—he was a good foot taller than she was—the way a besotted teenager gazes at her lover.

Astounding. But it lasted no more than a few seconds. As soon as the jacket was settled comfortably around her, she was her old self again, assailing Rowley. "In any case,

I'm ready to eat. It's almost noon. Where do we get this lunch you promised? It better be indoors."

Rowley chuckled. "Why, of course it's indoors. There's a charming little restaurant right in the cable car terminal building. I've booked the whole place for us. And yes, I suppose it would be best to straggle off to it before it gets any worse. It's just up the path, no more than a five-minute walk."

And off they straggled in twos and threes. They'd all had dinner together at the hotel the previous evening, renewing old acquaintances and making new ones. Among the old acquaintances for Gideon and Julie was Pru McGinnis, she of the short, flyaway red hair, the muscular washerwoman forearms, the thick, chapped, red wrists, and the overall build of a VW bus, big, square, and sturdy. Now a fellow at the august Franco-American *Institut de Préhistoire* in Les Eyzies, France, she'd been a student of Gideon's in the very first graduate course he'd ever taught, although she was only a few years his junior. A jolly, animated, resourceful New York–born woman approaching forty, she'd gotten an MA in physical anthropology under Gideon, then—to Gideon's disappointment—had switched to theoretical archaeology for her doctorate. He had been on her doctoral committee and had had to sit in on the defense of her dissertation: *Post-processual, Structural, and Contextual Paradigms in Archaeology, Considered from an Epistemological Perspective.* He hadn't understood a word.

Before moving on to the *Institut,* she'd taught for a few years at the University of Missouri, where she'd picked up a Western accent, soon gone, and a penchant for Western garb, which had stayed with her. Today she was in a tailored plum-colored cowboy shirt, a flouncy denim-and-gingham square-dancing skirt (sans crinoline), and worn, lizard-skin boots.

As a student, she had been criticized by one of Gideon's fellow instructors as being "insufficiently reverent," but Gideon had found her to be a breath of fresh air in an otherwise hidebound department. He had liked her as a pupil, been proud of her as a protégée, and now considered her a friend, as did Julie.

Like most first-time visitors to the Rock, the Olivers were fascinated by the Barbary apes that scrambled around them or sat hunched and glowering along the edges of the path, grooming each other or moodily eating handouts given them by the mostly British tourists despite the prominent signs warning of a five-hundred-pound penalty for doing so. And the snacks they fed the animals were as bad as the snacks they fed themselves: sweets, sweets, and more sweets—candy bars, muffins, sugared biscuits, and packaged cakes, with the occasional bag of flavored crisps to break the monotony.

"Cute li'l buggers, aren't they?" said Pru, who had been to Gibraltar before, having been one of the team on the Europa Point dig. When the dig had started, the professional team had been composed of nothing but archaeologists—experts in stones, but not in bones. But once they had unearthed their first evidence of human skeletal material, however—the proximal end of an ulna protruding from a crevice in the cave wall—Pru had been called in to perform the delicate exhumation. Gideon had been a little surprised at that, inasmuch as she had only that MA in physical anthropology, and, really, not much to recommend her in the way of experience as a "dirt archaeologist." But Les Eyzies, where she was working, had been relatively nearby, and Corbin Hobgood, Europa Point's assistant director, had been an old friend, and so he had brought her on. As a result, it had been Pru herself who had excavated the bones of the First Family. And a fine, careful job she had done, as far as Gideon could tell.

One of the monkeys ambled up to him with its sham-bling, quadrupedal gait, and, without bothering to look up at him, stuck out a demanding hand for a handout. When Gideon didn't oblige, the heavy-browed, cinnamon-colored creature tugged impatiently on his pant leg, almost send-ing him tumbling; like most nonhuman primates, they were strong for their size.

"Beat it, you bum," Gideon muttered, snatching the fab-ric out of its grasp.

Julie was shocked. "Gideon, that's not like you at all."

"Well, I hate monkeys," he mumbled, a little ashamed of himself.

Now both women stared at him, astonished.

"You *hate* monkeys?" Julie exclaimed. "I never knew that."

"Oh, I don't mean I *hate* them," Gideon said, chastened, "but I don't like them. Now, apes I like. Thoughtful, intel-ligent, adaptive. How can you not like a chimp—bright, eager to please, always ready to play? And how can any-one's heart not go out to a gorilla sitting in the corner of a zoo cage somewhere, all pensive and melancholy? But monkeys, no. Look at them—greedy, spiteful, malicious, contemptuous—"

"Contemptuous?" Julie said, laughing. "Pensive? Some-body's getting a wee bit anthropomorphic here."

"Okay, I plead guilty to that. Got carried away there for a minute. But look at them. Unlike apes, they—"

"But these *are* apes," said Pru, gesturing with the sun-glasses she carried in her hand. "Barbary apes. The sign says so. 'Please do not feed the Barbary apes.' " She clapped her other hand to her heart. "My God, somebody keep me from falling down. Did I just catch Professor Oli-ver in an error—about primates, yet?"

"The sign may say so, but the sign is in error," Gideon replied calmly.

"I could have told you," a laughing Julie said to Pru.

"The uninformed—for example, those with mere master's degrees in physical anthropology—may call them apes," Gideon went on windily, "and it's true that they're big for monkeys, they lack tails, they look a bit like baboons, and they have a baboonlike gait, but in fact they are monkeys, macaques, *Macaca sylvanus*, and they are among the nastier, crabbier, least amenable of their kind."

"With a diet like that, I'm not surprised," Pru said. She stopped walking to lean close to a couple of males, each in the process of sullenly, but extremely competently, opening up a package he'd been given. "'Cadbury Curly Wurlies,'" she read aloud from one label, "and 'Mr. P's Pork Scratchings.' No wonder they're crabby," she said, straightening up. "You'd be crabby too if you lived on a diet of—*hey!*"

A skinny, hairy forearm had snaked up just as she turned away, and long, spidery fingers had expertly plucked the sunglasses out of her hand.

"Come back here, you creep!" she cried as the animal scampered up onto a rocky ledge, its Curly Wurlies in one hand and Pru's sunglasses in the other.

"Those cost me $34.95, you . . . you little shit!"

Whereupon the monkey, staring contemptuously—*Yes, contemptuously*, Gideon thought—at her all the time, slipped the glasses more or less over its eyes and just sat there wearing them, safely out of reach.

The nearby tourists laughed and reached for their cameras.

"On second thought, I guess the little guys are pretty amusing at that," Gideon said.

THE tiny Top of the Rock Bar and Restaurant, hidden one floor below the big tourist cafeteria, was a cozy, olde

English sort of place with open-beam ceilings, a gleaming mahogany bar, and an inviting fire glowing in a small stone fireplace and casting feathery, flickering, orange reflections on the walls. On the front door was a sign stating *Reserved for Private Party*. There were only two small tables, and three or four stools at the bar, just about enough room for Rowley's group. Places had been attractively set for eight: three at the larger table, two at the smaller, and three at the bar. Everything looked wonderfully appealing to the chilled troupe looking yearningly in through the glass door.

There was only one problem. They couldn't get in. The door was locked, there was no response to their knocking, and the preordered lunch wasn't going to be ready until one, almost an hour away.

"That gives you all an opportunity to do a number of things in the interim," said Rowley, looking on the bright side. "If you just want to warm up over a cup of coffee or cocoa, the cafeteria upstairs is open, and there's a souvenir shop up there too, with some excellent books on the area. But if you want to brave the elements, you'd have time to go on down to the Apes' Den area, if that appeals to you. It'll be less windy there, and that's where you'll find the largest assemblage of them."

"Oh, goody, let's do that," Pru said sourly to Gideon.

"Good idea. Maybe you'll find the one that has your glasses."

"Or you could simply wander down the paths a ways," Rowley continued. "I'm afraid you won't have time to get to the Great Siege Tunnels or St. Michael's Cave, but there are some wonderful views. Oh, and there's an old Moorish sentry post still standing, not very far down the path to my left. Dates from the twelfth century. Not much to it, really, but you might find it interesting, or, er . . . well, that's about it, I suppose, given our time constraints."

"Buck and I will go up to the cafeteria," Audrey proclaimed. "Come, Buck." Without waiting for his concurrence, she headed for the steps.

Buck shrugged his brawny shoulders. "Yes, ma'am," he said with his tolerant, aw-shucks smile, and obeyed, shambling after her like a good-natured trained bear.

"That's Audrey's husband?" Julie murmured, shaking her head. "I can't get over it."

Gideon had been no less surprised at meeting Craig "Buck" Pope the evening before. To call it a marriage of opposites was to put it mildly. Audrey—whom Gideon knew fairly well, having worked with her several times, both on committees and in the field—was virtually unchanged in the ten years that he had known her. A tiny, bird-boned woman in her sixties, wiry and closed-faced, with long-out-of-date harlequin glasses resting on a blue-tinged, blade-like nose, and iron gray hair forced into an untidy bun, usually with a couple of pencils sticking out of it, she was everybody's image of a turn-of-the-century—the twentieth century—spinster schoolmarm, the kind that lived in somebody's rented attic and smelled of chalk dust. All she needed was a high-necked, frilled collar and a cameo brooch.

Buck, on the other hand, was a retired Army master sergeant from Oklahoma, twice Audrey's size, with a voice like a gravel spreader but a gentle manner. His formal schooling had stopped with a community college degree, but he was now an instructor in infantry field tactics at a military institute outside of Chicago. Outgoing, friendly, and a live-and-let-live type, where Audrey was severe, demanding, and inclined by nature to be censorious, he seemed utterly unsuited to her. But they had been married for at least twenty years—a late first marriage for both—and as far as Gideon could see, they got along splendidly. Buck treated her with a solicitous, old-fashioned courtesy, gentling her as he would a cantankerous horse, obeying her frequently imperious commands with what seemed like an indulgent if slightly amused affection, and in general, speaking only when spoken to.

But if he did open his mouth to say something when they were in a group—and this is what really came as a surprise—Audrey instantly took an adoring backseat, refraining from all interruption, correction, and disagreement. This was extraordinarily un-Audrey-like behavior, particularly astonishing coming from one of archaeology's leading and most outspoken feminists.

"And they get along like that all the time," said Pru, who had once worked with Audrey for over a year and knew her well. "Is a puzzlement. I never get tired of watching them together. Well, I think I'll go up to the souvenir shop, and then just stroll around for a while."

Julie not very hopefully suggested a cup of cocoa to Gideon, but as she expected, he was interested in seeing the Moorish sentry post.

She looked doubtful. "It's getting pretty cold. And look at that fog roll in."

Indeed, the weather had worsened in the last few minutes, and, although they were wearing fleece pullovers under windbreakers, the warmest clothes they'd brought, they were chilled through, Gideon no less than Julie. They'd been warned that, while Gibraltar town could be counted on for year-round summery temperatures—it could be considered part of the Costa del Sol if you wanted to stretch a point—it could get quite chilly on top of the Rock. But they had foolishly scoffed. They were used to hiking in the multiglaciered, seven-thousand-foot Olympics. A mere thousand-foot "mountain" was something to be sneered at. But they hadn't taken this fog, this cold, whirling, penetrating, wind-driven fog, into account.

"You go on and have your cocoa, sweetheart," Gideon said. "I'll only be a little while."

"Well, keep your mind on where you're walking, will you? They're not exactly big on guardrails up here, and visibility is getting pretty poor, and it's a long way to the bottom."

"I appreciate your wifely concern," he said, laughing, "but don't worry. I have no intention of falling off the Rock of Gibraltar."

"It's only that your mind has a way of wandering sometimes—now, you know it has—and if you're not paying attention to where you're going—"

"Julie," he said, taking her by both arms, and looking squarely into her eyes and speaking firmly, "go and have your cocoa. I promise you, I am not, repeat, *not*—going to fall off the Rock of Gibraltar."

FIVE

AND he didn't; not for almost fifteen minutes.

The Moorish outbuilding turned out to be on the very top of the long ridge that crested the main body of the Rock, above the footpath, so that to reach it he had to mount thirty or forty steep, high steps that had been roughly carved into the limestone. These he climbed, working his way around two monkeys that only grudgingly moved aside for him. He could practically hear them sigh in exasperation. In the middle of the top step was a third one, a particularly big one, baboon-sized, that looked as if he had no intention of letting Gideon or anyone else get by him. Gideon stopped and took an unopened bag of peanuts from his pocket.

"Here, pal," he said, making amends to all monkeys collectively. "I'm fresh out of Curly Wurlies, but maybe you'd like this? With my apologies for my earlier remarks, of course. And then perhaps you'd be kind enough to let me by?"

The monkey looked without interest at the bag and turned away his head.

"Monkeys *like* peanuts, don't you know that?" Gideon asked. "Here, want me to open it for you?" He pulled apart the top of the bag and offered it. The monkey glanced up into his face with a what-the-hell-do-I-have-to-do-to-get-rid-of-this-guy expression, sauntered a few steps away, turned his back, and sullenly sat down again.

"Be that way," Gideon said, turning his attention to the outbuilding.

It was old, all right, a small, cylindrical structure—room enough for only one man—with a conical cap of a roof and a narrow, arched entrance. The construction was a mix of roughly cut limestone, ancient mortar, cracked, crumbling cement of some kind for the roof and floor, and thin slabs of orange brick to create the curve of the doorway's arch and to patch the walls where stone blocks had come out or been destroyed. It was precariously sited right smack at the very edge—the *very* edge—of the near-vertical cliff that formed the long eastern wall of the Rock, so close that Gideon assumed that it must originally have been built at the back of what had been a rock overhang that had collapsed at some point along the way. The entrance and two small, high windows just below the interior roofline all faced out over the edge, so that the man in it could, on a clearer day than today, spot sails approaching from the Mediterranean many, many hours before they arrived. There were no openings on the other side, toward Gibraltar town, from which, of course, no hostile forces would have been expected.

The wind up here was so gusty and strong that it shredded the fog in places, and he caught a sudden, unnerving glimpse straight down over the edge. An almost perpendicular gray wall fell dizzyingly away, its upper reaches devoid of plant life other than a few scrubby wisps of broom clinging to life in tiny crevices, and a single, stubborn, gnarled Aleppo pine sticking straight out of the cliff about twenty feet beneath him. A thousand dizzying feet below, bathed in wispy sunlight, was a narrow, rocky beach, gray and desolate.

"Whoo," Gideon breathed, pulling back from the rim and laying his hand firmly on the solid little hut for safety's sake. A man who knew himself to be reasonably brave in most situations, he had no head—and no stomach—for heights. And the wind gusts did nothing for his sense of security.

What a miserably cold, solitary station this would have been, he thought as he bent his six-foot-one frame to gingerly squeeze through the entrance. Because of its proximity to the edge, it couldn't be approached from directly in front. He had to do it by standing on the side of the hut, chest pressed against it, getting a death grip on the margin of the doorway with his right hand, and more or less slithering along the surface and pulling himself inside; not a comfortable maneuver, but he wasn't about to quit now. Not that he didn't consider it.

Inside it was a little roomier than anticipated. He was able to stand to his full height and to stretch his arms almost fully out to the sides, but not above his head. It was as moldy and dank as expected, and it smelled like a bear cave after a long winter, but, as always for Gideon, it was filled with the fascination of ancient things and long-dead inhabitants. He was standing in an enclosure, he thought happily, in which watchful men had stood before America was on anybody's map, before the Magna Carta, before Galileo and da Vinci and Michelangelo, before the Gutenberg Bible, before—

He wasn't alone. As his eyes adapted to the dimness, he realized that the place was still occupied. Christ, no wonder it smelled like a zoo. Two sleeping, leathery brown bats hung peacefully by their feet from the uneven roof, and an owl he'd incompletely awakened grumbled and muttered and ruffled its feathers, and then sank its head into its chest to go back to sleep. More unsettling, less than two feet from his eyes, a now-wide-awake, nesting peregrine falcon rose menacingly onto its powerful yellow legs and hissed at him, its beak agape. Beneath it lay three rust-colored eggs.

Now, a peregrine falcon isn't much bigger than a crow, but it is a natural predator, it has a bad temper, and being confined in a small space with it is not recommended by bird books. It has the viciously hooked beak, the talons, and the ferocious yellow eyes of an eagle, and Gideon had read somewhere that when attacking its prey—or the presumed enemies of its young—it is believed to be the fastest animal in the world.

He didn't give it a chance to prove it. In a flash he had regrasped the margin of the arched doorway and heaved himself around to the outside, tottering momentarily but frighteningly on the edge of the cliff, his heart pounding away, as a wind gust snatched at him. The sooner he—

Before his mind could grasp what was happening, he was sliding down the face of the cliff, scrabbling desperately at the rough surface for a handhold that wasn't there.

My God, he thought dully, *I'm dead. Julie—*

Whump! "Ow! Oogh!" The breath was knocked out of him with a whoosh, and for a few seconds it took all his concentration to get his lungs going. Once that was accomplished, his mind started working again.

Why was he still alive? He opened his eyes.

He was sitting—literally sitting—in a tree, the lone Aleppo pine he'd seen from above, in which he was wedged remarkably solidly into a crotch between the trunk, the thick, blessedly sturdy trunk, and two not-quite-so-sturdy branches. Looking down, his eyes were caught by the twigs and stones he'd broken loose, tumbling and falling away from him, down the gray cliffside, bouncing off the wall, down, and down . . .

He stopped looking down.

What had happened was already becoming fuzzy. Had a gust of wind thrown him off balance? Had he been pushed? He tried to reconstruct the moment, the feeling just before his fall. Had there been a *thrust*? Had he felt hands on his hip? Had some windborne object struck him? Had there been a sound? Had he— He shook his head. No good. It had happened only seconds ago, but already the memory, if it was there at all, was dissolving, like the wisps of last night's dream.

As the helpless, mindless panic of his fall subsided and his breathing became more regular, he took stock of his situation. The trunk seemed solid enough. It hadn't seemed to give much when he landed on it, and he was relieved to see a set of thick roots twining into whatever earth they could find between heavy slabs of rock. The two branches supporting him were less conducive to serenity. They had given, all right, almost bouncing him back into space, and they were still quivering from the shock of it. When he shifted his weight to a less painful position, he felt them bend under him, and one of them gave out an ominous, thin, snapping sound.

He stopped shifting his weight.

Still, he wasn't dead after all; that was the critical thing. He breathed out a sigh. As long as he didn't move, he was safe.

By now his wits had returned to the extent that the thought made him laugh. Safe, as long as he sat in, or rather *on*, a dwarf tree sticking out of the side of the Rock of Gibraltar, a thousand feet in the air, with nothing at all between him and the stony beach at the bottom, and twenty feet of nearly vertical cliff face between him and safety of a more permanent sort at the top.

He tried calling out, but gave it up after his second "Hello . . . is anybody there?" (He felt too ridiculous to sit there in his tree yelling, "Help!") Whatever he yelled, he realized no one was going to answer anyway. If someone had actually pushed him, whoever had done it had probably already fled, and if not, he wasn't about to come to his aid. To reach anyone else, his voice would have to carry up and over the top of the ridge and down the long stone stairwell to the trail. And even if his voice did carry, which it wouldn't—not in this wind—who was there to hear him? If there was anybody out on the trail in this weather, Gideon certainly hadn't seen him.

All right then, it was up to him to get himself out of there. Time for a plan. Julie, in her park-ranger mode, said that the best plan, the best thing you could do if you were lost or in trouble, as long as you weren't in danger of imminent death, was to stay put. People would come and find you, especially if they had some idea of where you'd been going. And in this case, Julie knew he'd been headed for the watchtower, and Rowley knew exactly where it was. So how long would it be before they came looking? Well, at least another forty minutes: half an hour before they started worrying about him, and ten minutes to get here. After that, it would be another twenty minutes, because they'd have to go back to the cable terminal building and return with some rope. So, at a minimum, an hour, all told. Could he last that long?

Not a chance. Oh, the tree felt solid enough, even with that *crack* he'd heard, but the fact was, he didn't trust himself not to fall out of the damn thing. Balance had never been his strong suit. He'd fallen into more than one stream from more than one log bridge that his companions had crossed without a problem. And that had been from heights of three or four feet, not with a thousand feet of empty space under him and fierce, spiteful gusts of wind whack-

ing away at him. Some people were said to be seized by a
near-irresistible urge to jump when they found themselves
looking down from a height like this. Not him. All he had
was an irresistible certainty that he'd fall out of the damn
tree if he sat there long enough.

No, it was time to go.

He looked at the wall of solid rock that loomed above
him. Well, not exactly what you'd call solid rock, really.
Mostly, it was composed of what appeared to be a com-
pacted, gravelly clay of some kind, with outcroppings of
limestone pushing through it here and there. The Aleppo
had improbably grown from one such outcropping, winding its roots through and around the limestone to reach the
clay beneath. About fifteen feet above him—only five feet
below the top of the Rock—was another such outcrop. If
he could manage to pull himself up onto that and then
stand up on it—not a happy thought, but he could do it—
he'd be home free; he could reach the top from there and
pull himself up. The problem was getting to the outcropping in the first place. He could shinny the two feet from
where he was to the base of the tree and get up on *this* outcropping. From there, given his height, he'd easily be able
to reach up another eight feet.

Which left seven to be accounted for. Taking extreme
care not to look down again, he hitched himself along the
trunk an inch at a time, then leaned forward to test the clay
near the outcropping to see if it was soft enough to dig footholds in, yet firm enough to hold his weight. Firm enough
was definitely not the problem. The stuff was more like
breccia than clay: a conglomerate of little pieces of rock in
a coarse matrix that seemed to be some kind of hard sandstone. When he dug at it with his fingers—holding grimly
on to a root with his other hand and wrapping his legs
around the trunk as tightly as they would go—all he did
was tear a fingernail. And now for the first time he noticed

that he'd torn a couple of other nails on the way down, and scraped his knuckles as well. He'd hurt his back too, he realized, although it didn't feel like anything serious—just an abrasion or two and maybe a strained muscle, and a little bruising; nothing too bad . . . he hoped.

But that was something to worry about later. For now, he had to get back up, and the thing to do was obvious. If there was nothing that would serve as hand- and footholds, he would have to carve out his own. Fortunately for him, the tools were right there. The roots of the Aleppo, in their unremitting search for sustenance, had split and fractured the rock, leaving a couple of football-sized chunks lodged in their coils. Tugging the smaller chunk out (no easy task for Gideon, considering his nervous-making perch) he found that it would indeed do the job; by repeatedly pounding its broken edge against the sandstone, he was able to dig out a small cavity.

But it was far too heavy to be a useful tool, a good twelve or fifteen pounds; it took two hands to keep it going for more than a short time, and he most definitely didn't have two free hands. He was worried about his endurance too. What he needed was a smaller rock, but a quick probing of the outcrop showed that there was nothing that would do. The one other chunk that he could pull out was about the same size as the first one. All right, then, using both of them, he'd make his own. He'd spent a good many hours one summer teaching himself the craft of prehistoric stone-knapping, and although the art of fine-edge pressure-flaking had been beyond him (he'd spent more time applying Band-Aids than turning out arrowheads), he'd done pretty well with the less complex skills involved in percussion-flaking, which, at its most basic level, consisted of using a hammer stone to chip away at the edges of a core stone or "blank" to create a crude hand ax or chopper.

In simpler terms, you banged one rock against another until something gave.

It helped, of course, if the banger was harder than the bangee, and if the bangee was made of flint, or obsidian, or something else that would fracture along regular, predictable planes, but these were luxuries he didn't have. What he had were two pieces of limestone. Setting the smaller one on the trunk between his thighs, with its cleanest edge up and at a slight angle (if you struck the edge straight on, you'd just crumble it away), he delivered his first careful blow with the other one, his aim being not merely to break the rock in two, but with a series of well-placed blows to produce a finer implement, sharp-edged and shaped to the hand.

The first blow produced nothing; only a sharp little *clack*. He tried again. This time the hammer stone glanced off the core and drove painfully into his thigh. He winced. That was going to be another bruise. The hell with producing a finer implement, he decided. Any old chopper would do, as long as he could operate it with one hand. He tried another blow, harder. Nothing. Even harder. A tiny chip came off the wrong rock. Frustrated, grunting with the effort, he clenched his teeth and raised the hammer stone over his head—

"What in the world are you doing down there?" Pru McGinnis's wondering voice floated down to him from the top.

"Pru!" he cried, looking up. "Am I glad to see you!"

She looked down at him, thoughtfully chewing on her lower lip. "Umm . . . I don't suppose you could use a little help?"

SIX

"SO I look down and what do I see?"

Pru was zestfully regaling an enthralled, aghast Julie. "It was awe-inspiring, positively cosmic, as if I was watching the very dawn of mankind re-created before me. There he was, this primitive, hulking creature crouched in his tree, grunting, at the very moment of the invention of toolmaking. You could see the intense concentration on his face as he crudely hammered his rocks together, in preparation for coming down from his arboreal abode and standing erect upon the earth on his own two legs."

A subdued Gideon offered a modest correction. "Coming *up* from my arboreal abode, actually."

Which was the first time Julie relaxed enough to laugh. "But you *are* okay?" she asked for the third or fourth time.

"I'm fine, honey. A few dings, a few scuffs, but all in all, in pretty good shape for a guy who fell off the Rock of Gibraltar."

And now the laughter turned to relieved giggles. "'I

appreciate your wifely concern,' " she mimicked, dropping her voice an octave and adding a supercilious, mock-English accent, " 'but don't worry, I have *no* intention whatever of falling off the Rock of Gibraltar.' "

"I did not say 'whatever,' " Gideon muttered, but then ruefully laughed along with her. "Next time I'll pay more attention."

They were in the tiny bar-restaurant, midway through the simple, satisfying luncheon of roast chicken, chips, and salad, along with bottles of cold white Montilla wine from across the border. Julie, Gideon, and Pru were at the larger of the two tables, speaking quietly, preferring to keep their conversation private.

Between the two of them, Gideon and Pru had described how she had found him. She had been walking on the trail without anything in particular in mind when she heard a *clack-clack-clack* sound, "as if someone was banging two stones together." Curious, she had climbed up to the sentry post, looked down, and found Gideon doing exactly that. She had hurried back to the cable car terminal and located an employee who was able to get hold of a stout, twenty-five-foot electrical extension cord. The two of them had then run back and used the cord to "walk" Gideon up the cliff face.

"It was really exciting," Pru declared. "It was *fun!*"

"It was exciting, all right," Gideon admitted. "I don't know about fun. Maybe five years from now it might seem as if it was fun."

"And you still really think you might have been pushed?" Julie asked.

He shrugged. As time had passed, a conviction that he had indeed been pushed had first grown, then shrunk. On the one hand, it seemed impossible that he could have fallen off the Rock on his own, but wasn't that just what he'd done on those log bridges? No one had pushed him then;

he'd managed to fall off without any help. Maybe the same thing had happened here. There was that nasty wind, after all. "I don't know. I *think* I felt something . . . a push." He touched his right hip, just above the hip pocket. "Here." Another shrug. "I think."

"You don't sound very positive."

"I'm not. But I just can't believe I did it all by myself. I mean, did you ever hear of anybody accidentally falling off the Rock of Gibraltar?"

"Most people who fell off the Rock wouldn't be able to talk about it afterward," Pru pointed out. "You had a little luck on your side." She and Julie were both clearly disinclined to believe anyone had pushed him.

Julie gently touched the back of his hand. "No offense, sweetheart, but you're . . . how do I put this? You're really not very good with heights."

"Tell me about it," he said with a sigh. "All the same—"

"Gideon, listen. Let's assume for a minute that somebody really did push you. If that were true, it would pretty much have to be someone right here in this room, wouldn't it? Who else would have any idea where you were? Who else that you know would be in Gibraltar? Why would anyone else want to . . . well, kill you?"

"Why would anyone in this *room* want to kill me?"

"That's what I was wondering."

He nodded. "Yeah, you're right," he said. "I guess."

A few moments of meditative silence followed, until Pru, having wrested the last shred of white meat from her half chicken, jerked her head and gestured decisively with her fork. "Okay, I've thought it through, and I simply can't see anyone having pushed you. It doesn't hold water." She shoved her plate away and moved her wineglass nearer.

"Look," she whispered, leaning closer in. "Do you really believe someone here—one of these people—harmless, fusty, certified academics right down to their sensible shoes—not only *wanted* to murder you . . . well, on second thought, that part I can believe—"

"Thank you so much."

"—but went so far as to actually try to *do* it? No, that's straining credulity. Think about it. Aside from the guts it would take, he would have had to follow you down the trail, carefully keeping out of sight, then follow you up the steps, then—"

"That's not necessarily true. He could have heard me say I was going to go up there, and then gotten there before me and waited."

"Even so, he would have had to hide behind a rock or something until you went into the hut, then skulk up and crouch behind it, waiting for you to come out, then shove you over at exactly the right moment, when you were right on the edge—all without being seen, I might add—and then run back here before anyone noticed. And act as if nothing happened." She sat back. "That, if you'll permit me to say so, is a pretty bizarre hypothesis."

Yes, it was, but that hadn't stopped him from entertaining it. When he'd walked in with Pru only a few minutes late for lunch, after getting his bloodied knuckles washed and sprayed with an antibiotic, he couldn't help scanning the room, searching for a guilty face, or more likely, one that looked astonished at seeing him alive. He didn't find any. They all looked exactly like their everyday selves, with no special interest in him. And none of them did have any special interest in him, that was a major sticking point. Except for Pru, he knew none of them very well, and most hardly at all. His only connection to most of them was his lab work on the First Family and the subsequent paper that came out of it, and there had been nothing in those to provoke their antagonism. On the contrary, his phrase describing Gibraltar Boy—"a seeming phenotypical mosaic of Neanderthal and *Homo sapiens* traits"—had helped catapult almost everyone associated with the dig to vastly increased prominence. (When they quoted it, which they often did, the "seeming" usually fell by the wayside.)

All the same, he couldn't get the idea out of his mind. If he squeezed his eyes shut he could feel . . . he could almost feel . . . he could imagine he could feel . . . that quick, firm shove at his hip. . . .

"Well?" Pru pressed when nothing was forthcoming from him.

He came back to the present. "He wouldn't have had to be hiding while I was inside the hut," he said. "All the openings—the doorway, the little windows—looked out in the other direction, over the Med. He could have walked right up and stood there waiting for me to come out, and I'd never have known it."

"Even so—," she began impatiently.

"I know, I know. It's pretty unlikely."

"It's damn unlikely."

The waitress came and collected their plates. "What'll it be for pud?" she asked. "Choice of jam roly-poly, apple crumble, or gateau."

"Jam roly-poly for me," Pru said with enthusiasm. "And coffee."

"What'll it be for *what*?" asked Julie.

"Pud," Gideon said. "Pudding. Dessert. We're in the UK now."

"Oh. I'll pass. Just coffee, please. I'm still too keyed up for dessert."

Not Gideon. He had wolfed down the chicken and chips, but he was still ravenous. "I'll have the apple crumble. And coffee for me too."

"Okay, here's another possibility," Pru said as the waitress moved off. "Couldn't it have been the wind?"

"I doubt it."

"What about something blown *by* the wind?" suggested

Julie. She was trying to give him a graceful, reasonable out, a way of having fallen off the Rock of Gibraltar that wasn't his own dumb fault. "I don't know, a piece of cardboard, an empty carton? You said you didn't have your feet planted very firmly. Something like a cardboard carton might have been enough to —"

"Uh-uh. I thought about that for a minute too, but it was blowing the other way." He tipped his head in the direction of Adrian Vanderwater. "A *levanter*, remember? Not a *poniente*."

"All right, then, isn't it possible that when a gust hit you, you kind of leaned against it—you know, overcompensated—and then when it suddenly stopped, over you went in the other direction?"

"Yes," he said slowly, "I guess that is possible. I just think . . ." He shook his head, not sure what he had just thought. Who knows, maybe it had been the wind.

Their coffee and desserts were brought and placed before them. Julie grimaced at the pale, glistening mass on Pru's plate. "What is that, exactly?"

"Something you don't see in the States anymore," Pru said, scrutinizing it with obvious relish. "A roly-poly. It's a suet pudding. They flatten it and roll it up around a jam filling. Have you ever had suet pudding? Want a bite?"

"Um . . . no, I don't think so."

"Weenie," Pru said, getting ready to attack her dessert with the soup spoon that had been provided.

"You know what they called jam roly-polys in the eighteen hundreds?" Gideon asked. "Dead man's arm. Because they used to steam it—and serve it—in an old shirtsleeve."

"If that's meant to affect my appetite, dream on," Pru said, digging in.

Gideon was feeling pretty mellow by now. Not ordinarily a lunchtime drinker, he'd thirstily consumed two glasses of the cold Montilla, and the pungent, strong wine, more like a rough sherry than a dinner wine, had given him a pleasant glow. With alcohol coursing through a nervous system that had already been given a roller-coaster of an adrenaline ride only an hour earlier, he was seeing the world in a different light now. They were probably right. He'd lost his balance, that was all. And if they were willing to believe that the wind had a part in it, so was he.

It was perfectly credible. Why dream up some complex theory of who and why and how? What had happened to his adherence to Occam's razor, the principle of parsimony that he was always prating about to his classes, the idea that if you have a simple theory that satisfactorily explains the facts, you don't go around "unnecessarily multiplying uncertainties," that is, dreaming up more complex ones? He'd taken a heck of a tumble, he'd very naturally panicked, and the result had been a bout of rather absurd paranoia.

"You're both right," he said, methodically working away at his apple crumble, a palatable British version of apple crisp. "I overreacted."

"Well, it's no wonder," Julie said kindly, patently glad to see him returning to his logical, reasonable self.

"Hold it, I just had another thought," Pru said, scooping up the last of the puddled custard on which her demolished roly-poly had lain. "What have you got in that pocket, Gideon? I heard something crackle in there."

"I don't know." He reached in and pulled out the opened bag of peanuts. "These. Why?"

"And you said there were monkeys around?"

"Yes. In fact, I offered them to one of them, but—wait a minute, you think a *monkey*—"

"Why not? Grabbing for the bag and accidentally pushing you off balance? They're strong, you know that. And they could easily reach your hip. And if you offered the bag to one before, then he probably saw where it came from," she said. "It makes more sense than anything else, Gideon."

Another graceful out, this one provided by Pru.

He smiled gratefully at her. "It certainly does." And now that he thought about it, it did. It would account for the one thing the wind didn't account for: the touch on his hip that he thought—imagined?—he'd felt. It made sense. It explained things more simply and logically than having to construct a villain or even a cantankerous wind. He liked it. Thomas of Occam would have liked it too. He relaxed a little more.

"In fact, now that monkeys are in the picture," Julie put in brightly, "maybe it wasn't so innocent. I wonder if he didn't do it on purpose. Maybe you shouldn't have said all those nasty things about monkeys. They have feelings too, you know."

"I tried to apologize to the big guy on the top step," Gideon said, willingly going along with the change in mood. "The peanuts were supposed to be a peace offering. He wasn't buying it."

"Hey," Pru said, "maybe it was a desperado-type monkey, one of those bad-to-the-bone monkeys, a homicidal monkey. A sociopath monkey." Pensively, she put a forefinger to her pursed lips.

"Tell me, was he wearing sunglasses, by any chance?"

SEVEN

TINK-TINK. Tink-tink-tink.

The tapping of Adrian Vanderwater's fingernail on his glass had its intended effect. His fellow diners in the Top of the Rock Bar and Restaurant ceased their several conversations and turned amiably toward him.

With Adrian at the smaller of the two tables was his one-time student Corbin Hobgood, now an associate professor at Stanford and the man who had been Adrian's assistant director on the Europa Point dig. On the three bar stools were Rowley Boyd, Audrey Godwin-Pope, and Audrey's husband, Buck.

"Ladies and gentlemen," Adrian was saying, "I think we all owe a debt of thanks to Rowley and the Museum of Archaeology and Geology for their generosity in arranging this delightful outing and the superb lunch we've just enjoyed."

Wine and water glasses were lifted in Rowley's direction. "Hear, hear," came from someone.

"Yeah, but you could have done a better job with the weather," Pru said to general laughter.

"But what could I possibly have done about the weather?" Rowley asked earnestly, going off into a long, serious explanation of how, because of the conference programming, this was the only day that he could confidently assume that everyone would be free for an outing to the Rock. If it had been possible to arrange for a day with better weather, he would have done so, and so on. And on.

Gideon couldn't help smiling. He knew Rowley from having run into him at various meetings, and he had come to know him as a charming, cheerful, almost cherubic man. But he was also just about the most literal-minded person he had ever met. Irony was totally lost on him. In its April 1997 issue, *Discover* magazine had run a playful article about some Neanderthal musical instruments that had supposedly been newly discovered in Germany's Neander Valley, including a tuba (made from a mastodon tusk), a bagpipe (made from the bladder of a woolly rhinoceros), and a collection of hollowed-out bones that was dubbed a xylobone. The alleged discoverer of these instruments, "Adrian Todkopf," went so far as to theorize that the Neanderthals' fondness for music might well have accounted for their extinction: "Maybe their music scared away all the game. They would have produced an awful racket oompah-pahing all over the place."

To Gideon's knowledge, no one other than a handful of creationists took it as anything but the joke it was—except for Rowley Boyd. Shortly after the article came out, Gideon had sat, one of a half dozen mortified fellow anthropologists, as Rowley heatedly (for him) and at length attacked the article as preposterous . . . because, among other things, "the true woolly rhinoceros—*Coelodonta antiquitatis*—has never been associated with the Neander Valley!" When it was gently explained to him that the article was an April

Fool's gag, his response was a stricken, incredulous question: *"Why would anyone joke about something like that?"*

". . . but now," Adrian continued, as always serenely oblivious to the prattling of others, "inasmuch as all of us who are going to take part in this evening's festivities are here together, it might be a good time to finalize the program plans. Corbin, my boy, perhaps you'd care to address the details." There weren't many people who could call a Stanford professor "my boy" and get away with it, but Adrian was one of them.

"Certainly, Dr. Vanderwater," Corbin said soberly, having cleared his throat first. The minutely but heavily written-upon four-by-six card in front of him showed that he had already given the matter considerable thought. "As our first order of business, I suggest we agree upon a moderator for the event, someone to run things and keep us to a schedule."

"Can't you do that, Corbin?" someone suggested.

"I suppose so . . . yes," Corbin replied as guardedly as if he'd been asked to facilitate the next session of the UN Commission on Disarmament, "but I think it would be more appropriate to have someone of greater stature. Dr. Vanderwater, would you be willing to take that on?"

"Well, I don't know about 'running things,'" Adrian said jovially, tipping a few drops of Tullamore Dew into his coffee from his leather-covered flask, "but I'll be glad to apply the hook if people run on too long. That is, if the others would like me to."

This was met with generally mild acclamation and a little indifferent hand-clapping. Nobody gave much of a damn, it appeared. Except Audrey Godwin-Pope, Gideon observed. Audrey's head snapped up and her eyes glinted with something like indignation, but only for a moment, after which she'd joined in the tepid applause.

How like the three of them, a now thoroughly relaxed Gideon thought with amusement. For fat, rosy-cheeked Adrian, affable and avuncular, the limelight was his natural habitat, and wherever he was, in whatever group, he gravitated naturally to it. The idea that anyone might object would have come as a crushing blow to him. Corbin, on the other hand, was just the man you'd want in charge of the behind-the-scenes details; the more trivial they were, the harder he'd work. And Audrey—so capable and accomplished in her own right, and yet so sensitive to slights, real or fancied, so vigilant in protecting her status against all comers.

In a very real way, Adrian's happy association with the Europa Point dig was due to Audrey. As the Horizon Foundation's director of field archaeology, she'd been the one who had invited him to direct the dig when Ivan Gunderson had offered the site to them. It was no secret, however, that at first she'd been far from satisfied with what she considered to be Adrian's extravagantly expensive running of it. She had maintained close administrative oversight and they had quarreled several times over costs. Adrian had grumbled publicly about Horizon's penny-pinching approach to staffing and equipment, but Audrey, in control of the purse strings, had won every time, which must have infuriated Adrian. As soon as the First Family was unearthed and the news hit the media, however, hostilities were suspended, the coffers were opened wide, and everything turned rosy, but Audrey, who could hold a grudge for a long time, must have been hell to work for all the same.

Thankfully, Gideon had never been in that position, but he'd seen her in action in other situations. At a conference in Boston once, when she had made the arrangements for a dinner party of eight, including Gideon, at a Thai restaurant, the hostess had called for the "Garwin Poe" party.

"It's Godwin," Audrey had told her. "And Pope, not Poe."

"Madam, that is what I said."

"No, you said *Gar*win. It's *God*win. Godwin-Pope."

"Gardwin?"

"No, *Godwin*. G-o-d-w . . ."

And on and on, to the embarrassment of the dinner party and the consternation of the Thai hostess until the poor woman got it right. And this was a place Audrey had never been to before and was unlikely ever to go to again. So what was the point? But that was Audrey.

Along the same lines, a mutual acquaintance named Victoria Tarr had confided to him that, for a time, Audrey had stopped by Vicky's house for coffee once or twice a week. Whenever Vicky went in afterward to tidy up the guest bathroom in the event that Audrey had used it, she found that the toilet paper roll had unfailingly been reversed so that the new sheets unrolled from the top, instead of the less standard way that Vicky preferred it, with the new sheets coming from the bottom.

Once again, that was Audrey. Things had to be right.

Dry-stick appearance and prickly manner notwithstanding, however, Gideon had always liked her, in small doses at any rate, partly because of the wry, pithy sense of humor that would sometimes come peeking through the arid exterior. She had a pet parakeet, for example, which she had named Onan. Why Onan? "Because," she had replied drily, "he casts his seeds upon the ground."

She was also a surprisingly good mimic, even of men's voices, once she had a couple of glasses of wine inside her. "Who is this?" she would ask, looking suddenly up from her Chardonnay, and then proceed to skewer some colleague with wit and wicked accuracy. Gideon had once come in for a skewering himself. ("Greetings, sir, I am the Skeleton Wizard. If you will kindly show me your left *multangulum majus*, I will be glad to tell you who you are.") Gideon had laughed as appreciatively as everyone else.

In any case, she was someone to be reckoned with; a brilliant archaeologist, a more-than-competent administrator, and the author of over a hundred wide-ranging monographs. She was also a founding member and two time president of Sisters in Time, the feminist caucus of the International Archaeological Society. Forthright and free-spoken, she was in Gideon's opinion not well suited to her present position with Horizon, inasmuch as an important part of it involved getting money out of people, which necessarily involved tact and diplomacy, not her strongest points. Still, she'd been there for years now and seemed to be doing fine, so apparently he was wrong. Maybe it was the moderating influence of big, solid, benevolent Buck.

Corbin Hobgood he knew from having run into him at conferences and having served with him on a student-research grant program for AAA, the American Anthropological Association. In his late thirties, with pallid, shiny skin (in the field, no matter how steamy the location, he wore a broad-brimmed hat, long sleeves, and long pants to protect his melanin-challenged complexion), he had thick, black eyebrows that met in the middle and a jaw that was always shadowed, although he often shaved twice a day. He was, by all accounts—and Gideon's observations supported them—meticulous and hardworking, and he was reputed to be a decent field archaeologist as well. But he was a plodder, always drudging away, more at home with details and minutiae than with the provocative, exciting themes and patterns that made archaeology something alive. He was also cursed with a slow, nasal, maddeningly precise monotone that, depending on your mood at the time, could either put you to sleep or drive you up the wall.

But his positive traits—thoroughness, diligence, an exacting if narrowly focused intelligence—had worked in his favor, as had a certain tendency toward servility to authority that Gideon found unpleasant, but that some others apparently did not. He had been one of Adrian Vanderwater's last research assistants at Cal, and it was to his loyal, reliable former student that Adrian had turned when he was in need of an assistant director for the Europa Point dig. Corbin, for his part, had been born to be an assistant director. He accepted eagerly and was with Adrian from the beginning to the end of the excavation.

It had turned out extremely well for him. His association with Gibraltar Boy and the First Family had made his name. He had written several excruciatingly detailed papers on the dig, and two of Adrian's books on the subject listed Corbin as full coauthor (although Gideon had always assumed this was simply a generous gesture on Adrian's part; an expression of thanks for Corbin's probable assistance with bibliography, background research, data compilation, etc.). On the strength of all this, he was able to leave his position at Tunica State College in Mississippi, where he'd been locked into a disastrous specialty in ceramic techniques of the middle woodland horizon, and move into an assistant professorship at Stanford, where he had since acquired tenure and advanced to associate professor.

"Now then," Corbin said, having studied his card a few moments, "as to timing. I think we ought to keep the whole thing to no more than an hour and a half, so may I suggest that we all limit ourselves to fifteen minutes each at the most? Would fifteen minutes be agreeable to everyone . . . yes, Rowley?"

Rowley Boyd, looking uncomfortable, coughed discreetly and stood up, nervously sweeping back a few strands of lank, straw-colored hair from his forehead. "I just want to say that, ah, we might want to rethink tonight's event entirely. Ivan is . . . well, I don't know how to put it other than to say that he's not the man he was."

"As are none of us," Audrey said. "And your point is?"

"I only mean to say that, well, that he doesn't always . . . he's not always . . . we don't want to put too much, shall I say, stress on him, that's all I mean to say."

"I don't think there's much fear of that." Adrian laughed. "I've never known anyone to be overstressed by testimonials to his own eminence."

"No, you don't understand," Rowley persisted. "I'm suggesting that we eliminate the testimonials completely. Just present the awards and call it an evening. Keep it short. I say that entirely in his own interest."

Rowley was closer to Gunderson than any of them, and probably more in debt to him as well. Before the Europa Point dig, the Gibraltar Museum of Archaeology and Geology had been a virtually unfunded operation with a dedicated but unpaid part-time staff of a single archaeologist (Rowley), housed above a hole-in-the-wall Arab grocery store in George's Lane. Now it was in an impressive old naval headquarters building on Line Wall Road, with a salaried staff of eight, the finest cast of the First Family skeletons in existence, a collection of stone tools from the site, and three magnificent, life-sized dioramas of prehistoric life at Europa Point, including a torchlit, affecting scene of the burial in progress. All of this was thanks to Ivan Gunderson, only partly because of his initial excavation and subsequent donation of the dig site itself. More important, Gunderson, who now lived in Gibraltar most of the year (he had other homes in Palm Beach and Aix-en-Provence), had been extremely openhanded in his financial support of the museum. He was by far its most generous and reliable donor.

"Oh, bosh," Audrey said. "I spoke with Ivan by phone less than two weeks ago. He was very much his old self. He was very excited about the dinner."

But Rowley wouldn't be put off. "He has his moments, but I assure you, if you haven't seen him recently, you'll find him very much changed. He spends most of his time now, er, gluing pots."

That got everyone's attention. It wasn't simply the notion of the celebrated Ivan Gunderson sitting around gluing ceramic shards together all day, it was the very idea of *pots*. Gunderson had never had any interest in pots. The European Neanderthals and early humans to which he had devoted the last six decades of his life had never managed to make one. It had taken another 15,000 years before someone in Japan came up with the first pot.

"Gluing pots?" Adrian repeated dully. "What kind of pots?"

Rowley, twisting his hands around one another, looked miserable. "Any kind. I just get them from a ceramics shop in Ronda. I, er, break them up with a hammer and bring them to him and he glues them together. He puts them on shelves and forgets where he put them, and I take them away and . . . and break them again and bring them back, and he . . . well, he glues them together again. He never seems to notice."

There was shocked silence. Something squeezed Gideon's heart. "What does he imagine he's doing?" he asked quietly.

"I tell him I take them to the museum," Rowley said wretchedly. "Not that he asks very often."

"Is it Alzheimer's?"

"We don't know. I suppose so, but he won't see a doctor. He becomes angry if it's brought up."

Audrey was furious. "Rowley, for God's sake, I wish you would have told me this before. I'd never have arranged the damned dinner. Oh, the poor man. We'll have to cancel it. Oh, this is dreadful."

"Aw, honey," Buck said, "he'll love it, you'll see."

For once he had no effect on her. "Oh, poor Ivan. I had no idea—"

"No, no," Rowley interrupted, "Buck's right. Ivan is looking forward to it tremendously. He's been talking about it all week. It would be a terrible disappointment to him to call it off."

Audrey rounded impatiently on him. "So then what exactly is it that you're suggesting?"

"I'm suggesting that we have the reception and dinner as planned—moving things briskly along—and then present him with his awards." Here he was referring to the Horizon Foundation's V. Gordon Childe Lifetime Achievement Award in Archaeology, to be conferred by Audrey, and the annual Mons Calpe Medal from the Gibraltar Historical Association, which Rowley himself, as director of the museum, was to present.

"And then we simply call it a night and go home," Rowley continued. "No testimonials. It's really his awards that he's so excited about."

"No testimonials at all?" said Adrian bleakly.

Rowley offered an apologetic shrug. "Well, a few words with the awards, of course, but I really think it best that we don't do any more than that. He tires easily, you see, and when that happens, his mind tends to . . . his memory seems to . . . well, I fear that an hour of testimonial after testimonial would simply tax him too much." Another shrug, equally apologetic.

"It seems like the best thing to do," Gideon said, his spirits low. Others offered reluctant agreement. Everyone was disappointed. And depressed.

"As you may know, we have a similar situation arising in a few days, and we've been struggling with what to do about that one too," Rowley said by way of appeasement. "We've come to the same conclusion. No long addresses."

As Gideon knew, a public event was set for the day after tomorrow, at which the first shovelful of dirt was to be turned at what would eventually be the Europa Point

Prehistoric Site and Ivan S. Gunderson Visitor Center. Ivan, who had matched the public funding pound for pound, was supposed to make a speech and also have yet another award, the Honorary Freedom of the City of Gibraltar, bestowed on him by the territory's minister of culture.

Audrey was not that easy to appease. "I see," she said stiffly. "And assuming that we hold our own little dinner at all, can we be sure he's going to remember to come?"

"Absolutely. I'll be collecting him myself." Rowley hesitated. "He does have good days, you know. More often than not, actually. Perhaps this will be one."

"Let us fervently hope so," said Audrey with a roll of her eyes.

EIGHT

IT started off well enough.

The Rock Hotel, a long, white, six-story art deco building situated above Gibraltar town on the lower flanks of the Rock itself, and directly overlooking the Alameda Botanical Gardens, is by most accounts Gibraltar's finest, its register adorned with the names of royalty real, cinematic, and literary—Prince Andrew, Prince Edward, Sean Connery, Peter Sellers, Alec Guinness, John Steinbeck, Ernest Hemingway. Its particular gem is its marble-balustered Wisteria Terrace, a trellis-shaded patio set among lush plantings, filled with the sounds of birds, and looking out toward the wide bay with its tankers at rest, and in the distance, the gleaming rooftops of the Spanish town of Algeciras on the far shore. It was here that the participants gathered for cocktails and exotic canapés—lobster-and-fennel wontons, mini-éclairs with creamed prawns, ham rosettes on duck liver croutons—before going in to dinner.

Before that, most of them had already gathered in

Gideon and Julie's room for predrink drinks. Among the hotel's famous amenities (which included a bright yellow rubber duck in every guest bath and a supply of lollipops) was the provision each afternoon of a decanter of sherry and another of Scotch to every room. Gideon and Julie had earlier invited Pru to join them for a chat. She had been spotted carrying her Scotch decanter down the hall by Buck and Audrey and she had invited *them* to do the same, picking up Corbin and Adrian on the way. Even Rowley, who wasn't staying at the hotel, had stopped by for a few words with Audrey—and a small glass of sherry—before driving off to pick up the guest of honor. As a result, most of the attendees were already pretty well oiled—relaxed and good-humored—before they ever got to the Wisteria Terrace.

As was appropriate, Ivan Gunderson, urbane and smiling in the cream-colored, subtly beige-striped blazer and midnight blue silk ascot that had become his trademark dress, was the center of attention, and he performed brilliantly. Straight-up martini in hand, he graciously if somewhat regally mingled with the others, making sure to allow time for everyone. He had been quite charming on being introduced to Julie, bowing over her hand—for a moment Gideon wondered if he was going to kiss it—and wryly apologizing, in his elegant, agreeable tenor, for the boredom she was surely about to endure.

But it wasn't long before Gideon, whose lunchtime wine hadn't set well with him and was therefore one of the few not drinking, began to see that Rowley was right. Gunderson wasn't the same man he'd had last seen a couple of years ago. Age, lying confidently in wait for so long, had finally caught up to him with a vengeance. Oh, he still looked much the same; a little more stooped, a little more frail and tentative on his feet, but still the same tall, graceful frame that made any jacket look like an Armani, the same thick, scrupulously brushed mane of white hair, the same clear, ice blue eyes, the same kindly, appealing air of intelligence and reasonableness. But behind the polished surface, it became increasingly clear that a battle had been fought and lost. The witty, urbane Ivan Gunderson known to the world had been evicted, and a confused, forgetful, and probably frightened old man had taken up residence.

He was operating by rote now, and by instinct. He was still skilled at the little ceremonies of life; his remarks to Julie showed that. But he initiated almost nothing in the way of conversation. Say something to him with a smile, and he would smile back, and look amused and knowledgeable. Say it with a solemn shake of your head, and he would turn grave too, and shake his head as well, and commiserate with you in vaguely relevant terms. Gideon had warm and grateful memories of their early meetings, when the famous Ivan Gunderson had gone out of his way to be welcoming and helpful to the young, unknown physical anthropologist. It had been Gunderson who'd taken him in hand at the very first professional conference he'd attended, and had made sure that he was included in dinner plans and social outings. Through the years they had met a good dozen times, often at small, convivial dinners, but whether Gunderson now had any idea of who Gideon was was doubtful. Clearly, familiar words and phrases served as cues: *weather, archaeology, Gibraltar Boy, First Family, I believe the last time we met was in San Diego*—all would prompt replies, lively and seemingly pertinent, but at bottom no more than stimulus-response reactions.

He was good at it too, but after twenty minutes, the emptiness behind the words sank in for almost everyone, and Adrian's jocular suggestion that they go in and sit

down to dinner before they perished of hunger was greeted
with relief by all.

DINNER was in a private dining room where three tables had been arranged in the shape of a T in front of a
row of floor-to-ceiling windows. At the head was Gunderson, with Adrian to his right, and Audrey and Buck to his
left. At the table that formed the stem of the T were Julie
and Gideon, sitting across from Corbin and Pru. At the
bottom of the stem was Rowley, who had modestly turned
down the invitation to sit at the head table. Sun-dried tomato and couscous salads were brought out as soon as
they came in.

"Before we begin," said Adrian from behind his chair,
before sitting down, "I think it would be appropriate if we
all were to raise our glasses in memory of Sheila Chan, our
cherished friend and colleague, and my dear student, whom
we all mourn and miss."

"Sheila Chan," several others echoed. The glasses were
raised, sipped (Gideon's held tonic water), and set down,
followed by three or four seconds of silence, after which
the couscous salads were addressed and conversations were
resumed.

"Who's Sheila Chan?" Julie asked Gideon.

Gideon hunched his shoulders. "No idea. It's a familiar
name, though." He looked across the table at Pru and Corbin.
"Who's Sheila Chan?"

"You didn't know Sheila?" Pru said, surprised. "No,
that's right, of course you wouldn't have known her. But
you must have heard about what happened to her?"

A shake of the head from Gideon. "No. So, who was
she?"

"She was one of the area supervisors on the dig," Pru
said with the slightest of edges to her voice, "a hard worker,

competent—well, you knew her a lot better than I did, Corbin. Why don't you tell it?"

Corbin, whose mouth was fully occupied with cous-cous, nodded while he finished chewing, his long, gaunt, blue-tinged jaws working steadily, deliberately away, ten-dons popping and shifting as hard as if they were working on a slab of beef jerky. Finally he swallowed and sipped some water. "Yes, Sheila and I were grad students together at Cal, under Adrian."

Sheila had been two years ahead of him, he explained, although she never did finish up her doctorate because of, well, various problems. "Not academic, you understand, not at all; more . . . oh, personal. She was the sort of person—well, it's hard to describe—"

"No, it's not," said Pru. "She was impossible to work with. She couldn't get along with anybody."

"Oh, I wouldn't say that," said Rowley, who had been silent till now, his worried attention fixed on Gunderson at the head table. "I know she wasn't well liked, but she seemed nice enough to me. During the original dig, she spent some time at the museum—we had lunch together once—and I found her very stimulating company. An in-teresting person."

"You didn't know her that well," Pru said. "You never worked with her. Lunch isn't the same thing."

"Well, that's true enough," Rowley admitted, and went back to watching Gunderson. He leaned toward Gideon. "How does he seem to you?" he asked in a whispered aside.

"Hard to say, Rowley. All right, I think. I *hope*."

Rowley shook his head. "Oh, I hope so too." He had eaten no more than a third of his salad and was now back to gnawing on his unlit pipe.

"She had a chip on her shoulder like a two-by-four," Pru went on. "This lady walked around like a stick of dynamite just waiting for you to light her fuse. One of the reasons she didn't pass her comprehensives the second time was that she wound up telling her committee they didn't know what the hell they were talking about and stomping out."

"Not good," Gideon opined. "It's supposed to work the other way around." He was a little surprised at Pru's vehemence. There weren't many people she so actively disliked.

"It's not that I disagree with you entirely, but I think we should be a little more respectful of the dead," Corbin said.

"Oh, please," said Pru.

"She had a very hard upbringing, Pru, you know that." Corbin appealed to Gideon and Julie. "She never knew her parents. She grew up in foster homes, shuffled from pillar to post. No one ever adopted her."

"That's so," Pru allowed. "I suppose a childhood like that might have ruined even my sunny personality. Still, you have to admit, she went out of her way to make it hard to like her."

"She didn't make it easy," Corbin agreed, returning to his salad.

"Well, go ahead with the story," Julie suggested into the ensuing silence. "What happened?"

She had been unable to land a university position when she finished up her course work, Corbin went on. Things had been tight that year; he'd been lucky to land his own post with Tunica State—and of course Sheila's having an unfinished doctorate didn't help any. So she'd been teaching community college evening courses and working as a part-time consultant for an archaeological survey firm when Corbin, whose responsibilities as assistant director included staffing, brought her on as one of the site's three area supervisors, in hopes that it might flesh out her résumé a little.

"Her résumé wasn't the problem," said Pru.

Corbin ignored her. "It didn't do her much good, though, professionally speaking, even after the dig became famous. She never did hook up with a university. She applied for my spot when I left Tunica State and even they turned her down, along with everyone else. No one really knows why."

"*Au contraire*," said Pru. "Everyone knows why. Not only couldn't she finish her dissertation, but Adrian would never give his 'dear student' a decent referral."

"I don't know where you get your information," Corbin said prissily, "but I suppose everyone's entitled to their own opinion."

"Wait a minute," Gideon said as a few memories clinked into place. "Sheila Chan . . . I *did* know her, or at least we corresponded. She was the one doing a dissertation on Neanderthal genetic anomalies—on ankylosing spondylitis, in particular."

"Yes, that's right," Corbin said. "I'd forgotten, but as a matter of fact, now that I think of it, she told me how kind you'd been to her."

Julie had grown impatient. "But what was it that *happened* to her?"

"She died," said Corbin. He returned to his salad, apparently considering his contribution done.

"I know, but—"

"It was a couple of years after the dig ended," Pru said. "We were all back here—well, not *here*—most of us were at some of the cheap hotels downtown; Horizon wasn't picking up the tab then, and we were on our own nickel. It was called *Europa Point: A Retrospective*—a kind of mini-conference bringing things up to date on Gibraltar Boy and the First Family two years later; maybe fifteen contributors all together—people who had had some part in it—hey, come to think of it, why weren't you here, Gideon?"

"I remember being invited. Couldn't make it, I forget

why. But I did see the proceedings, of course. Excellent papers; a lot of good scholarship, well presented."

"Why, thank you, prof," said Pru, beaming. "I was program chair."

"Is somebody going to get around to what happened to Sheila Chan?" Julie pleaded through clenched teeth.

"She was killed in a cave-in," Pru said. "It was really bizarre. It was two days before they dug her out."

"That's awful," Julie said, "but why is it bizarre?"

"Because it was the Europa Point Cave itself where it happened. The whole hillside came down on her. It was like, you know, woo-hoo, the Curse of Europa Point."

"She wasn't supposed to be there at all, that was the sad part," Corbin said with a reproachful look at Pru. In his opinion, flippancy was out of place at any time, let alone when discussing a colleague's death. "It'd been rainy the year before, and the soil had loosened, and they had the site roped off because they thought there might be a landslide. After all, when you think about it, there had obviously been other landslides in the past, or we wouldn't have had to dig it out in the first place. But no, she paid no attention. She kept going there anyway."

"Actually, that wasn't the sad part," Pru said more pensively. "The sad part was that she had no relatives, nobody interested in having her body returned to them. She was cremated right here in Gibraltar, when they didn't know what else to do with her."

"That *is* sad," Julie said.

"Ivan paid for it," Corbin added. "He had her ashes scattered in the Strait."

"But why was she hanging around the site?" Gideon asked. "Wasn't the dig completed and closed down by then?"

"It was," Pru said. "That was the funny thing. But you know, I suppose there's always something that might have been missed. And she was *painstaking*, boy, I'll say that for her. Heck, she made Mr. Meticulous here"—a nod in Corbin's direction—"look positively slipshod. Hey, Rowley—"

Rowley started. He had gone back to watching Gunderson. "I'm sorry—what?"

"Did she ever tell you what she was after, fooling around in the cave? Apparently, you got along with her better than anyone else."

"But that was during the original dig. I don't think I said two words to her at the meetings the following year. I wasn't around very much."

"Of course you were around. You picked us up at the airport."

"Yes, I was *around*, but I spent almost all the time on a site survey on the west side, remember?"

"Oh, yes, so you did," Pru said.

"Another Neanderthal site?" Gideon asked.

"No, they were considering building a hotel, or perhaps it was a condominium, and the law requires that they get an archaeological evaluation before they do any digging. That's part of my job here. You never know what you might find. I've turned up two Neanderthal campsites that way in the past, and of course I was hoping for another, more permanent habitation."

"And did you find one?" Julie asked.

"Alas, no," said Rowley, turning apprehensive eyes on Gunderson again. "How does Ivan seem to you?"

THE salad plates were cleared and the main dish, grenadine of pork glazed with port wine and served with prune confit, was quickly brought. (The staff had been asked to be "brisk.") Over this aromatic dish, Corbin and Pru entertained the Olivers with the usual war stories about the personality conflicts and typical contretemps at the Europa

Point dig. By then, Gideon had unbent and had a glass of white wine, and the conversation was animated and entertaining.

At the head table, however, things were considerably more stilted. Gunderson's resources seemed to diminish by the minute. Audrey and Adrian, on either side of him, worked at trying to engage him in conversation, but Gunderson, eating with the single-minded avidity of the aged for their remaining pleasures, was in a ravenous world of his own, devouring his food as if he'd never have another opportunity. Gideon's heart sank further every time he looked up at him.

The only comment he was heard to make came when he had finished using a roll to mop up every last scrap of his dinner (an action that would have been unthinkable in the Ivan Gunderson of a few years ago).

"I don't remember my mother," Gunderson said suddenly and quite loudly, "but as I may have told you before, when my father remarried, his new wife brought her three grown daughters to live with us: Sally, Veronica, and Annie-Maude. So there I was, one impressionable young boy of eleven who'd never been around women, suddenly surrounded by a household of four of them. *Four* of them! Now that's enough to give anyone pause."

Everyone waited for whatever was coming next—a joke, an apocryphal story—but that was it. He reached for his wine and gazed uneasily about him, obviously wondering why everybody was looking at him.

Audrey cleared her throat. "Perhaps this would be a good time to get on with the ceremonies?"

Yes! Gideon urged silently.

Gunderson looked up anxiously. "We haven't had dessert yet."

"Well, why don't we begin our ceremonies while we await our dessert and coffee?" Adrian suggested mildly, and then, before Gunderson could reply, he said, "Rowley, why don't you start the festivities?"

Rowley hurriedly took his unlit pipe from his mouth, stood up, blushing, and made a warm, pleasant little speech about how much Gunderson had meant to the Territory of Gibraltar, recounting how the very first Neanderthal skeleton ever to be found anywhere, a female, had actually been discovered there in 1848, but no one had understood what it was until after a similar skeleton, a male, had turned up eight years later in the Neander Valley—*das Neander Thal*—near Dusseldorf.

"And so what might have been 'Gibraltar Woman' became instead 'Neanderthal Man,'" Rowley said, "robbing Gibraltar of its rightful place in the history of archaeology. That is, until the, ah, eminent gentleman seated there to my left came along"—he smiled down at Gunderson, who smiled back—"and provided the impetus and insight that led to the wonderful discoveries at Europa Point. We now not only have Gibraltar Woman but Gibraltar Boy as well—the justly celebrated First Family—catapulting Gibraltar back into the mainstream, indeed, the forefront of prehistoric archaeology."

He turned to face Gunderson directly. "Ivan, on behalf of the Historical Association, it is my great pleasure and honor to present you with this year's Mons Calpe Medal in recognition of your many contributions, moral, financial, and advisory, to the Gibraltar Museum of Archaeology and Geology."

He raised the award high for all to see—a gleaming Roman coin ("Mons Calpe" was the Romans' name for Gibraltar)—hung on a gold chain that was stitched down the center of a wide, red-and-white-striped ribbon. When Gunderson rose to accept it, head modestly bowed, Rowley placed it around his neck, draping the ribbon almost tenderly over his shoulders.

In a rattle of nervous applause, Gunderson shook hands with Rowley and faced the assembled guests. He looked genuinely touched. He also looked as if he might be back in reasonable form. All held their breath as he opened his mouth to speak.

"Thank you so much for this honor," he said smoothly and sincerely, at which the collective, inheld breath was released, "which I must in all honesty say is completely undeserved. It is Dr. Vanderwater who did the work and brought forth the great achievement; Dr. Vanderwater and his extremely accomplished staff—"

An imperial, benevolent nod and wave from Adrian, simpers from Corbin and Pru.

"—some of whom I am extremely gratified to see here tonight. But whether I deserve it or not"—a humorous twinkle lit his eyes—"I'd just like to see anyone try and get it away from me." He sat down smiling. "Thank you all for this wonderful, wonderful evening." Then, as an after-thought: "You've made an old man very happy."

The applause was heartfelt this time. People were moved by the occasion, and thankful and relieved that Gunderson had been able to handle it with his old flair. By now coffee and dessert had been brought, and at Audrey's suggestion, the presentation of the V. Gordon Childe award was held off until the almond crème brûlée had been disposed of. Gunderson reverted to the same intent, glitter-eyed greed he'd shown with the main course, and only when he'd scraped the sides of the fluted cup clean and finally lain down his spoon did she arise.

Her speech was as short as Rowley's, if not quite as warm. She brought the award, a gold-plated trowel on an onyx base, from the floor behind her and placed it on the table in front of Gunderson. "The directorial board of the Horizon Foundation has unanimously determined that this year's V. Gordon Childe Lifetime Achievement Award in

Archaeology be awarded to Ivan Samuel Gunderson in appreciation of his many contributions to the understanding of European prehistory, and his great success in sensitively interpreting it for readers and television viewers throughout the world. Congratulations, Ivan."

Again Gunderson stood, accepted the trophy, and shook hands. Again he faced his audience.

"Thank you so much for this honor, which I must in all honesty say is completely undeserved. It is Dr. Vanderwater who did the work and brought forth the great achievement; Dr. Vanderwater—"

The smiles on the faces of his appalled audience turned wooden. Troubled glances shot around the table.

"—and his extremely accomplished staff, some of whom I am extremely gratified to see here tonight. But whether I deserve it or not, I'd just like to see anyone try and get it away from me. Thank you all for this wonderful, wonderful evening. You've made an old man very happy."

What made it especially horrible was that he said it with all the same easy verve and informal good humor, even the very same stresses and pauses, the same twinkles and smiles at all the same places. Even the identical brief hiatus before the last, "spontaneous," throwaway sentence. He had no idea that he made the same carefully rehearsed speech only a few minutes before.

The attendees smiled and clapped, doing their best to cover their dismay, but Gunderson sensed that he'd done something wrong, although he didn't know what.

"And I . . . I just want to add," he began uncertainly from his seat, "that, that . . . the proudest accomplishment of my life has been the privilege, the privilege of, of having been . . . been instrumental in the discovery of, of . . ." Sweat streamed down beside his eyes in runnels as he desperately rummaged, in a disordered and inaccessible mind, for the words he wanted. ". . . the discovery of . . .

Guadalcanal Woman," he finally spat out wretchedly, "and Guadalcanal . . ." but his darting, panicked eyes showed that, while he saw from the expressions around him that he'd missed his target, he had no idea of where or how to find it. He looked anxiously, pathetically, at Rowley. "Did I misspeak? I misspoke, didn't I?"

"Not at all, Ivan," Adrian cut in with his warmest smile. "It was a wonderful speech, and a wonderful way to end the evening."

"Wonderful, wonderful," others echoed and there was yet another round of applause. Gideon joined in, but he could feel tears at the corners of his eyes.

"I'll drive you home," Rowley said, quick to seize on his cue. He too was on the edge of weeping. The good-byes were muted and hurried, and within a couple of minutes he was leading a shambling, confused Gunderson, clutching his prizes, out of the room. He looked fifteen years older than when he'd come in.

The remaining diners looked mutely, glumly at their coffee cups. "Guadalcanal Woman," Pru said softly. "Where did that come from?"

"He was back in 1942," Adrian said with a melancholy smile. "Ivan was in the Marines, you know. He spent more than a year in the South Pacific. A life-altering experience. He talked about it often."

"*Very* often," Audrey said drily.

"If he fought with the Marines at Guadalcanal, he had a right to talk about it," Buck said, in a rare reprimand to Audrey. "Guadalcanal. Jesus."

In the silence that followed, Pru let out a long, lip-flapping sigh. "Well. I don't think this was one of his better days," she said.

NINE

JULIE stretched, sighed, and let her head fall back on the pillow. "Let's be decadent this morning—"

"We've already been decadent this morning," Gideon pointed out, nuzzling the ear lobe nearest him.

She laughed. "Then let's continue in that vein, and order up a room service breakfast. We can have it out on the balcony in those lovely terry cloth robes."

Their room's generous balcony was two floors above the Wisteria Terrace, so the view was, if anything, even more grand than from the terrace. Through the French doors, which they'd left open during the night, they could see the winding paths and lush plantings of the public gardens just below, the bay a little farther out, and off to the left the Strait of Gibraltar and the dusky mountains of Africa, shimmering in their haze as the early morning sun found them.

"I'm for that," Gideon said. "How about if I order up a good, greasy, thoroughly decadent full English breakfast— the Full Monty?"

"I'm for *that*," Julie said. "I'm starving."

Over their mammoth breakfasts—fried eggs, bacon, sausage, grilled tomato, mushrooms, baked beans, white toast in a rack, marmalade, butter, and a cozy-covered pot of tea—they worked out their plans for the day.

"Well, you've got your lecture to give at noon," Julie said. "Where is that going to be again?"

"St. Michael's Cave. It's a set of natural caverns up on the Rock, and they use one of them as a lecture hall. That'll be over by one, and then we have a late lunch date with Fausto at one thirty."

Several years before, Gideon had lectured in an international forensics symposium for criminal justice personnel, held in St. Malo, France, and Fausto Sotomayor, then a young detective constable in the Royal Gibraltar Police, had been an attendee. Since then, he had been in intermittent touch with Gideon with one technical question or another, and they had become e-mail buddies of a sort, dropping each other a few lines now and then. They'd seen him briefly the day before, when Fausto, now much glorified—a detective chief inspector, no less—had insisted on driving them into town from the airport, and had invited them to lunch today at a downtown pub.

"What about before your talk?" Julie asked, spreading marmalade on a wedge of toast. "Are you free?"

"Mostly, but I did want to sit in on one of the paleoanthropological society papers at nine thirty. They're holding the conference down at the Eliott Hotel."

"What's the topic? Maybe I'll join you."

"The title is . . ." He consulted the conference program he'd brought out with them. "The title is—um, no, I have a hunch you won't be interested—'A Bio-Mechanical Assessment of Cranial Base Architecture in the Hominoidea.'"

She made a face. "Your hunch is correct. Tell you what: let's stretch our legs and stroll down the hill into town.

We'll have an hour or so, maybe get a cup of coffee some-where?"

He smiled. Tea was nice, very British and all that, but for both of them, a couple of cups of coffee in the morning were a necessity for comprehensive physiological func-tioning.

"Sounds good, Julie."

"And then I think I'll pick up a guidebook and just ex-plore the sights until we meet your friend for lunch."

"You don't want to sit in on my presentation?"

"Would you mind very much if I didn't? I *have* seen this one before."

"No, I don't mind."

To be honest, he preferred it that way. How could you be expected to enter fully into your exalted role as one of the world's foremost forensic scientists when the woman who told you when to take out the garbage was sitting in the first row watching you? "I'll see you at lunch then. The Angry Friar. Fausto says you can't miss it. On Main Street, in the middle of town. Right across from the Governor's Residence."

While they spoke, he had been leafing cursorily through the conference program, and now something, a boxed item on the last page of the schedule, caught his eye. " 'Close-of-conference reception,' " he read aloud, " 'proudly spon-sored by Javelin Press to celebrate the publication of *Uneasy Relations: Humans and Neanderthals at the Dawn of History: Implications for Today's World*, by Rowley G. Boyd. 5:00–7:00 P.M., Eliott Hotel Poolside Terrace (on top floor). Open bar and heavy hors d'oeuvres. Govern-ment and cultural dignitaries have been invited to attend.' " He looked at her. "What do you know, Lester really is do-ing his book launch here. I half thought he was kidding."

"*Uneasy Relations: Humans and Neanderthals at the Dawn of History: Implications for Today's World*," Julie repeated. "Now there's a mouthful."

"It sure is. I bet Rowley had a heck of a time talking him out of *Making It with a Neanderthal*, or *Caveman Sex*."

"But are these academics really going to show up for it, do you think?" Julie asked. "I mean, no offense to Rowley, but would these people be that interested in what he has to say?"

"What's that got to do with it?" Gideon said, laughing. "Free booze, free food—of *course* they'll attend."

Delivered with the meal was a folded copy of the *Gibraltar Chronicle* ("The Independent Daily—First Published 1801"), and now, while Gideon contentedly sipped his third cup of tea and continued with the program, Julie unfolded it to browse.

"Oh, boy," she said the moment she looked at it.

He glanced at her. "What?"

Mutely, she handed the paper to him.

And there it was again, big and bold, and apparently tracking him around the world like a vindictive ex-spouse.

PROMINENT SCIENTIST TO REVEAL "STUNNING" SCIENTIFIC FRAUD AT PUBLIC LECTURE TODAY.

"Aw, no," he groaned, scanning the piece. It was an abbreviated version of the overheated Affiliated Press release, with the addition of the title of his presentation: "'Mistakes' in Human Evolution."

"Well, look on the bright side," Julie chirped.

"There's a bright side?" he said dismally.

"Sure, there is." She stood up, leaned over to kiss him on the cheek, and headed inside. "I bet you'll have a heck of a crowd."

AT ten thirty, Gideon returned to the hotel for a final prep session before his presentation, then went downstairs to wait for Rowley, who had offered to have his administrative assistant, Henrietta, stop by the hotel at eleven to give a ride up to the cave to anyone who needed one. (Rowley himself had gone up earlier to make sure everything was in order for the lecture.) He found Buck and Adrian already beside the curving driveway, waiting for the lift. The others were there too, grouping up to walk into town so they could drop in on the society meetings for a few minutes before going up to the cave.

"Say, Gideon," Pru said wryly, "just in case we get tied up and don't make it to your, um, 'stunning exposé,' will you have abstracts of the paper you can let us have?"

Gideon sighed. "I gather you saw the article in the *Chronicle*."

"Hard to miss. Right there on page one."

"Well, the answer to your question is no. I do not have abstracts. I am not giving a 'paper.' This is going to be strictly off-the-cuff, seat-of-the-pants stuff. Miss it today, and there will never be another opportunity."

"Oh, well, then, we'll be sure to be there," she called merrily as she, Audrey, and Corbin started down the driveway. "Wouldn't want to miss *that*!"

At eleven on the dot a gray, mud-spattered Ford minivan pulled up beside them. "I'm Henrietta," the large, jovial driver jauntily proclaimed. "Climb aboard, gents!"

Buck instinctively took the front seat beside her; not only was he the biggest of the three, and needful of the most leg room, but riding shotgun seemed to suit him. Gideon and Adrian sat behind.

"Henrietta," Gideon said as she pulled out onto Europa Road, "do you happen to know how Ivan Gunderson's doing?"

"Ah. Ivan." Henrietta's round, jolly face sagged. "I haven't seen him today, but according to Rowley, he was quite destroyed by what happened last night. As soon as I drop you gentlemen off, I'm on my way to see him with a load of broken pots—that's the clinking you've been hearing from the back. We're hoping it helps him find his footing, but sometimes it takes days."

"Yes, that's typical of *dementia senilis*," Adrian averred. "But it was dreadful to see him in that condition."

"Well, you know—" Buck began, but Adrian hadn't yet relinquished the floor.

"Did I understand Rowley to say yesterday," he continued, "that Ivan is expected to give some sort of welcoming presentation at the Europa Point ceremony tomorrow?"

"Yes, he—"

"Will he be able to manage it?"

Henrietta shrugged. "God only knows. Rowley's going to make sure he writes it down, but . . ." Another shrug.

They climbed the flank of the Rock in silence for a few minutes, until Adrian slyly lifted his eyebrows and disingenuously said, "Bigger than Piltdown, eh?"

Gideon sighed again. He'd been expecting more of this, although perhaps not from Adrian.

"Yeah, hey, I saw the paper too," Buck said, turning. "What is that about? Aud says it's, like, some kind of stupid joke." His beefy face flushed. "Not that she meant—"

"I understand," Gideon said. "And it is a stupid joke. Not that you could tell from the way the article was written."

"Oh, I wouldn't worry," Henrietta said, unabashedly joining in. "I read it too. I think most people could tell you weren't being serious."

"The thing is," Gideon said, "some of these reporters take what you say and—"

"Indeed they do," said Adrian with a full-throated laugh, and Gideon got his first rich morning whiff of Tullamore Dew. "They take what you say in all innocence and twist it unconscionably. Of course it's irritating at the moment, but really, it becomes quite amusing with the passage of time. Let me tell you what happened to me once. It had to do with the relative chronology of the Mousterian succession at Peche de Dourre. Now, what I *actually* said was that the superpositioning of the Ferrassie variant was an unfortunate— "

And off he went on a convoluted story about Neanderthal lithic technology, stopping when the car stopped at the pay booth that marked the entrance to the Upper Rock Nature Preserve, which encompassed most of the popular visitor sites on the Rock, including St. Michael's Cave. But as soon as Henrietta was recognized and waved through, he took up where he'd left off.

Even Gideon, let alone Buck and Henrietta, had trouble following him. When the story had finally reached its conclusion (they knew because he had stopped talking for a full five seconds and was looking at them with a wry, expectant expression), Henrietta, after providing the appreciative chuckle that was expected, addressed Gideon.

"Tell us, then, will you? What will your lecture be about? Really."

"Well, why not wait to hear the full, unexpurgated version? I wouldn't want to spoil the anticipation for you."

"Oh, come on, give us a hint," Adrian coaxed. "Whet our appetites."

"Yes, do," agreed Henrietta. "What are these 'mistakes'?"

"We won't tell anybody," Buck said.

Gideon, a professor through and through, wasn't the sort of man who could easily turn down multiple requests for a lecture—even a prelecture lecture—from a captive and apparently sincere audience.

"All right, it's about what you might call the slipups, the bloopers, that have occurred over the years—over the eons—of human evolution."

Buck's open, honest face showed shock. "Can evolution make mistakes?"

"Well, not mistakes. Call them arrangements that haven't worked out quite as well as they might have, things that, oh . . ."

"What Gideon is referring to are what are known as vestigial organs," explained Adrian, ever ready to provide expertise and edification to the insufficiently educated. "You see, Buck, our bodies carry around these tag ends of structures that were at one time functional, but now serve no use, and in fact may do us damage. Our appendix would perhaps be the best example. All it can do for us now is to become infected. Our coccyx, which is no more than the rudimentary root of the tail we once had, would be another such example. Most of the time, these tag ends make their appearance early in our intrauterine development and then disappear—fortunately. How would you like it if you still had, pulsing at the sides of your throat, the gill slits that are found in the human embryonic pharynx?"

Gideon took advantage of Adrian's predictable pause for astonishment and appreciative laughter to barge in. "Uh, actually, Adrian, the subject isn't going to be vestigial structures. Interesting as they are," he added as Adrian's face clouded. The great man very much disliked being told he didn't know what he was talking about, however gently.

"No? What then?" he asked coldly.

"Mostly, the problems that resulted when we evolved from quadrupeds to bipeds," Gideon said, and then, at Buck's puzzled frown, added, "from four-legged animals to two-legged. You see, the difficulty is that we didn't get totally redesigned. Nature—evolution—doesn't go in for total redesign. Generally, it acts in a kind of piecemeal manner, fixing this or that up, but not taking into consideration how it affects other things. And getting up on our hind legs has affected a lot of other things, which is why we wind up with problems."

"I don't get it," Buck said. "What problems?"

"Do you mean like fallen arches?" Henrietta asked. "Varicose veins in the legs? Oh, Lord, I can tell you all about those."

"Yes, exactly. When we were on four legs, the blood from the leg veins had to overcome about two feet of gravity to get back to the heart. Now that we're standing erect, your heart is a good four feet above the ground. Sometimes it's too much for the venous pumping system. The blood can't make it back up, it collects in the leg, and the veins bulge—varicose veins."

"Oh, I get it. That's pretty cool," Buck said. "And fallen arches, what about them?"

"Ah, you see, our feet are unique in the animal world. In most four-legged animals, what they have are paws or hooves—nice, compact, simple structures wonderfully suited to running or walking. But primates were tree-dwellers to start, and almost all of them still are. So instead of four feet, they have what you might call four hands—a lot more useful for getting around up there. But ever since we humans started walking upright, our rear hands, so to speak, have been turning into paws to make walking more efficient. The problem is, they're not really either; useless for holding things, but not built too well, not compact enough, for efficient walking. Not yet, anyway. The result is fallen arches. And bunions. And most of the rest of our foot miseries."

"So you mean I got flat feet because I used to be a monkey?" Buck exclaimed with his deep, pleasant laugh.

"Closer to an ape, actually," Gideon corrected, unable to help himself.

"Ape, monkey, whatever," Buck said happily.

Adrian seemed on the brink of putting in his own

explanatory two cents' worth, but then remembered he was still miffed and sat silently back without saying anything, pretending to be engrossed by the passing scenery. And looking more like a big, sulky baby than ever.

"But what may be the biggest problem," Gideon went on, warming to his subject (once he'd gotten well launched, he was almost as hard to stop as Adrian), "is that the human pelvis has changed. See, when we walked on four legs the ribs were *underneath* our guts and took care of holding them in place, but once we stood up, that didn't work anymore, and the pelvis constricted to meet the challenge. It went from being a pair of wide, flat, open blades to becoming a sort of bowl with only a tiny opening in the base, that could support the internal organs."

"So why is that a problem?" Buck asked.

"Because while that's been going on at the bottom of the spinal cord, the thing on top of it—the brain case—has been expanding. In other words, the birth canal has been getting smaller, while the biggest thing that has to go through it, the infant's head, has been getting bigger. Giving birth hasn't been getting any easier."

"Tell me about it," muttered Henrietta.

"And yet at the same time that the skull has been expanding," Adrian said, finally unable to resist chipping in— he wasn't one to stay irked very long—"the *facial* skeleton has diminished in size. We no longer have a snout, which means there is less room for our teeth. But our teeth have *not* gotten any smaller, and as you can surmise, that has meant trouble. The last teeth to come in, the third molars or wisdom teeth, often don't have a decent space left, so they come in impacted, or crooked, or not at all. Good for the dentists, bad for the rest of us. I wouldn't be surprised if, in another half-million years, we only have twenty-four teeth or so. Instead of thirty-two. Wouldn't you agree, Gideon?"

With difficulty, Gideon restrained himself from pointing out that evolutionary change didn't work that way. It didn't work *toward* something. It worked *from* something, but even people like Adrian Vanderwater seemed to have a hard time getting that straight. It was the conditions of the moment that determined which genes would be favored and thus increase their proportion in the next generation. If the conditions changed, the "direction" of evolution would change. It had happened again and again, and was in fact the reason that most advanced life-forms were such seemingly patchwork products. It was a crucial understanding of the process that he freely badgered his introductory students into comprehending, but in this case he held his tongue. He was happy to have a cheerful, outgoing Adrian back with them and didn't want to spoil things. He groped for a reply that was truthful and yet wouldn't tick the archaeologist off again.

"I wouldn't be surprised," he said.

TEN

AT the visitors' entry to the cave, Henrietta's presence once again got them waved through without need of fees or passes. Rowley, accompanied by Audrey and Corbin, was there to greet them in the entrance grotto. "You know, Gideon, you're not on for half an hour," he said around the bit of his unlit pipe. "There's time for a look 'round if you'd like. I was about to give these two the tuppence tour. Can I interest you two in joining us? There's a lot of history here."

Only Buck took him up on it. Adrian rather frostily said he preferred to explore it on his own, inasmuch as he was already quite familiar with the history of St. Michael's Cave, and Gideon said he wanted to have a look at Cathedral Cavern, the natural amphitheater in which he'd be speaking. He found it at the end of a narrow passageway, approaching it from the rear: a breathtaking, echoing, bowl-shaped hollow with a hundred-foot-high concave ceiling from which hung tremendous stalactites made all the more spectacular and mysterious by concealed amber, green, and orange lighting. Over the millennia, many of the stalactites had reached the bottom and congealed, making great, crenellated, floor-to-ceiling columns, also impressively lit.

The audience section consisted of twenty rising rows of red plastic chairs, each row sited on a white-painted concrete tier. Altogether, there was seating for a good four hundred people. The stage was simply a natural rock platform, slightly raised from the rest of the rock floor. The temperature was a comfortable seventy or so, but it *smelled* cold—cold, and flinty, and a little musty, but not unpleasant. About the way a great stone cavern ought to smell.

The walls, the floor, the stage—everything but the chairs—were slick with moisture, and shallow puddles had formed in the hollows in the stone floor. At either end of the stage was a huge speaker, and in the center a lectern had been set up with a rubber floor mat behind it. Gideon went down the tiers and up to the lectern to get a sense of the place from there, something he liked to do before he spoke. He placed his hands on either side of the lectern and looked out at the empty tiers. "Ladies and gentlemen—"

"Can I 'elp you, mate?" inquired a voice straight out of East London.

He turned to see a man in bib overalls, wearing a leather tool belt from the pockets of which protruded the multicolored, insulated handles of a dozen pliers, wire-strippers, and screwdrivers. Hanging on the outside were a couple of meters or testers of some kind. Even Gideon, whose knowledge of such things was laughable at best, recognized him as an electrician.

"No, just checking things out. I'm the speaker today."

"Oh, glad to meetcher. M'name's Derek. Going to be showing any slides, are we?"

"Nope."

"PowerPoint?"

"Nope."

"Just gonner talk, then?"

"That's right. I'm pretty low-tech."

"Right, then. You'll be sure and finish up before two? I 'ave to set up for a concert at four."

"No problem there. I'll be out before one thirty."

"Right, then."

With twenty minutes to go until noon, Gideon went exploring on his own, wandering among the visitors through the multilevel caverns and looking at the exhibits—a replica of a Neanderthal skull embedded in stone, a Neanderthal family bloodily butchering the day's kill around a fire, a six-foot-thick slice of stalactite taken from a toppled giant. At five to twelve he headed back to the amphitheater, running into Rowley, Audrey, Buck, and Corbin also on their way in, returning from Rowley's "tuppence tour." They entered from the front of the hall this time, coming in alongside the stage.

The moment they entered, Gideon stopped dead in his tracks. Julie was right. The place was now completely filled, every seat taken, with a row of standees at the back, and more coming. Up front, several of them—journalists?—had reporter's notebooks open on their laps. Half of Gibraltar seemed to be there, buzzing with excitement. And all of them, he thought wretchedly, eager to be in on it when the Skeleton Detective set the scientific world on its ear.

"Oh, Lord," he muttered. "How am I—"

"Say, Gideon," Rowley said, frowning at the area where the lectern had been set up, "shouldn't they have a mat or something for you to stand on? The floor's wet, you might get a shock."

"You're right," Buck said. "All that electrical stuff, the mike and everything—you could get a hell of a shock."

"There *was* a mat," Gideon said, puzzled by the undeniably bare, glistening rock floor. "Somebody took it away."

"Some mad scientist, no doubt," said Pru, who had just come along, "who's determined to prevent you from revealing his dastardly scheme to the world." This with a sinister wiggle of her eyebrows.

"It's hardly a joke," Rowley said in mild reproof. "You're quite right, Gideon. I saw the mat myself, but it's obviously not there now. You'd better find something non-conductive to stand on."

Gideon, who knew next to nothing about electricity, knew enough to agree with that. A few moments' poking around behind the rocky stage turned up Derek at a worktable in a crowded little workroom—a work cranny, more properly—soldering something or other to something or other else.

"Derek?"

" 'Arf a mo'," Derek said as a pungent wisp of smoke rose from his work. Satisfied, he put down the iron and looked at Gideon. "Yair?"

"There was a rubber mat behind the lectern," Gideon said. "It's not there now."

"Course it's there."

Gideon made a motion with his hand, palm up. *See for yourself.*

Derek did and came back shaking his head. "That's them janitors for you. Couldn't do a job proper like to save their lives."

The janitorial staff, it appeared, was the bane of Derek's existence. A gaggle of creaky old duffers who should have been superannuated years ago. Careless, slipshod, lazy, apparently they'd thought that Gideon had already given his talk, so they'd begun clearing the stage, presumably to set up for the four o'clock concert. This was grumblingly explained as Derek located the mat—a rubber pad glued to a

slightly raised wooden platform—in a corner of the workroom, hauled it out onto the stage, and flopped it on the
stone floor behind the lectern. Then he busied himself with
checking the mike, setting the angle of the goosenecked
reading lamp attached to the lectern, and tinkering with
the connections.

"Can't be too careful when you're working 'round electricity . . . now what's this?" he said disgustedly "Will you
just look at this 'ere?"

He tugged at a black electrical cord, revealing a frayed
spot where the wiring joined the base of the lamp, and
clucked his disapproval. "Accident waiting to 'appen.
Should've been repaired long ago." With a complaining
sigh he unplugged the lamp and unscrewed it. "Now I'll
'ave to go and find you another one."

"That's all right," Gideon said, concerned that the audience might think they were having an argument. "I don't
need one, the ambient light's fine. I don't have notes to
look at anyway."

"Suit yourself. Good luck, then, mate, they're all
yours."

Gideon faced his audience. An expectant hush replaced
the buzz of conversation. He took a deep breath.

"Good afternoon and thank you all for coming. I guess
I'd better tell you right now that my subject isn't quite what
this morning's paper implied, but I, uh, hope you won't,
um . . ."

But his anxieties were needless. The talk went beautifully. No one got up and walked out upon learning that that
Piltdown Man was not to be left in the dust after all. They
listened with active interest, laughed in the right places,
and asked intelligent questions afterward. He was pleased.

But he was also troubled. While his archaeologist
friends filed upstairs to the St. Michael's Cave Café for a
snack, he sought out the technician in the workroom again.

"Derek," he said, "let me ask you a question. That lamp—if I'd touched it, what would have happened?"

"Touched it? Nothing. You'd've 'ad to switch it on."

"Okay, let's say I switched it on."

"Well, still nothing, probably. You'd've been standing on the mat, wouldn'tcher?"

"But let's say I *wasn't* standing on the mat—remember, the mat wasn't there at first."

At this Derek showed some interest. He set down the soldering iron he'd been using. "I see whatcher getting at. Well, that'd depend on the condition of the wiring in the cord, wouldn't it? Let's have us a look, why don't we?"

The lamp was on a second, smaller worktable crowded with what looked like material for the junkman—broken hand tools, rusty lengths of rebar, chunks of wallboard, a battered old electric sander. Derek brought the lamp back to examine it under the better light of the larger work table.

"Blimey," he said quietly, probing in the cord's innards.

"What?"

"Well, just look. There's only the two-'undred-forty-volt wire still in one piece. The other one, and the ground wire—they're frayed clear through."

This told Gideon nothing. "Which means what? I would have gotten a shock?"

"Well, you'd've *become* the switch, d'you see, and the current would've 'ad to pass right on through you to close the circuit. Now as long as you was standing on the mat, it would just've gone through your 'and, not—"

"But if I wasn't standing on the mat?" Gideon persisted. "If there *was* no mat? Could I have been killed?"

Derek astonished Gideon by guffawing. "*Killed!* Blimey, mate, you would have been *fried*. To a crisp," he added, in case Gideon had missed his drift.

ELEVEN

GIDEON was late for his lunch date with Fausto and Julie, and when he arrived he had a little trouble picking them out among the mob of diners—the *Grand Princess* was in port and the little town was jammed with two thousand day-trippers—but Julie spotted him and waved him over to a green-umbrellaed table on the open square that served as a dining terrace for the Angry Friar. They were at the very edge of the square, only yards from the diminutive, pillared Supreme Court building and the two not-so-diminutive, shining bronze cannons that ceremonially guarded it (pointed, strangely enough, at the handsome eighteenth-century brick facing of the Governor's Residence across the street).

"Hi, honey. How's it going, Fausto? Sorry I'm late." He had decided during the taxi ride down that the account of his narrowly missing getting fried to a crisp could wait until they'd gotten through a little small talk and some lunch.

"Oh, it's been fascinating," Julie said. "Fausto's been telling me about the local crime scene. You wouldn't like it here at all. No forensic work. They don't have murders."

"None?" Gideon asked, slipping into a chair. "Why, are they against the law or something?"

"It's a fact, Gideon," Fausto said. "Not a single homicide in the last two years. "Not one."

Almost everything Fausto Sotomayor said came across as a declaration; sometimes a challenge. Although a native Gibraltarian, he carried the ghost of a Spanish accent, a Castilian lisp that his forbears had brought over from the mainland, but there was nothing lilting or musical about it. Besides, he spoke a brusque, slangy American English rather than British (he had lived in New York City with his UN-diplomat mother during his highly formative teenage years), and he spoke it in crackling, to-the-point sentences. On first meeting him, Gideon, whose ear for accent was usually sharp, had mistakenly taken him for a Puerto Rican New Yorker.

"Statistically, one killing every four, five years. I been here twelve years, only had three. Practically no violent crime at all. Not one case of rape in ten years, how about that? How many international cities you know can say that? There's just, you know, the date rape thing once in a while."

Julie wasn't much of a feminist as feminists went, but this was too much for her. "Oh, just the date rape thing," she said drily. "Nothing to be concerned about."

"Come on, you know what I mean. Kids. Alcohol-related. But there aren't any sleazeballs lurking in the alleys waiting for the sound of high heels. No stranger rape. Women can walk around anywhere, any time of night. Now admit it, that's damn amazing, considering that thirty thousand people live here. All mixed races and cultures—jeez, we got Arabs, Jews, Catholics, we got Spanish,

English, Indians, Italians . . . and we got maybe five thousand transients coming through a day. And still . . . no place safer." He rapped his knuckles on the wooden table.

"Amazing. You must do a heck of a job of prevention," Gideon said honestly.

Fausto jerked his chin in agreement. "You better believe it."

Fausto Sotomayor had been a newly promoted detective sergeant when he had been sent to the eighth annual International Conference in Science and Detection some years earlier in St. Malo, France, at which Gideon had conducted the forensic anthropology sessions. One of twenty law enforcement people in the class, he had seemed to Gideon on first glance among the least likely to make it as a cop. Independently wealthy, no more than five feet five, quick-moving and quick-talking, rail-thin, with small (even for his size) hands (fingernails buffed and manicured) and feet (toenails buffed and pedicured?), he dressed in silk shirts and trim, expensive, perfectly tailored suits, and exuded a lithe, oddly graceful cockiness—Jimmy Cagney with a Latin accent—that clearly set the teeth of his bigger, slower, less fashion-conscious colleagues on edge.

After a few days, though, his more appealing side came through, at least to Gideon. He was intelligent and straight-talking—in-your-face might be closer to it—and on knowing him a bit better, the bantam rooster cockiness seemed less a reflection of a truly bellicose personality than a matter of comportment, of style, that he'd picked up somewhere along the way. It was, after all, hardly unusual in small men, particularly among those in the "manly" occupations. But underneath it, once you got to know him, Fausto was in fact fun to be around. The trouble was, not many of his fellow attendees had gone to the trouble (and really, why should they have?) of cracking through the flashy, gangsterish style and combative façade to see what was underneath. For that reason alone, Gideon had not predicted much of a future for him in the upper ranks of law enforcement.

And yet here he was, Detective Chief Inspector Sotomayor, a full-fledged DCI, so others had obviously seen something in him too.

They hadn't ordered their lunches yet, so a couple of minutes were spent perusing the outsized, plastic-coated menus. Fausto ordered curried chicken and rice, Julie, whose appetite hadn't fully recovered from their huge breakfast, ordered a bowl of gazpacho, and Gideon asked for a ploughman's lunch and a half pint of ale to go along with the beers the other two already had in front of them.

"So you've never had a chance to use any of the forensic material from the course?" he asked when the harried, sweating young waiter had taken their orders and run back to the kitchen.

"No. Well, just once. There was this case, oh, let me see, three, four years ago. There was this girl who'd been missing for a couple of days, and we finally found her, killed in a cave-in down at the south end. It wasn't my case—I was just an inspector then, but I was helping the DCI who was running it, so I was out there when they dug her out. A mess; all mashed up, bones broken, internal organs exploded, maggots coming out of her—sorry, Julie, hell of a thing to be talking about at lunch."

Julie laughed. "Are you kidding? Who do you think I'm married to? Go right ahead, don't give it a thought. Maggots, exploding organs . . . everyday mealtime conversation at the Olivers."

Fausto shrugged. "Yeah, used to be the same way at my house. Hey, could that be why I'm divorced? Anyway, she had plenty of ID on her, and enough face left so people could identify her, so no need for forensic anthro on that score. But you know what came in handy? Remember that Finnish guy who was there? The bug expert who you couldn't understand anything he was saying?"

"Professor Wuoronin," Gideon supplied. "A good entomologist. Knew what he was talking about."

"Yeah, him. Gave out a ton of material on bugs that feed on corpses, you know, the sacro . . . the scaro . . ."

"Sarcosaprophagous insects."

"Yeah, sarco . . . yeah, them. So I knew a blowfly maggot when I saw one, and I saw a zillion on her. All between two and three millimeters long, nothing longer, nothing shorter, which meant they were two to three days old, which meant I had myself a reliable time-of-death estimate."

"A *minimum* time-of-death estimate," Gideon reminded him. DCI or not, Fausto was still an old student and Gideon could get away with correcting him. Indeed, as Gideon saw it, he was morally obligated to do so. "The cave-in couldn't have occurred any *later* than two to three days before . . . but it could have happened earlier. You can't be sure of exactly when the flies laid their eggs."

"Yeah, yeah, I know, I know, but everything came together. Some passengers on the Morocco ferry, they saw the cave-in happen, so we knew exactly when it was. Two days before we dug her out."

"But then you really didn't need the estimate based on the maggots," Julie said. "Or am I missing something?"

"Okay, all right, you're right," a grudging Fausto admitted. "It was strictly corroborative. Jeez, what a purist." He grinned. "But it was fun, you know?"

"Mmm, I bet," Julie said. "Sure sounds like fun. Measuring maggots."

Their meals came. The waiter brushed away a few hovering black flies that had touched down on the food. The flies moved off but floated nearby in slow, hanging circles.

They seemed to be a general nuisance on the patio. Other diners were brushing at their food and their faces.

Julie made a face. "Um . . . would those be blowflies?"

"Nope," Gideon said. "Black flies."

"They don't feed on corpses?"

He shook his head and began on his ploughman's lunch, tucking ham, relish, and cucumber into a partially sliced-through hunk of baguette to turn it into a sandwich. "They do not."

"What do they feed on, then? No, wait, I don't want to know."

"A wise decision," Gideon said, biting in. "Mmm, good."

Fausto had tucked his napkin into the collar of his shirt—he was still a sharp dresser: mauve shirt, green tie, slick-looking olive brown suit—and was shoveling in chicken and rice, daintily but effectively. Julie was dabbing a spoon into her gazpacho, deciding whether or not she was really hungry at all.

"Fausto," Gideon said, "this would be Sheila Chan we've been talking about, wouldn't it? And the Europa Point Cave."

Fausto blinked. "Now how the hell would you know—oh, that's right, she was one of you people. She was here for the meeting they had back then. Did you know her?"

"No, just by e-mail." Gideon hesitated. "Was there anything suspicious about her death?"

Julie looked inquisitively at him over the rim of her glass. Fausto paused in lifting a forkful of rice to his mouth. "Why would you ask that?"

"Just some things that have been happening. Was there?"

"Anything suspicious?" He shook his head. "No. All cut and dried, everything kosher. Why?" he asked again.

"Fausto, did you ever hear of anyone getting pushed off the top of the Rock by one of the Barbary apes?"

"You mean on purpose?"

"On purpose or accidentally."

"How could they push you off accidentally?"

"Come on, just answer—"

"No, I never heard of it. Why?" He was getting irritated. In that way he was like any cop. He preferred asking the questions.

"Gideon thinks he may have been the first," Julie put in.

"The first to live to tell about it, anyway," Fausto said with a snort. "That's for sure."

"Gideon," Julie said, "I thought you agreed there wasn't anything suspicious about that."

"Well, I did, but then today at my lecture—"

"Oh, I forgot to ask," Julie said. "How did it go?"

"Just fine, absolutely great, except for the part where I nearly got electrocuted."

She started to laugh, but then saw he was serious. "What happened?"

Gideon told them.

"And your conclusion?" Fausto said. He had eaten most of his dish, shoved it away, and pulled the napkin out of his collar. Gideon had eaten about half of his ploughman's, Julie none of her gazpacho. Coffee had been ordered—tea for Fausto—and brought to the table.

"I don't know," Gideon said. "Everything might be explainable, taken one thing at a time—accident, carelessness—but to have been almost killed twice in less than twenty-four hours—"

"Brings to mind the Law of Interconnected Monkey Business," Fausto said, dropping three cubes of sugar into his tea.

Gideon was surprised. "How do you know about the Law of Interconnected Monkey Business?"

"You talked about it in the seminar. Goldstein's Theorem of Interconnected Monkey Business. Hell, it's practically my mantra."

Gideon's too. It was a "law" posited only partly in jest by Gideon's old professor and all-around mentor Abe Goldstein. When too many suspicious but seemingly unrelated things—too much monkey business—start cropping up in a short time, to the same people, in the same context, you can bet on there being some connection between them.

The three of them sat there looking somberly at each other until Julie said: "But why would anyone want to kill you?" The last time she had asked him that had been yesterday, after the incident on the Rock, when she had been trying to convince him that the idea was silly. This time, he was glad to see, it was meant as a serious question. It was her support, her backup, that he wanted, not her skepticism.

Fausto took it seriously too. "We'll want that lamp," he said, pulling a cell phone from his inside pocket. "I'll have one of my—"

Gideon lifted the lumpy plastic shopping bag he'd set down beside his chair. "I figured you would. Here it is. The wires haven't been cut, I could see that much. Not cleanly, not with a knife or a snipper. They look frayed, the same as the cord fabric, but whether they've been filed to look that way, or just worn through on their own, I don't know."

Fausto had opened the mouth of the bag, and without touching the lamp, was peering as well as he could at the torn area of the cord. "Can't tell. Maybe filed, maybe just frayed. We'll have to see."

"How long will that take? Do you have a lab here?"

"Yeah, we have a lab, but I'm not sure they'll know how to do this kind of thing. Might have to send it off to FSS—the Forensic Science Service Lab in London. If my people can handle it, I'll have the results tomorrow. If it has to go to London . . . who knows?" He studied his buffed and manicured fingernails, letting a beat pass. "Listen, maybe I should assign you some protection," he said casually. "Somebody to kind of keep an eye on you. Very discreet, of course. Just in case."

"That's a good idea," Julie said.

Gideon shook his head. "I don't think so."

"If you'd had somebody with you," she said, "that thing up on the Rock would never have happened. Even if it was just a monkey."

"No, but somebody trailing me around wouldn't have stopped what happened in the cave. That mat was removed when I wasn't even anywhere near it, and the lamp had been fooled with before I ever got there." *And not by a monkey*, he said to himself. "Assuming it *was* fooled with," he added to show he was being open-minded.

"But—"

"No, Julie, I think I just have to be careful, that's all. Whoever's doing it—if somebody's really doing it— obviously wants it to look like an accident, so he's not going to shoot me or stab me. I just have to watch my step."

"I gotta agree," Fausto said. "Change your mind, tell me."

"I don't suppose you'd consider our going back home?" Julie said doubtfully. "After all, you've had the testimonial for Ivan, you've made your public presentation, all that's left are the meetings, and I'm sure . . . no, I didn't think so."

"But you know," he said, "*you* might want to—no, I didn't think so."

"Whither thou goest," Julie said with a smile.

"What made you ask about Sheila Chan?" Fausto wanted to know. "Are you saying there might be a connection there?"

"I was thinking so, yes."

"That was two years ago. And you never even knew her. What's the connection?"

"Just that we both worked on the Europa Point dig—well, she worked on the actual dig, I worked on the bones in the lab later on—so it just seemed to me—"

"Not much of a connection," Fausto said.

"No, it isn't," Gideon agreed. It had sounded far-fetched to him even as he'd said it. He was getting carried away with the interconnectedness angle.

The phone that was still in Fausto's hand chirped. He flicked it open and listened. "Oh, hell, where? What do the fire guys say? Okay, have Matt check it out—ah, the hell with it, I better come myself. Twenty minutes."

He drained the last inch of his tea and stood up, holding his hand out for the bag with the lamp. "Gotta go."

"Something serious?" Gideon asked.

"Well, a death. Some old guy apparently smoking in bed, falls asleep, burns himself to death. Some people never learn. See you later. I'll call you soon as I know about the lamp." He handed them cards, shook hands with the two of them, snatched the check, barely evading Gideon's grab for it, then paused as he was leaving with the lamp tucked under his arm.

"Well, at least this is one dead body that you can't fit into your monkey business business."

As things would turn out, he couldn't have been more wrong.

TWELVE

LEFT by themselves, Julie and Gideon ordered more coffee and stayed on for a while.

"It's got to be your speech," Julie said thoughtfully, stirring cream into her mug. "Somebody read the articles and thought you were going to reveal *something*, and they didn't want you to do it."

Gideon smiled. "That's what Pru said. I just laughed."

"What did she think it was?"

"No, she was just kidding."

"Well, what do *you* think? Could that be it?"

He shook his head. "I'm at a loss, Julie. I can't say it hasn't occurred to me, but what could I say that would worry somebody so much? And anyway, can you imagine anybody taking those articles seriously? I mean, really imagine it?"

"Of course people would take them seriously. The newspapers took them seriously, didn't they? Why wouldn't the readers?"

"Okay, yes, the ordinary reader, maybe, but . . . look, the only people here who could possibly be affected by something I might 'reveal,' whatever the hell that might be, would be some of these archaeologists, right? What could I possibly know that they'd be that desperate to keep me from telling?"

"I've been thinking about that. Couldn't it have something to do with Gibraltar Boy and the First Family? After all, that's pretty much why we're all here. And you're the one who made the connection to Sheila Chan—to what happened to her.".

He nodded. "I did, yes, but that part of it seems pretty far-fetched to me now. As Fausto said, two years is a long time ago. A big stretch, even for interconnected monkey business."

"Okay, if you say so, but that still leaves you, and the more we talk about it, the more it seems to me it all has to have something to do with the Gibraltar Boy and the Europa Point dig."

"Maybe, but—"

"Look at it this way," she said intently. "If somebody really snuck up behind you on the Rock, and if somebody really set you up to be electrocuted . . . assuming there aren't *two* people trying to do away with you . . . it just about has to be somebody who's here for the meetings, one of your good buddies—who else would have been in both those places right then? Doesn't that imply rather strongly that it's got something to do with the Europa Point dig, with Gibraltar Boy?"

He considered this, sipping his coffee. "Julie, don't forget, I was never at the dig. I just did some lab work on Gibraltar Boy and I completed that almost five years ago now. I haven't been involved before or since. And what could I possibly say about him that was so earth-shattering anyway?"

"I've been thinking about that too. You could say that after much deliberation, you finally came to the conclusion that he really was just another Neanderthal, not the product of a mating between Neanderthals and humans. Wouldn't that shake up some of these people who've been—forgive the expression—living off the Neanderthal-human connection ever since?"

It was something he hadn't thought of. "Well . . . sure, but I *haven't* come to that conclusion."

"No, but they don't know that."

"And even if I had, other anthropologists think exactly the same thing and have said so, and as far as I know they're still walking around. I'd just be one more voice in the minority. I wouldn't have any way to prove it."

"No, but they wouldn't know that either. They might think you've come up with something new, especially on account of those articles. Besides, being the modest fellow you are, I think you underrate the impact of your opinion."

He smiled, finished his coffee, and sighed. "Julie, what do you say we call a moratorium on the subject for a while? I need to get my head clear. We may be seeing it all wrong. Let's be tourists for the afternoon. You've been out seeing the sights all morning. How about showing me around the town?"

"That's a good idea. It's a cute place. There's plenty to see."

She gave him a pale smile as they stood up. "Just make sure you look both ways when we cross the street."

INDEED, there was plenty to see, especially from a historical perspective. The actual sites of historic importance in the little city were few, but the very fabric of the town was an amalgam, or rather an accretion, of its own history.

At first glance it was a typical English market town with its fish-and-chips places, its pubs, its Marks & Spencer store, its red "Royal Mail" mailboxes. But if you raised your eyes to the upper story (almost all the buildings lining the narrow Main Street—now a pedestrian walkway—were two stories), you were in Spain: pastel-colored stucco façades; wooden shutters painted in vivid green, red, or blue; delicately filigreed iron balconies. And looking up the side streets, you might have thought you were in Moorish Iberia: narrow, cobbled, winding alleys; overhanging, flower-filled balconies that nearly met the ones across the way; tiny Arab fruit and vegetable markets that were little more than cubbyholes.

There was plenty of evidence of the long British military presence too. Aside from the big eighteenth- and nineteenth-century cannons prominently displayed all over the place—in front of government buildings, in the public gardens, along Line Wall Road—the street names made it hard to forget: Bomb House Lane, Horse Barracks Lane, Victualling Office Lane. And the main library, a stately, pillared nineteenth-century building of classical design, was still known as the Garrison Library.

And walls. Ancient, crumbling, fortified defensive walls and bastions, some British, some Moorish, a few Spanish, poked up all over the place, some lining the harbor, others snaking all the way down from the top of the Rock, and still others, along with the old city gates, appearing in bits and pieces throughout the downtown area. And looming above the town, on its own bleak promontory, visible from almost everywhere, was the ancient, brooding presence of the fortified square tower known as the Moorish Castle.

"Built during the Arab occupation," Julie told him. "Guess what it's used for now."

He shook his head. "Looks like a good place for a dungeon."

"Actually, you're right. It's the prison, it's the Gibraltar jail. It's been the prison ever since the Brits took over in 1704."

"Whoa," he said looking up at the grim, gray walls. "No wonder there's no crime here. Who wants to risk being shut up in a place like that?"

Still, for a man like Gideon, who happily lived most of his professional life in the past, it was all intriguing, but after a while the press of fellow gawkers—a second cruise ship had come in—began to wear on him—on both of them—and he asked Julie if she had found some quiet place unlikely to be full of noisy, excited tourists.

"As a matter of fact, I have," she told him. "And it's exactly your sort of place. You'll love it."

"My sort of place?" he asked curiously. "What exactly is 'my sort of place'?"

IT was an old burial ground, of course, and as devoid of day-trippers as Julie had promised. Trafalgar Cemetery was a small, triangular plot of land set flush against the base of the fortified, sixteenth-century Spanish wall known as the Charles V Wall. Originally laid out in 1798, Trafalgar Cemetery had at first been known as Southport Ditch Cemetery. A few yards above it, on top of the broad walls themselves, had once been another final resting place, the wonderfully redundantly titled Deadman's Cemetery. Later, that long, narrow cemetery had been converted to a rifle range, but Southport Ditch still remained, its name changed to Trafalgar Cemetery in 1805 to commemorate the celebrated naval battle that had recently been fought off nearby Cape Trafalgar and the sailors' remains—those that weren't buried at sea—that were soon to grace the plot. The body of Admiral Nelson, famously preserved in a cask of brandy, had also been carried to Gibraltar after the battle, but had remained only long enough to have the brandy replaced with spirits of wine, thought to be a better preservative, before going home to England for more fitting interment in St. Paul's Cathedral.

These facts were read aloud by Julie from *A Brief Historical, Shopping, and Dining Guide to Gibraltar* as they strolled the narrow, overgrown paths among the low, crooked old headstones. There was more, but she closed the book and slipped it into her shoulder bag.

"Gideon, I can't help thinking about it. In all honesty, how likely do you really think it is that these things that have been happening to you are, well, just accidents, coincidences? Of your being in the wrong place at the wrong time? On a scale of one to ten."

"Honestly? Maybe a two." Honestly, he thought it was zero, but no point in overworrying her.

"Me too," she said. "I guess we'll know more when Fausto finds out about the lamp."

"That should settle it. We may as well stop conjecturing until we hear from him."

"That suits me."

They stopped to read the timeworn legend on a squat headstone with a black iron cannon ball cemented into its top.

To the Memories of Lieutenant Thomas Worth and John Buckland of the Royal Marine Artillery, who were Killed on the 23rd November 1810 by the same Shot while directing the Howitzer Boats in an attack on the Enemy's Flotilla in Cadiz Bay.

"Now *that*," Gideon said, "is an example of being in the wrong place at the wrong time."

RATHER than walking back up to the hotel and eating with the others, they decided on dinner in the city. Julie turned to her guidebook for suggestions. Given the mood they were in after the half hour they'd spent in the cemetery, the Lord Nelson Brasserie and Bar seemed appropriate. "Located in the eighteenth-century Casemates Barracks building," according to Julie's guidebook, "and fitted out like the deck of a ship, with beams wrapped in sails, ceiling lights concealed in crow's nests, a painted blue sky, and historic paintings of the Battle of Trafalgar on the two-meter-thick stone walls, it is one of Gibraltar's most atmospheric dining places."

And so it was, but the boat-shaped bar and every table in the house were loaded with cruise passengers downing a last ale or stout before returning to their ships, so they sat outside on the pleasant terrace, situated at one end of the immense Grand Casemates Square ("the scene of Gibraltar's last public hanging," explained the ever-helpful guidebook).

Over smooth, soothing pints of bitter, their resolve to drop the subject of Gideon's near-death experiences melted away. "If we're right about it being one of your cohorts," Julie said, "then we're down to four people." She counted them off on her fingers. "Audrey, Adrian, Corbin, and Pru. No, make that five, with Buck. But Pru—" She jerked her head. "There's no way it could be Pru. I mean . . ."

"You're right, it's not Pru," Gideon said. "Definitely not."

"Definitely?"

"Definitely. It was Pru who hauled me up off the mountainside. If she'd pushed me over in the first place, she'd hardly have done that, would she. So, no, it's not Pru."

"Yes, you're right. That makes me feel better. So—wait a minute, we're forgetting about Rowley."

"Oh, I don't see how—"

"No, I know he hardly seems like a killer, but think for a minute. Didn't you tell me he'd gone up earlier to make sure things were set up for your lecture? He'd have had the perfect opportunity to get rid of the mat and all. And, *and*"—she was warming to her subject—"he would have been a familiar figure around there. No one would have been surprised to see him up on stage. He could easily have . . . no?" she said in response to the shaking of his head.

"Well, yes, he could probably have gotten away with it better than the others, but he's the one who pointed out the problem, who told me the mat was gone. He's the only reason I *didn't* get fried." *To a crisp*, his mutinous mind insisted on adding.

"Oh, you didn't tell me that," she said, a bit let down. "So that lets the two of them out. Pru and Rowley. So we're left with—who? Adrian, Corbin, Audrey, and Buck. I don't know—can you really see *any* of them as would-be murderers?"

"Mmm . . . well, Audrey, maybe."

Her eyebrows went up. "Audrey? Are you—"

"I'm kidding," he assured her. "Come on."

She smiled. "Well, I'm glad you're able to joke about it."

Gideon ordered a steak-and-ale pie for dinner. Julie, whose appetite had returned with a vengeance, ordered what she always did when she was truly, deeply hungry: the biggest hamburger they had, with everything on it. In Lord Nelson's case, the HMS Victory Burger was a truly monstrous concoction topped with representatives from every known food group: mushrooms, bacon, egg, cheese, onions, sausage, lettuce, and tomato. It took a knife and fork to get at it, but Julie demolished every morsel, along with the French fries that came alongside.

While they ate, they continued a generally unsatisfactory and wholly unproductive discussion of who and why, but they managed to end on a positive note.

"Okay," Julie said, "are you ready for the good news?"

"There's good news?"

"Yes, I just thought of it. If what's been happening is really related to those articles in the papers, then at least you can stop worrying. You've already given the speech and everybody now knows there *was* no big revelation. You can stop looking over your shoulder. That's good news, isn't it?"

"Very. I hadn't thought of it myself."

"Still, I imagine you'd probably like to know what it was all about."

"Know who's been trying to kill me? Oh, well, yeah, I suppose I have a certain mild interest in the matter."

THIRTEEN

BREAKFAST in the hotel dining room the next morning was somewhat strained, at least from Gideon's perspective. It's hard to relax and enjoy your kippers and eggs when you keep sneaking looks around the table wondering just which one of your merry companions has been trying to cut your life short. And—just in case it *wasn't* your now-completed and demonstrably harmless lecture that had elicited the attempts—whether he (or she) would be giving it another shot today.

The day before, while he and Julie had breakfasted on their balcony, everyone else had gone down to the dining room, pulled a couple of tables together, and eaten as a group. Apparently, this was to be the pattern for the rest of their stay, inasmuch as the pulled-together tables were waiting for them this morning, covered with tablecloths, with menus and place settings laid out, and everyone there.

If anyone noticed that Julie's and Gideon's moods were

subdued, it wasn't apparent. The conversation around them mostly concerned a controversial paper presented at the conference the day before, in which the author asserted, by means of a complicated mathematical model, that, had the Neanderthals been vegetarians instead of meat-eaters, their ecological niche would have been more bountiful, and they would have survived, possibly out-competing the invading *Homo sapiens* and causing *their* extinction. Audrey and Pru thought it made sense; Adrian and Corbin asserted it was poppycock. The discussion was spirited, peppery, and somewhat dogmatic, in the usual manner of academics quarreling over the arcane details of their discipline. Julie and Gideon were allowed to eat quietly without participating.

Midway through the meal, Rowley Boyd came in, slipped without saying anything into the vacant chair next to Adrian, and shook his head when the waiter asked if he wanted breakfast. Although the subject matter was something he'd ordinarily have jumped right in on, he sat, silent and grave, his chin in his hand, his forefinger slowly, meditatively tapping his lower lip, his downcast eyes on the table. His trusty pipe peeped unused from the breast pocket of his tweed jacket. Eventually, Adrian, apparently thrown off his rhythm by the mushroom cloud of gloom that had settled in beside him, asked with an impatient sigh if something was wrong.

"Yes," said Rowley, looking somberly up. His normally affable face was startlingly haggard and pinched.

The arguing came to an abrupt halt. A chill washed over the table like a surge of cold sea water.

"Wh . . . what is it?" Corbin said after a moment.

"Ivan's dead."

"Ivan Gunderson?" Corbin asked stupidly.

"No, Ivan the Terrible, for Christ's sake," muttered Pru out of the side of her mouth.

"But he was just here the other night! We were all talking to him!"

It struck Gideon, not for the first time, how often people responded like that to news of a death. "But I had dinner with him yesterday!" "But I just saw her this morning!" As if it was impossible for someone to be alive one minute and dead the next, although that was precisely the way it was. And yet he felt some of the same dull, hopeless denial. Gunderson dead? Impossible! He was here just the other day, wasn't he?

"How did it happen, Rowley?" Audrey asked tonelessly.

Rowley was searching the room for their waiter. "I, ah, believe I should like a cup of coffee after all."

"Take mine," Gideon said, sliding over his cup and saucer.

The cup was full, but Rowley drained it without setting it down, in two long gulps. "Thank you." He placed the cup on the table and breathed slowly in and out. His exhausted eyes were now focused on his hands, lying clasped on the table. "It happened the night before last, or rather very early yesterday morning, only a little while after I drove him home from the dinner. I learned of it only last night. I couldn't believe it. He'd been fine when I left him—well, perhaps a little disoriented, as you know, but—"

"Rowley," Gideon said. "What happened?"

"Sorry. He was smoking in bed. He did that, you know. He smoked a pipe too; he had a rack of Meerschaums, beautiful things that he used to get from . . ." He jerked his head and massaged his temples so hard the rubbing was audible. "His bedclothes were full of little burn holes. I warned him about it. His cleaning woman warned him about it. He promised to stop, but no, not him, he—"

"Rowley!" Audrey commanded. "*Will* you get on with it?"

"I'm trying to tell you!" cried poor Rowley. "There was a terrible fire. He died in his bed. By the time the fire people got there, his cottage was completely destroyed."

Julie and Gideon exchanged a quick glance—the fire Fausto had been called away to look into yesterday. Fausto's opinion to the contrary, it seemed that interconnected monkey business had apparently struck again.

While Rowley did his best to deal with his own emotions and the ensuing storm of questions, Gideon went up to the room to call Fausto. When he got there, the message light on the bedside telephone was blinking. The voice mail message from police headquarters was classic Sotomayor:

"Gideon. Fausto. Call."

Gideon reached him on the first ring. "Fausto, this is—"

"Gideon, sorry, can't tell you for sure if the lamp was messed with or not. Has to go to the lab in London. I express mailed it and put in a call to them to say it was urgent, but, you know, Gib isn't exactly at the top of their list, so I'm not sure how long it'll take. But we did lift some prints off it here. Four different sets, all pretty clear. Do you remember whether you ever touched it yourself?"

"I don't think I did . . . but I'm not sure. Maybe."

"Then I better get yours, just in case."

"Okay, I'll come over there a little later. But Fausto—"

"Now, I talked with that tech guy at the cave, Derek? Who says the work crew all swear to God they never moved that mat, that they don't know—"

"Fausto, that's not what I was calling about."

"What, this isn't important enough for you? Okay then, tell me, what did you call about?"

"The old man that died in the fire yesterday?"

"Yeah?"

"He was Ivan Gunderson, right?"

"Yeah. So how do you know his name? Is it in the paper already?"

"Ivan Gunderson was an archaeologist. He was one of our group. He was the one we had the testimonial dinner for the other night."

"No, uh-uh, this guy was an archaeologist, all right, but he was a resident of Gib. He lived here, had a house in the South District."

"It's the same person, Fausto. He owned several houses. One of them was here. It's where he spent most of his time the last few years."

Gideon heard—almost felt the breeze from—the long *whoosh* of Fausto's let-out breath. "So . . . ?"

"So, with Sheila Chan," Gideon said, "that makes two people connected with the dig who've now died in 'accidents.' Neither one with witnesses, let me point out. Add that to what now looks like an attempt to electrocute me, as well as—"

"But what's the dig got to do with you? You weren't on it, I thought."

"No, but I did the analysis of the bones from it—of Gibraltar Boy."

"Aw, jeez," Fausto said.

"Fausto, is there anything at all that caught your eye about the fire? Anything that made you think it might not have been an accident?"

"No, nothing, but I have to admit, I wasn't looking that hard. No reason to. According to Burkhardt—this lieutenant, fire department—it started on the bed, that much is for sure. And he was smoking, that's for sure too—or at least, what was left of his pipe, which wasn't that much, was right next to what was left of him, which also wasn't that much, which was on what was left of the bed, which was practically nonexistent. The whole cottage burned down to the ground, you know? Place was full of these glues and solvents—"

"He spent his days gluing pots."

"—so there were accelerants all over the place. Neighbors said it was more like an explosion than a fire. You know, *whooof!* Never saw a body burned like that. He looked like a piece of burned wood, all black and shriveled. I mean, this one gives new meaning to the term *fried to a crisp*."

Which is rapidly becoming one of my least favorite metaphors, Gideon thought. "Where is it now?"

"The body? In the morgue. The ME just finished the postmortem."

"Already?"

"Told you, we don't have much call for postmortems. Did most of it yesterday afternoon, wrapped it up this morning. Don't have his report yet—Figlewski, his name is—but he called me five minutes ago, soon as he was done. It's the usual. Died of smoke inhalation. No reason to think it's anything but what it looks like, he says."

"Uh-huh." Gideon hesitated. "Do you suppose I could have a look at it?"

"You want to look at the body?"

"Yes."

A dry, one-note chuckle. "Trust me, there's not a lot to look at."

"Still."

"Sure, why not? But what are you looking for?"

"I don't know, but I'd like to have a try. What shape is the skull in? Is any of it left?"

"Ah, you want to know if somebody bashed him over the head or something first, then started the fire to cover it. Am I right, or am I right?"

"You're right."

"Well, I can answer that for you right now. The answer's no."

"Uh-huh. And how did you establish that? If I'm not being too inquisitive."

"I established it," said Fausto, "with state-of-the-art, high tech information I received at this seminar I once took from this famous professor."

"Ah, well, then it must be reliable. Come on, Fausto, explain."

"What is this, a test? Okay." He paused to gather his thoughts. "In this seminar I learned that, in a fire, a skull can explode from the heat. But only if it wasn't broken to start with, you know? Because if there was a hole or a crack in it already, there would be a vent for the steam pressure from inside to escape?"

"Yes, that is what I said, but—"

"Well, there sure as hell wasn't any vent, because his skull looks like an exploded coconut. The top's completely blown off, all the way down to the, what do you call 'em, right under the eyes, the cheekbones—"

"Malars."

"Right, all the way down to the malars in front, and in the back, all the way down to the bone in the rear—"

"The occiput."

"I know, dammit, I was just gonna say that. Let me finish a sentence, will you?" He waited to see if Gideon meant to comply, then went on. "The occiput, what's left, you can really see how it just burst open, you know, because there are these kind of flaps of bone, bent outward, like—"

"And from all this you surmise?"

"I surmise," said Fausto, bristling at Gideon's tone, "that since the skull exploded, there was no preexisting opening in it to vent the pressure, and therefore no preexisting cranial trauma. Would that be correct, Professor Oliver?"

"No, that would be incorrect, Detective Chief Inspector Sotomayor."

"Whaaat?" This exclamation was followed by a few seconds of aggrieved silence, and then a shouted: "You're the frigging guy I learned that from! I was practically quoting you! I still got my notes, I—"

"Yes, but things change, my good fellow. New things are learned. Old assumptions are discarded. That is the nature of science. That is the essence of empiricism. One must be ready to cast off even the most cherished beliefs if they are contraindicated or unsupported by the evidence."

"Yeah, right. In other words, *you* screwed up. When you were showing us all those fancy diagrams with those line-of-force arrows that explained everything? You didn't know what the hell you were talking about. That's what you're telling me."

"You could put it that way," Gideon agreed.

He was far from the only one who'd been wrong. For decades the "exploding skull" hypothesis had been a cornerstone of forensic investigations involving burned bodies. The idea was that steam pressure built up inside the skull from the boiling (or rather, roasting) brain, eventually blowing apart the sealed vessel that was the cranium, much in the way that an unpunctured potato explodes in the microwave. But if the cranium was *not* sealed, that is, if there were preexisting openings—bullet holes, blunt force fractures—then the steam would safely escape through these vents without blowing up the skull—in the same way as it safely escapes through the skin of a fork-punctured potato. Thus, the reasoning went, while an unexploded skull was not proof positive of the lack of preexisting injuries—the effects of fire were not that predictable—an "exploded" skull was a good indication that it had been whole to begin with.

But when this intuitive, reasonable-sounding hypothesis

was finally put to the test only a few years ago in a study involving the experimental burnings of scores of cadaver heads, it turned out not to hold up. Skulls did not explode like hot potatoes. They might fragment or warp because the heat had deformed them and made them brittle, or because a stream of cold water from a fireman's hose hit the sizzling bone and cracked it, or because debris fell on them, or because they broke while being recovered. But explode—no, not a one.

"Well, that's a hell of a note," Fausto grumbled when Gideon had finished explaining. "So how much else of what you told us am I not supposed to believe anymore?"

"Fausto, except for this one thing, I promise you, you can rely with implicit faith on every word I uttered."

"Uh-huh. Until they turn out to be contraindicated or unsupported by the evidence."

Gideon nodded. "I couldn't have put it better myself."

"Okay," Fausto said with a sigh, "so where does all that leave us?"

"Right where we were before. Would it be all right for me to have a look at the body?"

"Pick you up in twenty minutes," Fausto said and clicked off

FOURTEEN

THE Gibraltar morgue was in St. Bernard's Hospital, which stood at the northern end of the city in what was called Europort, a modern, waterside complex strikingly different from the cozy, matey, "'ere's mud in yer eye" ambience of Main Street. Here were the high-end, balconied luxury apartments with their three-year waiting lists, and the tasteful, polished wood and brushed stainless steel headquarters of the colony's financial, insurance, and investment companies. Here too were the not-quite-so-refined offshore gambling and tax haven centers that had lately become main sources of Gibraltar's income.

Fausto drove them there in his pride and joy, a gleaming black, low-slung sports car—a Lamborghini Diablo, he said, clearly expecting a gush of admiration and astonishment from Gideon (in this he was sorely disappointed)—that was perfectly suited to the DCI's diminutive size, but required Gideon to sit with his feet off the floor and his knees jammed up against the dashboard. It also required some planning and a few contortions to get in and out through the butterfly-wing doors. And of course, Fausto drove it like any sports car enthusiast, which is to say like a maniac, careening joyfully around the narrow streets and tight corners of the old town, pedal to the floor. Gideon twice thought it was all over, but somehow they did make it. The hospital itself was brand spanking new, a smooth, cream-colored monolith of seven stories, of which Gideon was to see none. The hospital garage in which Fausto parked was underground, and the morgue was a floor below that.

Dr. Kazimir Figlewski was waiting for them in the anteroom. Instead of the roomy hospital scrubs favored nowadays by most pathologists, he was wearing an old-fashioned black rubber apron over a sleeveless undershirt. He was a skinny, smiling scarecrow of a kid with a wild thatch of stiff, blond hair that sat on the top of his head like a nest, and big, round, flaming red ears that stuck out like a pair of mug handles. His pale, bare, unmuscled arms were covered in light brown freckles.

Gideon was visited by one of those intimations of his own advancing age that had begun popping up lately. When did they start making doctors this young? Fausto had told him Figlewski was somewhere in his late twenties, but since when were people in their late twenties as young as this?

"I am greatly happy to meet you, professor," Figlewski said. His accent was what you might expect from someone named Kazimir Figlewski, throaty and Slavic, with long, broad, gliding vowels. He grinned and thrust out his hand.

Gideon, somewhat fastidious (many a small-minded colleague would say squeamish) around fresh remains (less than five hundred years old, say), couldn't help sneaking a look at the proffered hand. Shaking hands with a man—a boy—who had just finished poking around inside a dead body didn't appeal to him (some pathologists still worked without gloves part of the time, after all), but the hand looked clean and white enough. He took it.

"Thanks, Dr. Figlewski, same here."

"Please, you call me Kaz."

"And I'm Gideon. I hope you don't think I'm horning in, Kaz."

"Oh, no, please. Fausto warns me you are coming." He laughed. "I mean he *tells* me you are coming, that you think maybe we got some foul play here. That's great—I mean, I am wery interested to see what you do, how you do this. Is a great honor to meet you. I read your papers wery much in journals. 'The Bone Doctor.'" He grinned.

"Close enough," said Gideon, smiling.

"We don't never have a real forensic scientist come here before, you know. No reason for it. Last murder we have is two years ago. This is before I start working with police."

This is before you finished medical school, Gideon thought. "Yes, Fausto told me," he said.

Fausto had also told him that Figlewski wasn't really an ME in the American sense of the word. While his formal title was "forensic medical examiner," he was simply a local pediatrician who had a part-time contract with the Territory of Gibraltar; what might be called a police surgeon in a small American town. He spent a great deal more time clucking over infected ears than he did in the autopsy suite. Fausto thought highly of him, though, and with reason. He had emigrated from Poland to England as a fifteen-year-old speaking no English. Despite this language handicap, thirteen years later he had a medical degree from the University of East Anglia, and last year he had come to Gibraltar, answering the call for doctors to work in the new hospital.

"But I already do some traffic fatalities," he said, lest Gideon should think him inexperienced.

"Your first burn case, though?"

"On dead body, you mean? Because peoples, especially so many kids, always coming in—"

"On a dead body, yes," Gideon said. "An autopsy."

"Well . . . yes, this is true, but thermal injuries, they are covered in forensic course they send me to in London. But if I miss something, or if you have tip for me, I am standing all ears."

Probably not the best metaphor in the world for you, Gideon thought with the slightest of smiles, but he had already taken a liking to this chatty, earnest, slightly goofy young Pole. At least he had the right attitude for a forensic pathologist. In Gideon's experience, medical examiners and pathologists, unlike their police and prosecutorial brethren (to say nothing of the defense side), had little sense of turf, little desire to protect their jurisdictions. This wasn't the first autopsy he'd horned in on, and almost always he'd been warmly welcomed. They were scientists, not advocates, that was the difference. Nothing to support, or justify, or protect. They were more interested in teaching—and learning—than in proving or vindicating.

"Well, I don't know how many tips I can give you," he said. "I've never actually performed an autopsy myself, you know." (*And with luck I never will*, he added silently.) "I generally work with skeletal remains."

"Sure, you bet, the Bone Doctor."

Twice was too much for the irascible Fausto. "*Skeleton Detective.* For Christ's sake, Kaz."

"Skeleton Detective, Skeleton Detective," Kaz repeated, slapping himself on the side of the head to drive it in.

Continuing to bat himself on the temple—"Skeleton Detective, Skeleton Detective"—he led them out of the pleasant, fabric-walled anteroom, through a small, plain room lined with metal file cabinets, and with a large scale that took up most of the room implanted in the linoleum-covered floor; here, gurneys with bodies on them would be weighed and measured before being autopsied. A door on the far wall led into the tile-walled autopsy room itself—"Welcome to my world" said Figlewski—and the moment it opened Gideon was reminded of why he hated fire fatalities so much; maybe even more than decomps (although it was a close call).

The thing was, badly charred bodies *smelled* wonderful— walking into an autopsy room with one of them on the table was like walking into a weirdly sterile-looking steakhouse. And then you got up to the table and had to face the thing that lay on it. For Gideon, the war between the appetizing smell and his notoriously hair-trigger gag reflex made for a queasy and unsettling time of it.

"I told you," said Fausto, referring to the paucity of re- mains lying on the slanting, zinc-topped table.

Gideon nodded, trying to quiet the churning in his mid- section. Once he got down to work, it would pass, but for the moment, what was left of Ivan Gunderson was pretty off-putting. As Fausto had said, the body, lying on its back, looked more like a charred chunk of wood—a piece of driftwood that had been used more than once as part of a campfire on the beach—than what had once been a human being. That was the bad part. It was also the good part, in that there was nothing at all in this blackened, desiccated hulk to make him think of Ivan. It might have been any- body. It might almost have been anything.

As Fausto had told him, there was nothing that anyone could call a face. Only the back parts of the palate and mandible were left, with a few heat-shattered molars. This was a common result in fires. The human face and cranial vault are "protected" only by some of the thinnest muscles in the entire body. Lower down, along the sides of the head and in back, where the heavier musculature of the jaw and the neck do afford some protection, both soft and skeletal tissue generally fare somewhat better. And this was the case here. The base of the cranium, thick to begin with, and shielded by dense muscles as well, was still present, but only as an empty, bowl-shaped basin with some blackened soft tissue—not soft anymore—still left on the outside. If there had been any brain tissue left inside, which was unlikely, Kaz had removed it during the autopsy.

As for the rest of the body, Fausto had been right about that too. There wasn't much to see. One of his more lyrical anthropologist friends, Stan Rhine, had likened the appearance of a body as badly burned as this one to a derelict old sailing ship, dismasted and cast up on a beach somewhere, its curved, broken old ribs jutting up from the sands. The image had stuck with Gideon, and in Ivan's case, it was particularly apt. "The body was burned beyond recognition" would have been putting it mildly.

"Well," Gideon said, steeling himself. He stood a couple of feet from the table, looking down at it.

Kaz was on the other side of it, watching expectantly. Fausto was leaning back against a stainless steel sink four or five feet away, his arms folded. Gideon doubted that this tough little cop was worried about his stomach. More likely, he didn't want to chance getting anything nasty on his pale blue, nubby linen suit or the soft, immaculate French cuffs of his buff-colored silk shirt. Gideon wished he could work from five feet away too.

"Tell me what you know so far, Kaz," Gideon said.

"Well, we establish already that he is alive at time of fire—"

"How do you know that?"

"Elevated carbon monoxide level in blood. He is still breathing when fire started, for sure."

Gideon looked down at the dried, crusted remains. "You were able to get blood?"

"Blood, yes, even urine. There was congealed mass of soft tissue in pelvic cavity—liver, colon . . ."

"And you already have the results?"

Fausto answered for him. "Told you, there isn't too much going on here. Getting lab results in a hurry isn't a problem."

"What was the level?" Gideon asked.

"Fifty-five percent," said Kaz.

"Enough to kill a man his age," Gideon said.

"Oh, yes, for sure."

"So is that your best guess? He died of smoke inhalation?"

"Oh, yes. For sure."

"Okay, what else?" Gideon edged a step closer to the table. He liked to approach these things in stages, working his way up to the corpse. For him, it made it easier to take, like getting into cold water a few inches at a time, getting used to the shock, and then going in deeper.

"Else?" Kaz scratched his head. "Not so much, really. Uh, he was lying on back, in bed, during fire—I find pieces of melted, what do you call it, springs from bed, buried in soft tissue on back of hips and shoulders. And, well . . ."

"How sure are you that it's him—Gunderson?" Gideon asked, looking down at the body, his hands still in back of him. It wasn't that unusual for unrecognizable remains to turn out to belong to other people than were first assumed. While the fact that he had been found in Gunderson's bed made it likely that he was indeed Ivan Gunderson, it wasn't exactly proof. And nobody had identified this body by looking at it, that was for sure.

"One hundred percent," Fausto answered for Kaz. "That's one thing we're sure about."

"Was his teeth," Kaz said. "Mostly broken or gone, yes, but two back ones, upper molar threes, are still okay, and we bring his dentist here first thing this morning to see them. A positive identification."

Gideon shook his head admiringly. "You guys do work fast," he said. Another step closer to the table.

"Wasn't that hard," Fausto said. "Total of twenty-four dentists in Gib. Took about fifteen minutes to find Gunderson's. And he wasn't doing anything else this morning."

"So where you go from here?" Kaz asked. "You can do something with . . . with this small remains?"

"It doesn't look good, does it?" Gideon said with a sigh. "Is this it, then, Kaz? They didn't come up with any more pieces of him?"

"No more pieces, but I got some of his liver and other organs"—another gesture of invitation toward the refrigerator—"if you want—"

Gideon fended him off with upraised hands. "*No!* I mean, I wouldn't know what to do with them. I meant bones. Especially pieces of the skull."

Kaz shook his head. "I'm sorry, they find only this."

"The cottage was a mess," Fausto said. "Hardly anything standing. Roof collapsed, debris everywhere, all as burned up as he is, tons of water sloshed all over everything. Take you a year to try to find any bone at all, let alone from his skull. This is it, I'm afraid."

Gideon nodded. He had made it all the way up to the table now. "Well, let's see what we can see," he said, not very hopefully.

"You would like lab coat?" Kaz asked. "Pair gloves?"

"I would *love* a pair of gloves, Kaz."

Kaz gave him two pairs—since the advent of AIDS, wearing two sets instead of one had become common—which Gideon slipped on, not that the remains of Ivan Gunderson would be likely to pose any threat in that regard. Beside the table was a steel tray in which Kaz's simple

autopsy tools lay on a cloth: probes, scalpels, and the ubiq-
uitous, wicked-looking, foot-long knife known familiarly
as the "bread knife." All the classic old instruments. Scissors, favored by most young pathologists nowadays, were
not present. Gideon selected a dental pick, spatula-shaped
at one end, hooked and pointed at the other, and bent over
the ruins of the skull. Fausto stayed where he was, back a
few feet, leaning against the sink. Kaz, anticipating edification, leaned keenly over the table from the other side.
Gideon, for his part, would have been happy to edify, but
the pickings looked slim; he might well be wasting everyone's time.

He turned his attention to what was left of the skull,
gently probing with the pick end of the probe. "So what
we've got here is the base of the cranium from about the superior nuchal line on down," he mused aloud, "with some of
the heavy musculature—sternocleidomastoideus, masseter,
trapezius—still adhering to the lower portions. . . ."

Gingerly, he touched the gray-white, exposed bone with
the tip of the probe. Bits of it crumbled away. "Upper parts
are deeply burned, heavily calcined in places, graduating
inferiorly to singed, buff-colored bone, and then to—"
With the spatula end of the probe he prodded the surface
of the burned musculature. The crusty top layer flaked off
at the first touch, exposing a deeper stratum of red meat,
much like—he couldn't help thinking it—the middle of a
rare, charcoal-broiled steak. When a bit of that too was
picked and prodded away, fresh, ivory-colored, unharmed
bone showed through. "—to muscle-protected, unburned
bony tissue from about the zygomatic process and the su-
pramastoid crest on down. The burned, exposed bone
shows marked deformation at its upper margins, and there
are two roughly parallel, roughly vertical linear fractures
about three inches apart in the squamous portion of the temporal bone, both originating at the upper, burned, broken

edge of the vault. The anterior one runs down in the general direction of the external auditory meatus, and the posterior one toward the occipito-temporal suture—" He poked a little more with the probe. "—or maybe the posterior portion of the mastoid process. It's hard to see; the inferior portions of both fractures are hidden by the neck and jaw musculature."

He was speaking basically for his own benefit. He worked better when he talked to himself. But Kaz was understandably under the impression that they were having a conversation.

"This cracking and warping," he said sagely, colleague to colleague, "are, of course, what we would expect in thermal destruction of such magnitude, both from heat itself, and also from falling debris."

"Well, yes, sure," Gideon said, his eye caught by something about the anterior fracture, the one that ran down in the direction of the auditory meatus—the opening for the ear. "But, you know, there are cracks . . . and there are cracks . . ."

"Ah, yes?" Kaz looked at him with a puzzled scowl. "Cracks and cracks?"

"Mmm." Gideon fingered the crack in question. "You notice anything different about this one?"

"You mean compared to other one?"

Gideon nodded.

The young man stared painfully hard at it, working to come up with something. "Is a little wider than other?" he tried at last. "Almost like silver is missing from."

Gideon frowned. "Pardon?"

"Almost like silver is missing," Kaz repeated patiently and very slowly. He was used to his accent causing problems. "Silver. Of. Bone." *Silwer. Awv. Bawn.*

"Silver of . . . ?" a befuddled Gideon began.

"*Sliver*, for Christ's sake," Fausto intervened. "What's

the matter, you don't understand English?" Drawn by curiosity, he had come up to the table for a look too, although he kept his hands in his pockets to protect those taintless French cuffs.

"Silver, silver," Kaz agreed. "Of bone."

"Oh, yes, *sliver*," Gideon said. "It does look like that, Kaz, as if a sliver, a splinter, has popped out. But that's not why the crack is wider. It's wider because—"

"Because the sides of it are all eaten away," Fausto said, peering at it. "The other crack, it's got these clean edges. You could fit the two sides right back together. But this one, you couldn't. The sides are all, like, eroded."

"Exactly," Gideon said.

"Which means?"

"Well, let's look at a little more of it before I go out on a limb. I want to see the whole length of the cracks. Kaz, would you mind removing the soft tissue around the base of the skull?" he asked brightly. "I'd do it myself, but I'm sure you'd be better at it."

A snort from Fausto, and a contemptuous "Yeah, right." Meanwhile, he himself had now returned to his spot a good five feet away.

"And be really careful with it, will you, Kaz? We don't want to damage it any more than it already is."

Kaz's mobile features pulled together and darkened. "I will try my best," he mumbled, believing his professional competence had been called into question.

"Sorry, Kaz," Gideon said quickly. "I didn't mean *you* had damaged it. I can see what a good job you've done with it so far. I know you'll be careful. I don't know what made me say that."

He knew what had made him say it, all right. He knew that pathologists, with their natural focus on organs and soft tissue, could be downright careless about bone. Many a nick or scratch on a skeleton that had first been taken to be a sign of foul play had turned out in the end to be nothing more than the slip of a pathologist's knife during the autopsy. And many a genuine sign of antemortem trauma had been obliterated or made unusable as evidence in the same way.

But Kaz was a meticulous dissector, his long, deft fingers slicing, tugging, and delicately scraping away with skill and control. In a few minutes the lower right-hand side of the skull was as clean as a scalpel could get it.

"Nicely done," Gideon said truthfully, which mollified Kaz, assuming that his re-reddening ears could be taken as an indication.

Gideon leaned over the broken skull, breathing as shallowly as he could. Kaz's scalpel had released a fresh puff of barbecue-grill aroma. But one quick look made him forget all about the odor. He'd come up with something, something crucial. A familiar and irrepressible feeling of satisfaction, almost of triumph, ran through him.

"All right, men, we've got something here. Look at the fracture, the one we've been talking about, where it runs into the unburned bone, where the muscle was covering it before you cut it away, Kaz."

"Okay, we're looking," Fausto said, growing impatient. "Come on, my attention span isn't that great. Why don't you just tell us what we're supposed to see?"

"Because I'm a professor. This is what I do. Come on, look at the crack. What happens to it?"

Fausto sighed. "Nothing happens to it. The damn thing goes down into the, what do you call it, the ear-hole thing."

"The auditory meatus."

"Whatever. And it disappears in there."

"Very good. Now compare it to the other fracture, where *it* runs into the unburned bone that was under the muscle."

Kaz's brows knit. "I don't—"

"There's nothing to compare, dammit," Fausto said through clenched teeth. "The other crack doesn't run down that far."

Gideon straightened, stripped off his gloves, and tossed them on the tray. "Bingo," he said.

FIFTEEN

FOR almost two hundred years the Alameda Botanical Gardens have been a peaceful, restorative haven where the people of Gibraltar could go to get away from the congestion, dust, and bustle of the city. Lovers—moony teenagers and shuffling old married folk—still stroll hand in hand among its lush plantings, stately civic memorials, and nineteenth-century cannons, planning their futures and recalling their pasts.

Strolling there hand in hand, Gideon told Julie about the burned body in the morgue.

"So he *was* murdered," she said thoughtfully.

"I'm pretty sure."

"And does Fausto go along with you?"

"Oh, yes. He was setting up some interviews when I left him. Rowley's at the top of the list."

"He suspects *Rowley*?"

"No, but Rowley drove Ivan home that night. He's

probably the last one who saw him alive before the killer. He probably knows Ivan better than anyone else too."

"Does Fausto have anybody he suspects? Do you?"

"No. Do you?"

She shook her head. "No, I'm trying to imagine a reason any of these people would want to kill him, and I can't come up with one."

"I know. I would have thought he didn't have an enemy in the world. I'm sorry you didn't know him before; he was impossible to dislike. But then, we know next to nothing about his outside life. There's more to him than archaeology. Family, acquaintances, old enemies, maybe . . ."

"I know. But if you add in the attacks on you, and Sheila Chan's 'accident,' it just has to have something to do with Gibraltar Boy and all that—which means something to do with these people—your friends."

"Julie, we have no compelling reason to think what happened to Sheila *wasn't* an accident, and as for the supposed attacks on me, the jury's still out, right? There's no hard evidence anyone really attacked me."

"Yeah, right," Julie said, which, in reality, pretty much summed up Gideon's sentiments too.

They walked a few more steps. "You could really tell he was murdered by comparing the cracks in his skull?" Julie asked.

"More or less."

"That's remarkable. Every time I think I know all your tricks you come up with another one."

"But unlike most magicians, I always tell how I did it."

"Whether I want to know or not." She dug him in the ribs with her elbow. "You know I'm kidding. Tell me."

"What do you say we sit down?"

They chose a lichened stone bench in a grove of small but ancient oaks, poplars, and spiky palms, with the clean, white façade of the Rock Hotel, and the immense Rock itself, looming above them through the foliage.

"There were two keys," he said. The first had been the form of the fractures. One was narrow, with sharp, clean-cut margins. As Fausto had said, if there hadn't been any warping of the surrounding temporal bone, the edges would have fit together perfectly. That was fairly typical of thermally induced fracturing.

"The skull just splits open from the heat?" Julie said.

"No, not exactly. It happens primarily because the organic content of the bone is destroyed, which delaminates it—the external table separates from the diploe and shrinks and cracks. Continue the heat, and the same thing happens to the internal table, so then you get a fracture all the way through."

She frowned. "Isn't that what I just said?"

He laughed. "I suppose so, yes. In any case, there's nothing suspicious about that one. But the second crack, the anterior one, ah, that one was wide open, with margins so worn and eroded—so burned—that they no longer came close to matching each other."

Long used to this kind of conversation, Julie was characteristically quick on the uptake. "Meaning that the second crack was exposed to the heat for a longer time, so it must have come first," she said.

"Right. Presumably it was there before the fire started."

"But how do you know it wasn't just a question of the way he was lying?"

"The way he was lying?"

"Sure. He was lying on the bed, right? Which was where the fire started. Maybe that part of his head—the part that had the eroded crack—was against the mattress, so it took more of the heat for a longer time. Couldn't that be the reason for the difference?"

"Well, it could, yes—although the two cracks were awfully close together for a differential rate of burning. But, yeah, you could be right, it's possible. Fortunately, there was another key. And this one was the clincher."

It was the simple fact that the fracture in question ran all the way down the temporal bone to its very bottom and disappeared into the auditory meatus, he explained.

"I don't understand," Julie said.

"No, of course not. Neither did Kaz, neither did Fausto. This is more new research, something we didn't know until a few years ago. The thing is, when a skull cracks from the heat of a fire, it's only the burned part that fractures. The crack won't extend into undamaged bone. That's the way it was with the second crack; it ended at the point where the sternocleidomastoideus had covered the bone and prevented it from burning. Just stopped short."

"But the other one didn't stop short," Julie said, nodding. "When the doctor stripped off the muscle, there it was underneath . . . meaning it had to have been there before the fire started. A traumatic injury of some kind."

"Bingo," Gideon said for the second time in an hour. "Blunt force, from the look of it, although the actual site of the blow was gone."

"That's interesting, but didn't you say that the doctor said he died of smoke inhalation? Was he wrong, then?"

"No, I don't think he was wrong, but neither am I. I'm assuming Ivan was whacked over the head with something— probably lost consciousness; I hope so, anyway—and then the fire was set to cover it up, and Ivan, just about dead already, took in a few whiffs of smoke and that was the end of it. If whoever did it knew the place was full of glues and solvents, which he probably did, he also knew it would go up like a haystack. He figured Ivan's body would be beyond any useful forensic analysis. And he was damn near right. I was lucky to find anything at all."

Julie suddenly shivered. "Ivan's body," she echoed. "It's funny, I forgot for a while there that we were talking about a real person, a nice old man we were chatting with just a couple of nights ago."

"I know," Gideon said with a sigh. "I forget too."

They were quiet for a few seconds, watching a gecko skitter across the path and into the bushes, taking in the bird calls—warblers, wrens, blackbirds—breathing in the flowery air. The sights, sounds, and smells of life.

Gideon looked at his watch. "The groundbreaking for the Europa Point visitor center thing is at two o'clock. Want to come?"

"You mean they're still planning to have it? Weren't they going to present Ivan with another award?"

"Yes, they'll do it posthumously. But you know, aside from that, this will be my first chance to see the actual cave site. They haven't been letting anybody down there since the path to it collapsed when they had that cave-in a few years ago."

"When Sheila Chan got killed."

"Right. But Pru says it's not really that hard to get to, and nobody really stops you. She's going to show me around it. So I'm going. What about you?"

"Sure, I'd like to come."

"Did you pick up the rental car, or will we need to get a taxi? I promised Pru a lift."

"No, I have the car. It's back at the hotel. A bright red Honda. But I could use some sustenance before then," Julie said. "How about lunch?"

"Sure."

"Any preference?"

Gideon thought for a moment. "Anything but steak," he said.

SIXTEEN

THE farther one goes from the center of Gibraltar town, the less English the landscape becomes. Driving south toward Europa Point in their rented red Honda, Gideon and Julie watched as the buildings—modest, single-story homes mostly—became more and more Spanish, with red tile roofs predominating, and pastel-colored stucco walls replacing stone ones. Even the Rock itself, along the diminishing flank of which Europa Road took them, became rockier, drier, more austere; putting one more in mind of the stony windmill country of *Man of La Mancha* than of William Blake's "green and pleasant" England. After a mile and a half or so, the Rock petered out altogether, plunging into the sea at Europa Point, the very tip of the peninsula.

This was not quite the southernmost point of Europe (Punta de Tarifa, a few miles to the east in Spain, had that honor, being one-tenth of a degree of latitude lower), but it was supposedly the closest point in Europe to the coast of

Africa (also by one-tenth of a degree), and it was, as Adrian had volunteered on the plane, the historic point at which General Tarik and his invading Moors had first set foot on the continent thirteen hundred years before.

This information was provided by one of the line of informational posters set up on easels at the cleared, windswept cliffside site that was to become the Ivan S. Gunderson Visitor Center. Pru, on reading it, tilted her head to gesture behind her and said, "Looks to me like they've returned."

She was referring to the blindingly white Ibrahim-al-Ibrahim Mosque, the gleaming new dome and slender minaret of which dominated the area, dwarfing the red-and-white lighthouse that had stood for almost two hundred years, serving as a sentinel over the narrow neck of water that separated the tranquil Mediterranean from the roiling Atlantic.

Other than the lighthouse and the mosque, there wasn't much on this craggy, blustery plateau that swaddled the tail of the Rock. Down near the water, of course, was the famous rock shelter itself, the Europa Point Cave—still mostly buried under the landslide that had killed Sheila Chan—but up here there was little to see. A parking area, some low, winding stone walls, a few trails, a historical marker, a few nondescript outbuildings, and a lot of desolate, rocky land swathed here and there with scraggly ground cover. A bus had come with a load of Asian tourists who wandered disconsolately around, obviously wondering why this desolate spot was on their tour, and politely trying to look interested as their guide pointed out Africa across the water and chattered away.

The group of archaeologists and anthropologists that stood at the cliff-top site of the dedication wasn't much larger—perhaps thirty in all—and certainly no more animated. They had dutifully wandered the line of posters, looking at historical notes, architect's renderings, and photos and paintings of Gibraltar Boy and his human mother. They had solemnly watched as the governor-general turned over a gold-plated shovelful of earth, as the Freedom of the City Award, Gibraltar's highest honor, was posthumously bestowed on Ivan (accepted in his place by Rowley), and as a bronze plaque with Ivan's profile in bas-relief was unveiled by the deputy minister of culture, to be installed later in the entrance rotunda of the center.

And they had stood, shifting from foot to foot, listening to the inevitable speeches. The governor-general made one, the minister of culture made one, Rowley made one, and the president of the historical association made one, all extolling the manifold virtues of Ivan Samuel Gunderson. Adrian made one too, of course, and of course it was the longest of them all. Once he'd delivered the obligatory eulogy, he lapsed into one of his mellifluous, erudite lectures, going on—and on, and on—about ecological conditions at Europa Point in the Pleistocene's waning years, forgetting, or more likely ignoring, the fact that almost everybody in his audience knew as much about it as he did.

"Inasmuch as the northern ice sheets had not yet melted, the sea levels would have been far lower at that time. Thus, our cave dwellers would have looked out, not on the water we see today, but on a marshy seaside plain harboring a rich array of game—rabbits, birds, foxes. Fish, shellfish, tortoises, all would have been there within easy reach for the taking. Up here on the coastal plateau there would have been horses and deer, and higher up on the Rock they would have found ibex. Taken all together, our First Family and their clan surely lived what would have passed for a life of ease in—"

Gideon's attention wandered. He peered down the face of the cliff trying to pinpoint the location of the rock shelter but couldn't find it. The particular part of the cliff face they overlooked was not a clean, vertical wall of rock plunging straight down to the sea, in which a cave would have been easy to spot, but a wide, deeply eroded gorge that had been more or less dammed up with mounded earthen detritus that ran all the way down to the water in a sloping incline. Clearly, the cave-in of four years ago had been only the latest, and probably not the last, of the Europa Point land disturbances.

"Pru, what do you say?" he murmured. "Could you show me around the site a little?"

"You mean right now, this minute?" she asked. "Please"—she inclined her head toward Adrian, who showed no sign of approaching this close, and cathedraled her fingers in front of her chest—"say yes."

"Yes," Gideon said, smiling. "Adrian's not going to notice."

"That's for sure. Julie, you want to come too?"

"What? No, I think I'll give it a skip. Actually, I find what he's saying pretty interesting."

"That's because you're the only one here who hasn't heard it before."

Corbin, protected from the sun by a floppy, broad-brimmed hat that was tied under his chin, was standing nearby. She tapped him on the shoulder. "Hey, Corb, I'm going to show Gideon around the site down there. Wanna come?"

He turned. "What is there to see? It's not there anymore."

"Well, you know, just give him some idea of where stuff was, that kind of thing. Come on, you were the assistant director, you should be the one to give the tour."

Corbin's lips pursed. "What I was, was the chief deputy director."

"Whatever. Come on already, you've heard this crap from Adrian a million times."

"Adrian is a very great archaeologist," Corbin said reprovingly. "He's always worth listening to."

"Yeah, yeah," said Pru. "Come on, Chief Deputy Director, let's get a move on."

Corbin glanced with something like amused resignation at Gideon—*What can you do with a woman like this?*—and said, "Very well," with a put-upon but amicable sigh, and led the way.

Julie touched Gideon's arm as he followed. "Be careful," she whispered. "Watch your step. Pay attention when you're climbing around. Don't stargaze."

"How can I? No stars."

"You know what I mean."

"Yes, I know what you mean. Don't worry, I'll be careful. I promise not to fall off."

"Now where have I heard that before?"

With the path to the cave blocked by debris from the most recent landslide, getting to it required slipping under a "Danger—Do Not Cross" ribbon, clambering over some broken stone walls, and negotiating the rough earthen fill, most of which was covered with a slippery, uneven mat of ground cover. Pru, in jeans and wearing cowboy boots with heels that dug in, managed it easily, but Gideon, in Rockport joggers, and Corbin, wearing brown oxfords, had to slip-slide their way down to the relatively level ledgelike area that was almost at the bottom. Once there, Gideon could see the cave, which had been invisible from above; a cavern perhaps fifty feet wide and, in the parts that hadn't been obstructed by the recent landslide, about twenty feet deep.

"So this is it," he said with the near-mystical pleasure he always felt at times like this: *Here, where I stand right now, on this rocky ledge, on this very spot, Neanderthal creatures—almost but not quite humans—once worked, and played, and went about their lives.* On the cave ceiling, toward the rear, he could make out the sooty smudges from their fires, still plainly visible after 24,000 years.

"What's left of it," Corbin said. "Well, let me give you the two-bit tour." He walked them up and down the ledge, explaining the excavation strategies they'd resorted to (rock shelters were trickier than ordinary digs on open land), what kind of grid system they'd used, where they'd found various materials: a firepot over here, a couple of Mousterian tools over there.

"Where was the First Family burial?" Gideon asked. Corbin, dyed-in-the-wool archaeologist that he was, was deep in his analysis of the stone tool technology, and it looked as if it might be a while before he got around to the human remains.

"Unfortunately, you can't see it anymore," said Pru. "It was in a crevice about a foot off the floor of the cave, over there, under all that mess." She pointed at an area to the right, where the overhang had come down altogether, so that it was no longer a rock shelter at all.

"We lost about half the cave in the landslide," Corbin said. "There was another fifteen meters of it right there, but that's where the worst of it hit. Unfortunately, it was where most of the important finds were made. What a shame to see it covered over like that; such an important site."

"Well, I gather they're planning to dig it out again for visitors," Pru said.

"Good luck," Gideon murmured, looking at the mass of earth in front of him. "That's a lot of dirt." It was as if one of those monstrous, three-story-tall earth-moving machines had been excavating some vast crater somewhere up above, and had dumped its huge bucket down here time after time, with the express purpose of burying the rock shelter. The enormous pile of soil, now pocked with struggling vegetation, completely plugged up any access to this part of the cave.

"What are those, do you know?" he asked, pointing at an unlikely row of a half dozen evenly spaced holes dug into the base of the pile. Five were deep but relatively small; about four feet in diameter. The fifth, the last one in the row, was big, a good ten feet in diameter and ten feet deep. All had been made some time ago, their margins no longer sharp-edged. And all had been dug with tools, not naturally formed; the piles of backfill lay all around them.

Before the question was out of his mouth, he realized what they were. "Is this where they dug Sheila Chan out?"

Pru responded with a somber nod. "Yes."

"Interestingly," said Corbin, "they do it the way we might do test-trenching. The smaller holes, those were a uniformly spaced series of exploratory probes. The deep one—"

"Is where they found her," Gideon said.

"Yes," Pru said again. "I was here. Well, not down here, but up above, with some of the others. I stayed the whole dreary, cold, rainy miserable day. You were there most of the time too, weren't you, Corb?"

"I was. I felt as if it was my . . . responsibility, as if I owed it to her somehow. I suppose I hoped, in some obscure way, that, by being there, by simply assuming they would find her, that somehow—" He finished with a shrug.

"You understand, Gideon," Pru said, "at that point we thought—we hoped—she still might be alive."

"Ah," said Gideon. He had gone up to the largest hole and was fingering its weathered margins. He picked up a chunk of backfill from it and broke it easily apart with his hands. A mixture of claylike earth with a little humus and some gravelly rock fragments mixed in. Pretty ordinary soil, in other words. But something about it had started the gears of his mind turning. Something gnawed at him, just out of reach. . . .

"But of course, she wasn't," Corbin said gravely. "She was buried so very deeply. In fact, they were about to go on to dig the next probe when someone spotted her outstretched fingertips just coming through the dirt, way down in the hole."

"Me," Pru said. "I spotted her."

"How deep in the hole?" Gideon asked. Why he wanted to know he wasn't sure, but there was something . . . something . . .

"Pretty deep," Pru said, "and even then it was only her fingers we could see. The rest of her was much deeper, probably eight or ten feet down, so of course there was no chance."

Gideon rubbed his palms together to get the dirt off them. A gritty residue remained. "Do you happen to know what the cause of death was?"

Pru looked strangely at him. "Offhand, I'd say that having had a hundred tons of dirt come down on her might have had something to do with it."

"No, I mean the actual cause of death, the immediate cause. Asphyxiation? Brain injury? Crushing chest injuries?"

"I have no idea. Why is it important?"

"Just wondering," he said vaguely.

It was the best he could come up with.

BACK at the top, Adrian, the final speaker, had finished up and the ceremony was winding down. Pru went to join Audrey and Buck, who were climbing into Rowley's van for the ride back. Corbin, who was driving Adrian, waited politely while his mentor accepted compliments and answered questions from a few hangers-on. Julie was waiting for Gideon, sitting on one of the rough stone walls at the edge of the cliffs, looking out over the glittering Strait.

"The mountains that rise before us," she intoned, "are part of the chain known as er-Rif, geologically speaking a component of the great cordillera that once stretched southward from the Iberian Peninsula into what is now Africa, which was not separated from the European continent by the Strait of Gibraltar until the Tertiary."

"Good gosh," Gideon said, "you keep listening to Adrian and maybe you can start giving me some competition at Trivial Pursuit."

"Nobody can give you competition at Trivial Pursuit. Gideon, you got a call from Fausto on the cell phone. The lab said the wires in the lamp cord were definitely filed, not just worn down."

He sat down beside her. "So somebody really did try to kill me."

"Are you surprised?"

"No. But I can't help being astonished."

"The difference being?"

"There's an old story, supposedly about Noah Webster, the dictionary guy, in which Webster's wife catches him in some hanky-panky with the maid. 'Mr. Webster, I am surprised!' she says. 'No, my dear,' says Webster, '*I* am surprised. *You* are astonished.' However, I've also seen it attributed to Samuel Johnson, and even Winston Churchill, so the provenance is dubious, to say the least."

"See?" she said, laughing. "You're in no danger of losing your Trivial Pursuit title belt." She turned serious. "But I know what you mean: maybe it doesn't *surprise* you, but you still find it hard to believe."

"Exactly."

"Yes, me too." She reflected for a moment and stood up with a sigh. "Anyway, Fausto wants you to come in and get fingerprinted so they can start working out whose prints are on the lamp. I told him I'd drop you off at the police station on the way back to the hotel."

"Do you know where the police station is?"

"I saw it yesterday while I was wandering around on my own. A great old red-brick building with Gothic arches, very Victorian . . . easy to imagine Inspector Lestrade coming out of it on his way to meet with Sherlock Holmes."

She waited a few seconds for him to get up as well, but he was lost in his thoughts, frowning, staring at nothing.

"Gideon? Are you there? Shall we go?"

He finally stood up. "Definitely. I wanted to talk to Fausto too. There's something funny about that landslide."

"What?"

"I don't know." He shook his head slowly back and forth. "But something."

SEVENTEEN

THE Victorian building downtown turned out to be merely a substation with a sergeant in charge. DCI Sotomayor was to be found at police *headquarters*, which were situated on Rosia Road, about a mile north of town. Following the instructions they were given, Julie located Rosia Road, which angled away from Main Street and ran down toward the waterfront. "I think it's that building over there," she said, pulling to a stop.

"You mean the one with the all the police cars out front and that big sign over the entrance that says 'Royal Gibraltar Police Headquarters?' Hmm, you just might have something there."

"Very funny. Don't be tedious."

Laughing, he leaned over to kiss her. "We can't be more than half a mile from the hotel. I'll walk back. Think about where you want to have dinner."

"Let's just have it in the hotel with the others," Julie said. "I think it would be good to know what's going on.

Also," she added with a smile, "I'm more comfortable when we have them all in sight."

"Okay, see you back there in an hour or less."

Getting out of the car, he found himself in an area of old buildings, mostly housing salty-sounding businesses: ship chandleries, nautical charts, marine hardware and coatings. The rusted street sign on the wall beside him told him that the alley at whose head he was standing was called South Dockyard Approach, and it led down behind him, predictably enough, to a sprawling dry dock operation. The two-story police headquarters building in front of him, like others nearby, was made of big, gray, rough-cut stone blocks. Above the Royal Gibraltar Police Department sign was an older one that said *New Mole House,* which suggested that the building had originally had something to do with the docks; possibly, he thought, it had been the customs house. He guessed it dated from the early 1800s. (Later he was to learn that he was a century off. It had been built in 1904 as an office of the Ministry of Defense.)

The front entrance had been constructed as a *porte cochere,* an arched opening big enough to admit a large horse-drawn vehicle. A handsome gate of metal grillwork closed off the inner courtyard, a tranquil Spanish-style patio with ornamental cactuses and palms, enclosed by four white-stuccoed, balconied walls. Within the entryway vestibule, what had been the old gatekeeper's stall was now a little office with a desk, behind which sat a sat a smiling, crisply dressed young policeman, his starched white shirt and blue tie immaculate, his blue tunic draped with perfect symmetry over the back of his chair.

"How may I be of service, sir?"

"My name is Gideon Oliver," Gideon told him through the grated window. "Chief Inspector Sotomayor—"

"Oh, yes, sir, you're to be fingerprinted and then

escorted to the chief inspector's office." He made a brief telephone call, then produced a visitors badge, which was given to Gideon to be hung around his neck. No more than twenty seconds after he'd replaced the phone, another constable appeared at the gate, unlatched it, and took Gideon to a booking room where he had his fingerprints rolled by a female constable, also white-shirted and blue-tied, who absentmindedly hummed throughout the task. It took him a moment to recognize the tune: "It's a Small World, After All."

"I understand you're some sort of scientific detective," she said, finishing up.

"Yes, you could say that."

"What do you detect?"

He pursed his lips, put his thumb and middle finger to his forehead, and put on a detecting expression. "Tell me, been to Walt Disney World lately?"

Her jaw dropped. "That's amazing. Disneyland, actually. In Paris. Just last week. But how did you know?"

"Ah, we're not permitted to divulge our techniques."

His fingertips cleansed with a waterless cleaner, he was taken down a corridor to Fausto's office, which was on the ground floor, overlooking the courtyard. He was expecting something expensively furnished—carpeting, framed prints and posters, modern sculpture—to go along with Fausto's flashy, expensive taste in cars and clothes, but instead he found the Universal Cop's Office: linoleum flooring; scarred, unmatched furniture, most of it metal; walls completely bare of decoration unless you counted charts, bulletin boards covered with overlapping notes and memos, and maps with pins stuck in them; shelves filled with codes and procedure manuals; desk neat and almost bare. And no sculpture at all, modern or otherwise.

"Pull up a chair," Fausto said. He too was in shirtsleeves (in his case, silver gray silk, shot through with pale gold stripes), the French cuffs of which had been turned back in two meticulous, clean-lined folds. His tie, diagonally striped in soft pastels, was, as always, a perfect match.

"Fausto, where do you get your clothes, anyway?"

"Shirts from Prada, suits from Armani, ties Ferragamo. Why, you want to dress like me?"

"Are you kidding? I couldn't afford it."

"Sure, you could. I get them over the Internet. Doesn't cost as much as you think."

"Even so, I'm a professor; I'd never get away with looking like a Mafia drug lord."

"You're right," Fausto agreed, preening a little. "It takes a cop to do that."

Gideon took the offered chair. "So tell me about the lamp."

"Not much to tell. They found the cord fabric and the wiring had both definitely been filed down—"

"To make it look as if they'd just frayed."

"Unless you can come up with a better reason. They were even able to tell me what he used." He glanced at an open writing pad on his desk. "A steel bastard-cut half-round file, probably the eight- or ten-inch variety."

"Oh? Is that any help? I mean, is that an unusual kind of file?"

"I was hoping the same thing, but nope, it's just a file; find 'em in any DIY outfit."

"So where do you go from here?"

"First order of business is to try and match the prints on the lamp. We got four sets, okay? We already identified three of them, guys who had a legitimate reason for handling it—that guy Derek, and two of his crew. That leaves one unidentified set. If yours match it, then we got pretty much bupkis. If they don't—well, I'm not sure what we have, but it's a place to start. Get prints from some of your pals, to begin with."

"Uh-huh," Gideon said vaguely. With two-thirds of his mind, he was still trying to put his finger on whatever it was that had been bothering him about the landslide.

"Listen, Gideon, are you sure it wouldn't be better if you had a little protection? There's no shame in it. I mean, now that we *know* for sure somebody messed with the lamp, that changes things, you know?"

Gideon waved him off and told him about Julie's hypothesis: the attacks on him had been motivated by fears about what he might be going to say—to "reveal"—in his lecture. But now the lecture was over and done. Everybody knew there was nothing to reveal.

"You agree with that?"

"Yes, I do," Gideon said. "I still have no clue as to what they thought I was going to say, but I do believe that's what it was about, yes. And if you notice, nobody's tried to kill me since."

"Yeah, a whole twenty-four hours now."

"Closer to twenty-eight. Fausto, what about Ivan? Are you getting anywhere with that?"

"Just getting started, trying to nail down the basic facts. We did a few preliminary interviews, just short ones, with the director at the museum, Rowley what's-his-name— Boyd—and with some of your friends at the hotel. Well the one with the old fat guy, Vanderwater, that one wasn't so short; pretty hard to have a short interview with him. That guy can really *talk*. But then I know Vanderwater, I should have set aside more time."

"How do you know Adrian?" Gideon asked.

"From the Sheila Chan thing. I did some of the interviewing when she disappeared—mostly, the same people who are back now."

"I don't understand. You said there was nothing suspicious about it. Why were you interviewing people?"

"Because the whole thing started as a misper, so—"

"As a what?"

"A missing person case. Britspeak. Nobody knew where she was for two days before we figured out to look at the cave-in to see if she was there. And she was."

"Oh."

Gideon could feel the gears of his mind engage again and almost, but not quite, mesh. Sheila Chan . . . missing for two days . . . what was it about that that wasn't right, that didn't fit? She had been on his mind ever since the visit to the cave and now he felt he was on the very edge of catching hold of whatever it was that was eluding him. It was almost as if a snap of his fingers might flick it into focus. He snapped his fingers. Twice. The thought, if it was a thought, stayed out of range.

"Anyway, back at the ranch," Fausto said, looking at him curiously, "apparently this Rowley guy got him out of there about eight o'clock because his mind was wandering a little."

So, obviously, was Gideon's. With an effort he concentrated on what Fausto was saying. "That much is true enough. Except that it was wandering a lot, not a little. By the time Rowley got him out of there it was back on Guadalcanal in World War Two."

"Okay, so he gets him home to his cottage a little before nine, offers to make a pot of tea for him but gets turned down—Gunderson says he wants to go to bed—and Boyd goes home himself. Gunderson, he says, was in an 'excited, confused state of mind.' Now, we know the fire started around four A.M., give or take twenty minutes, so that means the attack happened sometime between nine and four. Obviously."

"Probably a lot closer to four, wouldn't you think?" Gideon said. "I don't see his killer hanging around for five or six hours after smashing his skull in before starting the fire. What about motive, Fausto? Getting anywhere there?"

"Nah, to hear them tell it, they all loved the old guy. *Everybody* loved the old guy."

"Well, everybody I know did," Gideon said, "including me. Maybe it was a stranger—you know, a robbery gone wrong?"

"Yeah, right."

"Pretty unlikely, I admit, but was there any sign of forced entry?"

Fausto laughed his rat-a-tat laugh. "Are you kidding? Maybe if any of the doors were still standing we'd know. The damn place burned to the ground. All those solvents."

"Right, I forgot."

The telephone on the desk chirped. Fausto punched a button and picked it up. "Anything?" He listened for a couple of seconds. "Shit. Thanks anyway, Rosie."

He hung up, grumbling. "The prints on the lamp. They're yours, all right. So . . . no leads there after all."

"Too bad," Gideon said, but his mind was off on its own again. The attempts on his life seemed long ago and trivial, hardly worth bothering about; comic-opera stuff, involving, as they did, broken-down old lamps and theories about homicidal monkeys. It was Sheila Chan that was eating at him. Something didn't fit about Sheila, or the cave-in, or both, and it was maddeningly, frustratingly, dancing around just out of reach. If he could only . . .

Fausto had returned to Ivan. "Boyd was able to give us a bunch of contacts that might turn up something. Gunderson's solicitor, his housekeeper . . ."

Whatever was nagging at him necessarily had to be in the context of either what Fausto had told him during lunch at the Angry Friar the day before, or what he'd heard from Pru and Corbin at the testimonial dinner the night before that—because that was all he'd *ever* heard about the cave-in and Sheila; that was his entire context, but it had been enough to set his antennae quivering when he saw the actual site, the actual dirt of the landslide. Both conversations together couldn't have totaled more than fifteen minutes. How hard could fifteen minutes be to reconstruct? Start with Fausto. Fausto had told them—Julie and Gideon—that he had been on the scene when she'd been dug out, that she'd been much crushed in the slide, that the maggots found on her indicated a time of death two to three days earlier, that some passengers on the Morocco ferry had seen—

"The maggots!" he cried, practically jumping out of his chair.

Fausto, caught in mid-sentence, blinked. "The *what*?"

"The maggots, the maggots!" Gideon repeated, and this time he did jump out of his chair, waving his arms and striding excitedly around the room. "The maggots!" he exclaimed yet again. "How could I miss it? Where was my mind?" He whacked himself in the forehead, much as Kazimir Figlewski had that morning, but harder than he'd meant to. "Ow!"

Fausto calmly watched this extraordinary performance from his chair. "So are you planning to let me in on this brainstorm anytime soon?"

Gideon returned to the desk and leaned over it, supporting himself with both hands. "Fausto, she was murdered," he said intently. "She—"

Fausto threw up his hands. "Oh, hey, give me a break, will you? Give it a rest already. We got this great record of one murder every five years, and you show up, and in *one day* you're telling me about two murders that we never noticed? What, I don't have enough on my plate? I'm telling you, if you'd been around these last five years I'd have had a homicide every other day. I mean, what is it with you? Every time you look at somebody dead, you—"

"Fausto, shut up and listen. She was not killed in the

landslide. She was already dead when it happened. The cave-in was a cover. Like the fire was a cover for Ivan."

"You see? Right there—that's what I mean," Fausto said with a pained expression. "For you, any time there's a—" He sighed. "Okay, all right, I know you're gonna turn out to be right. Just give me a minute to get used to it. I'm just, what do you call it, venting." He sat there shaking his head, then laughed, a mixture of incredulity and amusement, and followed it with one more sigh. "All right, I think I can stand it now. Let's hear it. Tell me, why was she not killed in the cave-in?"

EIGHTEEN

SHE wasn't killed in the cave-in, Gideon explained, because if she'd been killed in the cave-in there wouldn't have been any maggots.

"No maggots," Fausto said dully. "Uh-huh."

"No maggots," Gideon repeated. "Look, maggots are the larvae of flies—"

"I know that."

"—which hatch from the eggs that the flies lay on dead things—"

"I know, I know. Jesus, Gideon, tell me something I don't know."

"Well, what you obviously don't know is that flies do not lay eggs on dead things when they're covered by three, or four, or five feet of earth. You don't find maggots on people buried by landslides. How would the flies reach them?" He waited for that to sink in.

"Oh. I never thought of that," Fausto said quietly.

"Well, why should you? But *I* should have thought of it

the minute . . . damn, how could I miss that?" He raised his hand for another crack at his own forehead, but thought better of it.

Fausto scowled up at him. "So this means . . . ?"

"This means that Sheila Chan spent some time above-ground between the time she died and the time the cave-in buried her."

"You mean she laid around dead for two days? Those maggots were two days old."

"No, no, no. Just long enough for the flies to get to her and lay their eggs. Once they did that in the open air, where they could get to her, the maggots would be able to survive underground."

"How long would that take? For the flies to get to her and lay their eggs?"

"No way to tell, but not very long. Maybe five minutes. In a climate like this, almost certainly inside of a couple of hours."

"So you're saying she was killed somewhere else," Fausto mused, "then brought out to the cave, and buried under the cave-in?"

"Not necessarily." Gideon dropped into his chair again, quieter and more reflective now. "Corbin and Pru told me she'd been hanging around the site even though she wasn't supposed to."

"That's true."

"Okay. I think we can assume everybody knew it, so my guess would be that someone got to her right there, that she was killed right where she was found, and then they triggered the cave-in to cover her. That'd be a lot simpler and a lot safer than carting a dead body around in a car."

Fausto nodded. "Yeah, I guess."

"This cave-in business, though . . . I'm out of my element here. Is it really that simple to trigger something like that? How would you do it, dynamite?"

"Dynamite, gelignite, something like that. And the cliff was unstable to begin with, from all the rain we had. So I'd say it wouldn't have been that hard, no."

"Can you just buy explosives in Gibraltar, or do you need to get a license or something? What I'm wondering is, could there be a record of who bought any around that time?"

"Well, yeah, you need a license, but you have to be a construction or demolition company to get one. If I remember right, there are only two companies that have them. I can check that angle out. Problem is, if the guy had any brains, he'd have skipped the license thing and sneaked the stuff in from Spain, or even better, Africa. If I were him, that's what I would have done. I love my country, but I have to say we're about the easiest place in the world to smuggle anything into. Or out of. But don't get me started on that."

Gideon leaned back in his chair. "Fill me in on the case, will you, Fausto? When did you know she was missing? What made you check out the cave? Do you know if she had any—"

"Whoa. I told you, I was just helping out. It wasn't my case, so I don't have all the details in my head."

"Well, can we talk to the guy whose case it was?"

"Sure, if you want to go to the Falklands. But we ought to be able to get what information there is right here." He picked up the telephone. "Conrad, I need the file on Sheila Chan. It'll be in the dead files. Thanks."

He hung up and rotated his chair to face Gideon. "I can give you the general picture while we're waiting, though."

The call to the police had come from Corbin. Sheila had been scheduled to present a major paper at the conference, but she had failed to show up for it. Moreover, no one seemed to have seen her since the morning of the day before. Concerned, Corbin had already checked with the desk at the Eliott Hotel, where she'd been staying, and had learned that her room hadn't been slept in the previous night and no meals had been charged to her account since breakfast on the morning of the day before.

The police had taken it seriously, and in conducting their interviews, it hadn't taken them long to put together two highly pertinent facts: (a) the cave-in at Europa Point had occurred exactly two days earlier, only a few hours after anyone had last seen Sheila, and (b) despite the clearly posted warnings, she had been spending a lot of time at the risky site. Guessing that she might have been caught in the slide, and hoping that she might be alive under the rubble, they had quickly mobilized an emergency rescue squad to dig for her. And after four hours of burrowing holes in the dirt, they had uncovered those shrunken, reaching fingertips.

"Uh-huh. I don't suppose there's going to be an autopsy report in that file?"

"I'm pretty sure there isn't. Why would we do a postmortem on something like that? It was all pretty cut and dried, no suspicion of foul play . . . or so we thought."

"That's what I figured. And the body was cremated, so I can forget about actually looking at it." He sighed.

The case file Fausto had asked for was brought in and laid on the desk: an unpromisingly thin manila folder with CASE CLOSED stamped on the front. As Fausto opened it, the telephone rang again. With a cluck of irritation he picked it up. "Chief Inspector Soto—" He listened, rolling his eyes. "*Again?* Can't *you* handle it?" A long, melodramatic sigh. "Okay, yeah, I'll deal with him. Hell, no, I'll come down there. Once we let him in we'll never get rid of him."

He stood up, unfolded his cuffs, and effortlessly slipped in the links (something that Gideon had never gotten the knack of; invariably, it took him half a minute of fumbling) and shrugged into his Armani jacket. "Got one of our best customers out front. This time he's griping about his neighbor's budgie driving him nuts. I better talk to him."

"Budgie?" said Gideon.

"Budgerigar. Bird. Parakeet." He fluttered his fingers in front of his mouth. "Tweet-tweet?"

Gideon looked at him in surprise. "A complaint about a parakeet? I wouldn't have thought—"

"Yeah, I know, not exactly DCI material, but this clown's sister is married to the chief minister, who happens to be my boss's boss, so . . ." He spread his hands.

"Say no more. I understand completely."

Fausto slid the file across the desk. "Help yourself. Not much there, though." He squared his trim, narrow shoulders and stalked out the door, his mutters fading away as he headed down the hall. "I'm gonna kill him. This time I'm gonna . . ."

Gideon opened the file and fanned out the thin sheaf of papers inside. There was an initial report from the investigating officer, a case summary, a list of Sheila's outgoing telephone calls from the hotel, a number of uninformative interview accounts (Adrian, Corbin, Pru, and Audrey had all been contacted during the brief missing-person phase, as had the Eliott Hotel staff), and various forms and records. Only one of them held his attention for more than a few seconds.

ROYAL GIBRALTAR POLICE
PROPERTY RECORD FORM
LISTING OF PERSONAL EFFECTS
    Case # 2005-44
    Name of deceased: Sheila Laura Chan
    Property recorded on: 24 August 2005
    Property recorded by: Anthony Burns, Sgt., Jesse Figueroa, Clerk

Found on and in immediate vicinity of deceased:
Cash:
GBP £24.77
US $5.59
Jewelry:
"Swiss military" wrist watch, ankle bracelet.
Clothing:
Deceased was clothed in shirt, cap, walking shorts, belt, socks, sandals, underwear.
Other:
Trowel, sunglasses, ballpoint pen, wallet, comb, purse, credit cards (Visa, MasterCard), other cards (California Driver's License, Social Security, Berkeley Public Library, Safeway, Pier 1).
Found in deceased's lodgings, Room 434, Eliott Hotel:
Cash:
None.
Jewelry:
None.
Clothing:
3 shirts, 2 prs walking shorts, 1 pr jeans, 1 pr slacks, 1 pr walking shoes, 1 pr running shoes, 1 pr bedroom slippers, 4 sets underwear, 3 prs socks, 1 pr pyjamas.
Other:
Suitcase, ballpoint pen, gel pen, Hi-Liter pens, nail clippers, scissors, 2 plaster vertebrae, 2 books (*The Neanderthal Legacy*; *Neanderthals & Modern Humans in Late Pleistocene Eurasia*), shoulder bag, purse, lipstick, toothbrush, toothpaste, floss, sunscreen, 4 bottled drugs and medicines (aspirin, Ambien, Prozac, multivitamins, Lipitor).
Is property of evidentiary value?
No.
Released to:
No known relatives or claimants. Property donated to local charities or destroyed, 29 August 2005.

He was still studying this sheet, intently and protractedly, when Fausto returned, hanging up his jacket and coming to look over Gideon's shoulder. "Find something interesting?" He slipped out his cuff links as deftly as he'd inserted them, and crisply refolded his shirtsleeves.

"Uh-huh," Gideon said thoughtfully. "A couple of things. What were these, do you remember?" He tapped one of the entries with his finger: *2 plaster vertebrae.*

"Oh, yeah. They were models, not real. What about them?"

"It says at the bottom it was all given away or destroyed. There wouldn't be any way of tracing what happened to them, would there?"

Fausto slowly shook his head. "Not if it doesn't say there. Why, you think they might be important?"

"Well . . . yes. Considering how light she was traveling—how little else was on that inventory, they must have been important—maybe something to do with the paper she was going to give. You have to admit, they're funny things to carry around with you and keep in your hotel room."

"Oh, I don't know. I wouldn't be surprised to find them in *your* hotel room."

"That's a point," Gideon admitted with a smile. "But you know, what's equally interesting is what isn't there."

"What *isn't* there?" Fausto said, scowling down at the sheet.

"Let me ask you, can I assume this inventory is absolutely complete? I mean, would it include every single thing you found on her, or at the hotel?"

"If she had it, it's on the list. Why, what isn't there?"

"Think about it a minute. She was going to give a presentation, right?"

"Right, yeah."

"A major paper, you said."

"Yeah . . ."

"So . . . ?"

"So how about just telling me?" Fausto said irritably. "I guess I'm just too dumb to see it on my own."

"Where's the paper?"

"The paper," Fausto echoed. "What paper, I don't—"

"Fausto, these were professional, highly academic meetings. At a conference like that, people don't just get up and talk off the tops of their heads, the way I did at the cave. Everybody *reads* their papers. Aloud."

"That must make things really stimulating."

"It's awful, but that's still the way it's done. Well, where's the paper? For that matter, where are her notes? She'd almost certainly have had notes with her. Maybe handouts too. And chances are, she would have brought her laptop with her, full of background material and details, and maybe so she could make a PowerPoint presentation. Where's any of that?"

Fausto took the folder from him, went around the desk, and sat down again, studying the inventory form line by line. "I see what you mean. Not there, all right."

"Someone took them," Gideon said flatly.

"*Maybe* someone took them. Let's not get ahead of ourselves. That's one of *your* mottoes, isn't it?" He was thumbing restlessly, abstractedly, through the rest of the file, not really looking at it.

"Fausto, look at the facts. One—" He ticked the point off on his thumb. "—Sheila Chan's all set to give a big paper, but before she can do it she gets killed and all her notes disappear. Two—" This one on his index finger. "—*I'm* scheduled to give a big speech, and somebody does his best to kill me . . . and comes a lot closer than I like. Three—" The middle finger. "—Gunderson's scheduled to make some kind of speech at the Europa Point ceremony, but somebody kills him before he can do it and burns his house down to boot. Are you telling me you don't see a pattern here?"

"I don't know . . . yeah, maybe, okay." Fausto nodded his reluctant agreement, then unexpectedly produced his bark of a laugh. "Hoo boy. Talk about interconnected monkey doodoo. Little did I know that archaeology was such a dangerous profession. Thank Christ these meetings are only once every four or five years. Otherwise we'd be up to our eyeballs in homicides."

"You probably *are* up to your eyeballs in homicides," Gideon said a little grumpily. "You just don't know it because you don't have an obliging expert like me around to help you out."

"Yeah, that must be it," Fausto said, thinking. The file was still open on his desk. He was drumming his fingers on the topmost form. "Look, I think the place to start with Chan—" He snapped his fingers with a sharp *clack* that Gideon, an ineffective finger-snapper, envied. "Hey, I just remembered—I think I might know—come on."

In a flash he was out of his chair, through the door, and hustling down the corridor with his quick, short, decisive steps, heels clicking on the linoleum tiles. Gideon followed, his longer legs allowing him to keep up with a more moderate stride. They went to the booking room, where Gideon had been fingerprinted. The woman who had rolled his prints was sitting at a metal desk, still humming while she used a metal ruler to pencil lines onto a flow chart. As they came in, she stopped humming and sat up straight. "Can I help you, Chief Inspector?"

Fausto's eyes were hunting around the room, searching for something, not finding it. "Rosie," he said after a moment, "you used to have a kind of little vase in here. You made it out of a couple of plaster vertebrae that were part of the property inventory from the cave-in out at Europa Point. I don't see them."

Rosie swallowed. "Inspector Pullen said it was okay to take them, sir," she said nervously. "I did ask. I mean, I know that's not according to the books, but they were just going into the dustbin anyway, and I thought they'd be cute for, you know, a single rose or something, so I just glued them together—"

"I know, I know," Fausto said in what was as close as he ever came to a soothing tone. "There's no problem. I just wanted to know where it is. Professor Oliver here wants to have a look at them."

"It's not here anymore."

Damn, Gideon said to himself.

"It's at home."

Ah, Gideon said to himself.

"My ten-year-old—she's interested in bones. She wants to be a medical illustrator—she has it on her desk now. She uses it to hold her favorite pen." She was half out of her chair. "Do you need it right now, sir? Shall I run home and collect it?"

Fausto looked at Gideon. "Gideon?"

"No, not this minute," Gideon said. "If you bring it in with you tomorrow, I'll come by at some point and have a look at it."

"So how come they decompose?" Fausto asked as they walked back to his office.

"What?"

"How come they decompose?" Fausto asked again. "Bodies that get buried where the flies can't lay their eggs on them? Why don't they just shrivel up or something? What, the worms get into them? Is that what does it?"

"As a matter of fact, no. That's a bum rap that worms have had to live with for centuries. When people first saw maggots wriggling away on corpses they thought they were worms, and it seems to have stuck. But worms don't eat dead bodies."

"But bodies still decompose, no matter how deep they're buried. What makes that happen? What's the cause, technically? Why don't they just turn into mummies? Is it the moisture, or . . . ?"

"Oh, I see what you mean. No, you already have all the enzymes and bacteria needed to do the job crawling around inside you—well, enzymes don't crawl—right now. When you're alive they help you digest and assimilate foreign substances   food, primarily. When you're dead they help digest and assimilate *you*."

"Sort of like recycling."

"Exactly like recycling," Gideon agreed after a moment's thought.

NINETEEN

"YOU know," Gideon said, with his feet up on the railing of the balcony, his hands comfortably clasped at his belt buckle, and a tumbler of Scotch and water on the table beside him, "this interconnected monkey business thing—well, the term is meant to be funny, of course, but it's not as obvious or as simple—as simplistic—as it sounds. When Abe would get to talking about it, he very quickly got over my head in mathematics, but basically, what he was describing, as much as I could understand of it, was an application of set theory. The sets of people involved in the events, or the events themselves, or the places they happen, or the circumstances they happen in, are all subsets—A, B, C, and so on, of a larger set of people, or events, or whatever: S. And what you're searching for when you're trying to make sense of what's going on is whatever it is that the particular subsets involved have in common; that is, the intersection that they all share; that is, the set of all things that are members of A, B, and C. At the same time, of course, you want to exclude intersections that . . ."

He frowned, paused, and sighed. "Julie, I have absolutely no idea what I'm talking about. I got lost about two sentences ago. Is this making any sense at all?"

"Well, let's just say I still understood it pretty well ten minutes ago, but the more you talk, the fuzzier it gets."

"Ah, well, math never was my strong point, was it?"

"Don't feel bad about it. It makes you more human. If you were perfect, you'd *really* be hell to live with."

He raised a lazy eyebrow in her direction. "I don't know that I appreciate the emphasis on that *really*."

It was a little before dusk. They were on the balcony of their room at the Rock, looking down on the green palm fronds and winding paths of the Alameda Gardens just below, and farther out, across the Bay of Gibraltar, at the hazy, amber-tinted coast of Spain. Another glorious sunset over Algeciras was on the way. As before, the preprandial miniature twin decanters of sherry and Scotch had been waiting for them when they'd come in, golden and beckoning in the slanting, late afternoon light, along with a pair of stemmed glasses and another of small highball glasses. Although they'd passed on them the previous two days, today they flung open the French doors and took them out onto the balcony to unwind before dinner.

There was plenty of unwinding to be done, what with the latest twists and turns in the matter of Sheila Chan's demise. They had split the contents of the decanters, each starting with a small glass of sherry and then moving on to the Scotch, and Gideon was halfway through his Scotch by the time he'd finished telling Julie what had developed.

"Anyway," she said now, "if what we're looking for is what all these bizarre things have in common—Sheila's murder, Ivan's murder, the attacks on you—it's pretty obvious, isn't it? The Europa Point dig—Gibraltar Boy, the First Family, and all that."

"Yes, that's true enough, but *everything* that's happening here right now has that in common. Every archaeologist in town—and there must be a hundred of them—is here for the meetings, and the meetings are in commemoration of Europa Point. So it doesn't tell us anything. See, you want to *exclude* those intersections that *every* subset shares simply by virtue of being part of the larger set, S—"

She gave him a warning look.

"What we're looking for," he said, "is something that applies more specifically to Sheila, Ivan, and me."

She sipped her Scotch and gazed across the bay. "I can't think what that would be."

"I can. I was talking to Fausto about it. We were all just about to make speeches, presentations."

"Speeches? Mmm . . ." She thought it over. "Sounds pretty tenuous to me, frankly. Aren't there lots of people here for the Society meetings who are giving speeches?" She shook her head doubtfully. "I don't know, Gideon. . . ."

"It was your idea, Julie. You were the one who suggested someone was trying to stop *me* from making a speech. I just applied it more generally."

"My idea? Oh, well, then, on sober reconsideration, I have to say I think it has a lot going for it."

"So do I, and the more I think about it, the more it seems to make sense. Sheila's notes had been taken, and Ivan's, if he had any, would have been burned up in the fire, if they weren't also taken. Someone must have been afraid of what they might contain."

"One problem—nobody stole *your* notes."

"Nobody could. I didn't have any. And consider my case a little further. In the twenty-four hours before my speech, somebody tried to kill me twice. An average of once every twelve hours. Now it's been given, and I don't have another one to make, and, heck, nobody's been trying to kill me for *days*. Well, almost days."

"Knock on wood," she said, searching for something wooden to knock on but having to settle for the glass-topped table. "But yes, I think you must be right. I hope you're right." She reached over to graze the back of his hand with her fingers. "It would mean you're not in danger now."

"The crucial question is," Gideon mused, "what could any of us have possibly said—what did the killer think we might have been going to say—that was so earth-shaking it was worth murder?"

"No, the crucial question is, just *who* thought it was worth murder?"

Gideon sipped his drink and slowly nodded. "Got a point there, pardner."

Julie took a stab at her own question. "Well, for starters, as far-fetched as it may seem, we know it has to be one of the people staying here at the Rock; one of our own group. Except, of course, for Rowley and Pru."

"Why are we excluding them?"

She turned to look at him. "We talked about this before, don't you remember? It was Pru and Rowley who *kept* you from getting killed."

"Me, yes. But that doesn't mean—not that I believe it, you understand—that they had nothing to do with Sheila and with Ivan."

She stared at him. "Hold on a minute. What happened to all those interconnected subsets? The law of interconnected monkey business—"

"Is not infallible. It's not a law, it's a model, a guide. Everything doesn't always connect that neatly."

"But surely you don't—"

"I'm just saying it's possible, Julie, not probable. Fausto's going to be running the investigation. I wouldn't want to see him rule out anybody at this stage. If you remember, Pru had some pretty harsh things to say about Sheila at the testimonial dinner."

"But that hardly means—"

"No, of course it doesn't. But it's not something that I feel I can keep from him. He has to know."

"Well, you're the expert," she said unconvinced, "but—oh, wait a minute, I just thought of something. There must be other people we're not even thinking of, archaeologist types who live here. I mean, we know Rowley because he hangs around with us, but what about other archaeologists, maybe people who work at the museum, people we don't know about? They would have been here back when Sheila was killed too . . . oh, no, wait a minute, that doesn't fly because they could have killed Ivan any time these last five years. Why wait till now?"

"Because—"

"Because he wasn't giving a speech," she supplied, and then promptly supplied the countering argument as well. "But surely, he must have made *some* presentations in five years. He was obviously a cultural bigwig here. Although—" She pursed her lips, mulling everything over. "I don't know, what do you think?"

"I think this is making my neck ache." He tipped up his glass, drained the whiskey, and smacked his lips. "It's six thirty, dinnertime. Let's go down and have a look at the cast of suspects."

INDEED, the entire cast was assembled and waiting, Rowley having joined them this evening. The group had been put in the main dining room tonight, a big, handsome space with buttercup yellow walls, a long row of tall, arched windows looking out on the bay, and a rousing, thirty-foot mural of Nelson's great victory at the Battle of

Trafalgar, full of smoke and cannon flashes, covering most of the rear wall. The burgundy-vested, bowtied waiters, all of whom appeared to be Spanish, couldn't have been too crazy about looking at that every time they went back through the swinging doors to the kitchen, but if it bothered them they didn't show it.

When Julie and Gideon arrived, two of the waiters were just going around the table delivering appetizer and salad orders. After they'd finished, one of them took the newcomers' orders. Julie asked for bouillabaisse and chicken piccata; Gideon went for the "Taste of Morocco" menu, ordering a roasted tomato and onion salad, followed by lamb stew.

As they'd expected, the rambling conversation around the table was about Ivan Gunderson. Who could have killed him? Why? And how could the police even tell he'd been murdered, anyway? Weren't his house, his body, reduced to ashes?

This last question was directed at Gideon, the only certified, bona fide forensic practitioner in the group. Gideon looked up from his plate and chewed while coming up with a way to evade answering the question—without quite lying, if he could help it. Nobody here knew that he'd been to the morgue that morning and had himself been the one who had made the homicide determination. Nobody here knew that Sheila's death was now reopened as a subject of investigation, let alone that he, Gideon, had also been the instrument of that. There was a lot they didn't know, and it seemed to him an excellent idea to keep it that way.

He swallowed the mouthful of honey-sweetened lamb, prune, and almond. "Well, you know, arson investigators are pretty good at that. They look for the starting point of the fire, the use of accelerants, and so on."

"Accelerants?" Rowley said. "You mean fuels? My goodness, the place was full to the brim with inflammables—glues, solvents, cleaners. It's a wonder the whole peninsula didn't go up in smoke."

"Those pots he was gluing," Audrey said somberly. "I can't get them out of my mind. I simply cannot make myself imagine Ivan spending his days, hour after hour, meaninglessly gluing pots together." A brief, somber laugh. "And then regluing them when you brought them back to him."

Gideon went back to eating, relieved that the subject had moved on.

"I keep thinking of him too," Adrian said with a rumbling sigh. "Of the man he once was; so witty, so . . . nimble—and then of how he was on that last night . . ." He shook his head. "Iwo Jima Boy, Okinawa Boy, whatever it was. So very sad."

He trickled a little Irish whiskey into his coffee and screwed the cap back onto the flask. It occurred to Gideon that Adrian's flask never seemed to empty. He never had to upend it, but merely to tip it a bit. A magic flask; now, how did he do that? Did he carry a second flask to top up the first?

"It was Guadalcanal Boy," said Corbin sadly.

There was only the clinking of silverware against china for a few moments, and then Buck spoke. "You want to hear something that's really weird?" Buck was normally so quiet when he was around them that all heads turned in his direction. "He was never there. At Guadalcanal. I have a Marine buddy, a retired lieutenant colonel, who fought at Guad. He has a Web site that lists the survivors, every last one. No Gunderson. I checked with him, and he double-checked, and he says it's so. Gunderson was in the Pacific, all right, at Tarawa—which was bad enough—but not at Guad. Now how do you figure that?"

It was a moot question, but for Adrian there were no moot questions. "One of the prominent features of *demen-*

tia senilis, you see, Buck," he began kindly, "is a loss, sometimes only intermittent, of the ability to distinguish between—"

He was interrupted by the appearance of George, one of the competent, agreeable reception desk clerks, carrying a small, neatly folded, brown paper bag. "Oh, I thought I'd find you here, Dr. Oliver. This was left for you a few minutes ago. I took the liberty of bringing it in to you rather than saving it for you at the desk. The lady said she thought it might be important." He put the bag on the table in front of Gideon.

"Thanks, George." Curious, he opened it without thinking and began to take out the object inside, but the instant he saw what it was, even before it was all the way out of the bag, he caught his breath, dropped it back in, and rolled up the top; casually, he hoped.

But not quickly enough. "What *was* that thing?" Audrey demanded.

"I have no idea," he said with a shrug. (He considered the possibility of an apathetic yawn as well, but discarded it as lacking subtlety.) "Probably a present from an admirer—somebody who was at the lecture."

"It was a vertebra, wasn't it?" Audrey persisted. "Two vertebrae. Were they human?"

"Looked like it."

"People send you human vertebrae as presents?"

"You should see the kinds of things people send him," Julie said.

TWENTY

BUT no one had ever sent him anything quite like this before, and he wasn't about to let the rest of the table in on it. His large hand now lay protectively over it. He could barely make himself sit still until he could give it a more careful going-over in private. Already he was beginning to think he must have been mistaken in what the quick glance he'd had at it had told him. But if he was right . . .

"I've taken the liberty of ordering after-dinner coffee and drinks to be served in the bar this evening," Adrian said, observing that people were beginning to stir. "I thought it would be more comfortable. Shall we go?" As they got up he gestured jocularly at the bag. "Don't forget your bones."

"As a matter of fact, I think I'll drop them off upstairs so I *don't* leave them somewhere. Wouldn't want to shock anybody who happened to pick them up."

Gideon's chances of forgetting and leaving them somewhere were about as likely as his forgetting his ears and leaving them somewhere, but he didn't like the interested looks the bag was getting. While the others shuffled slowly into the Barbary Bar, he retrieved his key from reception (room keys were attached, not to the metal or wooden tags most European hotels used, but to happy little "Barbary ape" plush dolls; another whimsical touch, like the lollipops and the rubber ducks), and punched the elevator button for the second floor,

Alone in the elevator, he quickly had a look at the contents of the bag. Indeed, the vertebrae were just what he'd thought they were. He was sure of it now. *My God, this is the most exciting, most unexpected—* He caught a sidewise glimpse of himself in the elevator mirror and couldn't help laughing. Hunched greedily, almost lasciviously, over the open bag, he looked like Silas Marner ogling his hoard of golden coins. And like Silas Marner, it occurred to him that simply leaving them in his room might not be the best idea in the world. When he got to his floor, he didn't get out but hit the button for the lobby. Once there he went back to the reception desk and had George put the bag in the hotel safe. Then, his head spinning with speculation and conjecture, he took a couple of deep breaths and went to find the others.

In the Barbary Bar, with its evocative, *Casablanca*-like ambience—rattan armchairs, soft, amber lighting, potted palms, slowly spinning ceiling fans—the talk soon devolved to nostalgic, humorous stories about Ivan. After half an hour everyone moved out through the open doors to the Wisteria Terrace and settled in again for more of the same. To wistful, indulgent laughter, Audrey did a couple of her impressions of Ivan, notorious among archaeologists for his less-than-delicate field methods. ("Oh, no need to fool with a silly trowel to dig those remains out; I'll just hire a backhoe. Much quicker.")

By then Gideon was more than ready to go, but he

didn't want to seem eager to get back to the vertebrae so he stuck it out. Finally, at about ten thirty, the last of them to leave—Buck, Audrey, and Corbin—finally made their good nights and went upstairs.

"Now," said Julie, fixing Gideon with a razor sharp look, "what is going on? What's so important about those bones that you've been on pins and needles ever since you got them?"

His face fell. "Have I been that obvious?" He knew all too well that dissimulation wasn't his strong suit, but he'd prided himself on having carried things off pretty well this time.

"Maybe not *that* obvious, except to someone who knows you inside out the way I do, but take my advice and don't ever go in for professional poker playing."

"You think they noticed?"

"Probably not. They were too into their Ivan stories. Now tell me; what's going on?"

"Let's go up. I'll pick up the bones and show you."

"Oh, let's stay out here a while longer, Gideon. It's so lovely now that everybody's gone. Mmm, just smell that air."

"Nice," he agreed, not that he'd noticed until she mentioned it. Okay," he said, standing up. "I'll bring them out here. Get ready. This is going to knock your socks off."

A minute later he was back with the bag. He gingerly removed the vertebrae, cradling them carefully in both hands, and placed them on the table between them. It was his first chance for anything more than a hurried look, and although the soft, diffuse lighting on the terrace was anything but conducive to a close examination of skeletal remains, that's what they were going to get. Julie, understanding, left him to it and sat back with her eyes closed, inhaling the velvety air, lush with the perfumes of the night-blooming plants from the gardens below. "Mmm," she said again. .

"Mmm," he echoed automatically, but for all he knew the air could have smelled like a lion house on a rainy day. All of his concentration was focused on the extraordinary object in front of him as he slowly rotated it on the table-top.

It was the "vase" that Rosie, the constable at New Mole House, had taken home for her daughter, constructed of two adjacent thoracic vertebrae glued together, with a circle of aluminum foil Scotch-taped to the bottom to close it up. The foil and Scotch tape were quickly removed and discarded to make the examination easier. The vertebral foramens—the central holes that, all taken together, created the long, narrow, bony tube in which the spinal cord resided—provided an opening big enough for a few flower stems or a couple of pencils. The upper of the two bones was creamy white, the usual color of biological-supply-house skeletal casts. The lower one was a more muddy and uneven gray-brown, tinged with red. It was this lower one that had so captured his attention. After a few minutes he surfaced and began to speak.

"These are T9 and T10, the ninth and tenth thoracic vertebrae," he said slowly. They're located about . . ." He reached around her to touch the middle of her back. "Here. The top one—"

When she burst out laughing he thought he'd accidentally tickled her, but it wasn't that. "Oh, it's *cute!*" she cried.

"Cute?" He stared wonderingly at her, and then at the vertebrae. "Oh, the face. Yeah, I suppose that's pretty clever."

Rosie's ten-year-old daughter had apparently gotten a head start on her medical illustrator career by "illustrating" the upper vertebra, painting a clever little cartoon face on it. Viewed from the rear, the flat, smooth superior articular processes (where the inferior articular process of the eighth vertebra would have abutted) were now two round, googly eyes, the transverse processes (where the right and left eighth ribs would have attached) were a pair of donkey's ears, and the long, tapering spinous process (which, with its fellows, would have constituted the knobby, spiky length of the spine) was a tapering snout, with a curli-cue mustache and a goofy, big-toothed grin at the bottom.

"Sorry," Julie said, "I didn't mean to spoil the big moment." She suppressed a final giggle. "All right, you have my full and earnest attention. The top one is . . . ?"

"The top one is an exact reproduction of the ninth thoracic vertebra of Gibraltar Woman, as perfect as a cast can get. It's part of a set of First Family casts made by France Casting in Colorado, the only sets that were authorized to be made from the original bones. I bought one of them myself for the lab."

"Uh-huh. And it's special because . . . ?"

"It's not special at all. It's the other vertebra, the T10, that's special."

She looked at it, turned the little vase in her hands, tried to determine what was special about the T10. "Sorry," she said with a shrug, "I don't—"

"It's special for two reasons. First, because, unlike the T9, it's not a cast at all. It's the real, honest-to-God bone."

"It is?" she said, running her fingers gently over the rough, splintery surface. She was intrigued now. "This bone that I'm holding is actually from Gibraltar Woman herself?"

"Absolutely. See here, where the end of the transverse process is broken off? That delicate, lacy, sort of filigreed-looking stuff underneath? That's interior bone, cancellous bone; no mistaking it. You can't get results that fine with a cast."

"But I thought all the actual bones went to the British Museum."

"They did."

Her eyes widened. "This was stolen from the British Museum?"

"No, ma'am," he said airily, "it was never *in* the British Museum."

"But if the bones all went to—" She put the bones down with an exasperated little cluck and a cautionary glance. "Gideon, if what you're trying to do is confuse me "

"I'm sorry, honey," he said, laughing, "just trying to enhance the narrative tension—you know me. Look, the crux of it is—and this is what's *really* special about it— Gibraltar Woman didn't *have* a tenth thoracic vertebra."

"If that's supposed to unconfuse me—"

"The remains that were excavated at Europa Point were far from complete; you know that. They included the first, second, fourth, fifth, seventh, and ninth thoracics, and that's about as far down as Gibraltar Woman goes, really. Below that level, there's hardly anything left of her, just a fragmentary fifth lumbar and a bit of sacrum. Oh, and a piece of acetabular rim."

"But no T10? Are you sure?"

"Am I sure? Julie, I ran the damn study, didn't I? I worked over these things for three weeks. I know every nook and notch and foramen in her body. Well, in every bone in her body. Well, in every bone that was left. And this one wasn't left."

"Well, then, it has to be from someone else." Her forehead puckered. "Doesn't it?"

"No, it's from her, all right. The ankylosing spondylitis makes that clear."

She sighed. "I knew that at some point in this life I was going to have to learn what ankylosing spondylitis is. It might as well be now."

"It's not that complicated. *Spondylos*, vertebra; *itis*, inflammation; *ankylose*, to fuse, to grow together into one."

He picked them up to show her. "See here, where they've been glued together—this crack that runs between them?"

"Uh-huh. Where the two of them meet."

"Yes, but normal vertebrae don't really meet. They're completely separate bones. In the living body they're separated by a disk of pulpy soft tissue—"

"Umm . . . the intervertebral disk."

"Right, and each intervertebral disk has a kind of tough, cartilaginous ring around it—the *annulus fibrosus*—that keeps the soft stuff in the middle from squirting out, like toothpaste squirting out of a tube, when you put pressure on the spine—which you do every time you stand up, and even more when you sit down. Well, sometimes the *annulus fibrosus* calcifies, turns to bone, so that the two vertebrae above and below it become fused together, and the result is—"

"Ankylosing spondylitis." She took them from him. "Bony bridges that connect one vertebra to another, like these."

"You got it."

She made a slight flexing motion of the vertebrae. "You know, they—oh!" To her unmistakable consternation, they came apart with a little *pop*, so that she was left holding one in each hand. She practically flung them away from her, down onto the table, as if they'd burned her. "Oh, my God! I didn't mean—I don't know why I—" Even in the dim light, he could see that she'd paled. "Gideon, I've broken—"

"Shh," he said with a smile, "you haven't broken anything, sweetheart. Come on, relax that wrinkled brow." He leaned forward to smooth her taut forehead with his hand. "You'll wear out that sexy little *musculus frontalis.* "Look—" He picked the two pieces up to show her. "They just separated where Rosie glued them, that's all. No harm done. See? They'd already been broken before."

"Whew," she said, melting back into her chair. "Is that ever a relief. I could already see the headlines: 'Wife of Well-Known Anthropologist Destroys Priceless Scientific Relic.'"

"No, no," he said laughing. "In fact, it makes the point I'm making even better than before. Look at how the edges match up. They hardly needed the glue." His tongue between his teeth, he put the two segments gingerly together—they virtually clicked into place—and held them up for her to see. "The broken edges of the bridge make a perfect match, even without the glue, even though one is a cast and one is real bone. Which would never happen if they were from two different people."

"Which is how you can be so sure that they're both really from Gibraltar Woman?"

"Yes, it's a real break. Under ordinary circumstances, if I had a T9 and a T10, I might be able to say for sure that they *didn't* go together—different ages, different sizes— but I wouldn't be able to say with certainty that they *did* go together. But in this case I can—and they do."

Thoughtfully, she fingered the vertebrae again—*very* tentatively this time. "It must hurt."

"Sure, and give you a hunched, miserably stiff back as well. And lung and heart problems go along with it. Eye problems too. Basically, it's a kind of arthritis, really, very incapacitating when it's as severe as this."

"But she was only in her mid-twenties. I would have thought this was an old person's disease."

"Well, most kinds of arthritis are, but not this. In fact, her age is one of the things that pointed specifically to ankylosing spondylitis. It's not wear and tear or anything like that, you see; there's a strong genetic component to it, and it affects primarily young adults—mostly men, usually, but sometimes . . . well, as you see . . ."

"How awful . . . a young mother . . ."

He nodded his agreement. He was suddenly tired—depleted, depressed—and he could see that Julie was too. No wonder, it was going on midnight, and it had been a very long day; the session at the morgue, which seemed to have been a week ago, had been only this morning. In addition, their predinner drinks and dinner wine had caught up with them. Still, they soldiered on, raising the obvious questions: Where had that T10 come from? Well, from Europa Point, obviously, since that was where the rest of Gibraltar Woman had come from. But how had Sheila gotten it? Had she dug it up long after the dig was formally closed down, when she'd been prowling around the cave with a trowel? Had she found it before the dig was ever started and kept it a secret? Did she find it *during* the dig and surreptitiously make off with it? And for all of those questions—why? And why did she have it in her room at the conference? Did it have something to do with her murder? Well, they were pretty sure they knew the answer to that; it did. But what?

But they had run out of steam and weren't getting anywhere, and they knew it. Besides, by now it was getting chilly out on the terrace. "It's late," he said. "Why don't we leave this till morning, when we're fresh? What do you say we call it a day?"

She nodded. "I'm for that. I'm exhausted."

AT the reception desk they had the young night clerk, who had come on when George left, put the bag back into the safe and asked for the key to room 205. She went sleepily to the wall of grinning plush monkeys on hooks, reached toward them, and stopped, hand in the air.

"It's not here." She turned back to them. "Are you sure you don't have it?"

"No, I left it right here about seven o'clock, with George."

The clerk—her name plate said "Kayla"—scanned the rows of monkeys. "I don't see it. Are you *positive* you didn't take it with you?"

"Believe me, I'd know about it if I had a monkey in my pocket."

Kayla was still staring at the wall. "Did you actually *see* him hang it, or—"

"No, I didn't see him hang it. Look, can we get another one until you find it? We're pretty bushed."

Once upstairs (inasmuch as the Rock Hotel used vintage metal room keys, not electronic cards, Kayla had to go up with them to let them in), Julie went yawning to the closet to get her nightie. Gideon, who had meanwhile brushed his teeth, came out of the bathroom to see her standing at the open closet door with a frown on her face.

"Lose something?" he asked.

Instead of answering, she said, "Gideon, have you worn your sport coat since we got here?"

"No, why?"

"You didn't rehang it after I put it in the closet?"

"No, why are you asking?"

"It's been hung backward on the hanger."

He came over to stand beside her. His gray Harris tweed hung neatly from a wooden hanger. It looked fine to him. "What's wrong with it? I didn't know you *could* hang a jacket backward on a hanger."

"Sure, you can. Look at it, it's hung so that the wooden shoulder supports slant backward instead of forward. I would never in a million years hang a jacket like that."

"You're as bad as Audrey with her toilet paper," he said, laughing. He placed his hand on his heart. "I solemnly swear that I, Gideon Paul Oliver, did not—" He suddenly understood what she was driving at. "Somebody's been in the room—they took the jacket down and rehung it the wrong way!"

She nodded. "And that explains why the key was missing."

A hurried search, followed by a more thorough one, found nothing gone, although a few more details seemed to prove the entry of an intruder: a pen that she was certain had been lying on top of a postcard was now beside it; the bed skirt, which had been neatly in place when they'd left for dinner, now had a couple of twisted ruffles, as if someone had lifted it to look under the bed. It was odd, but nothing new, that Gideon, who could be so wonderfully, scrupulously observant when it came to some old bone, spotted none of these homely details but had to take Julie's word for them.

"They were after the vertebrae," he said, flopping into an armchair.

"But they were in the safe, not here."

"Yes, but when I left with them after dinner I was going to leave them here. I *announced* I was going to leave them here."

Thoughtfully, she took the chair beside him. "So, one more time, it *has* to be somebody from the group who did it. They're the only ones who would have heard you say it."

"Of course. They're the only ones who know about the vertebrae at all."

"Well . . . George knows . . . at reception?"

"Sure, but he's the guy that put them in the safe for me."

"Right," she said, nodding. "I didn't really think it was George anyway. I just . . . I don't know."

"You just keep wanting whoever is doing all these things *not* to be one of these people—one of our friends. I feel the same way. But it's one of them, all right. There's no way around it anymore." He leaned back, hands behind his head, and tried to twist the kinks out of his neck. "And now the vertebrae: How do they fit in? And where the heck did that T10 come from?"

There was a discreet tap on the door. When Gideon went to answer it he found a smiling Kayla there, holding out a plush monkey with the key to 205 dangling from it.

Gideon took it. "Thanks, where did you find it?"

"On the floor, in the Barbary Bar. It looks as if you must have dropped it there after all."

"No, I didn't have it there."

"Well, then, you must—"

"Let me ask you something, Kayla. What time did you come on tonight?"

"When I always do. Ten o'clock."

Ten o'clock. Everybody would still have been out on the Wisteria Terrace at that time.

"And were you away from reception at all?" He said it with a pleasant smile, so she wouldn't feel threatened.

His pleasant smile failed him. Kayla immediately turned defensive. "No! I stay there the whole time."

"You're up here now. You came up with us a little while ago."

"Yes, but only for a moment. It's my job to—"

"Kayla, relax. You're not in any trouble. You didn't do anything wrong."

"You think someone took the key when I wasn't looking? You think someone was in your room when you were downstairs? Has something been taken?"

"No, nothing's been taken, but someone's been in here. And yes, I think he did get the key when you weren't looking. Think now. You never left the desk?"

"Well, I did go to the loo once, but other than that, I never . . . oh, there was one other time—someone telephoned to say that there was a lorry blocking the driveway, but when I went out it was already gone."

"Ah."

"But I couldn't have been away for more than thirty seconds."

Time enough to snatch a monkey, Gideon thought. "What time would that have been?"

"Oh . . . ten forty-five, or maybe a little after."

Ten forty-five. Just after the session on the terrace broke up and the others were all on their own. "Okay, thanks a lot, Kayla."

She hesitated. "Did you want me . . . shall I call the police?"

"No, don't worry about it; I'll take care of it."

She looked much relieved; police calls at the Rock Hotel were obviously infrequent and best kept that way, especially on her watch.

"You *are* going to call the police, aren't you?" Julie asked as the door closed. She had changed into her nightie and returned to the armchair.

"I don't think so," Gideon said, returning to sprawl in his chair again. "Not much point to it. It's after midnight. I'll tell Fausto about it in the morning. It can wait till then."

"Are you sure that's wise? Isn't it better to check for fingerprints and things as soon as possible, before we muck them up?"

"Yes, but what good would fingerprints do, or DNA, for that matter? Everybody who could possibly have done it has already been in the room."

"They have?"

"Yes, the first night, remember? Everybody came by and sat around for a while before the testimonial, schmoozing and knocking back their drinks."

"Oh, that's right," she said, barely managing to cover a yawn. "Well, I still think we ought to report it."

"Report what? That somebody broke into our room and hung my sport coat backward?"

But she had dozed off in the chair, bare dimpled knees drawn up, chin resting on her hand, dark curls falling over her face. For a long while, he sat there and took her in.

"You're sure pretty," he murmured. "Too bad you're asleep."

"I can be awakened," she said without opening her eyes. "If there's a good enough reason."

TWENTY-ONE

JUST as unpacking their clothes on arrival was Julie's job, as called for by their informal but not-to-be-messed-with division-of-labor agreement, the provision of morning coffee was Gideon's task. Up a little before seven, he brewed a heavenly smelling pot in their room and carried two mugs of it back to bed, where the upturned corners of Julie's mouth and her gently quivering nostrils, if not her tightly shut eyes, showed her appreciation and receptivity. (Julie was one of those people who had a hard time speaking in complete sentences, or any sentences at all, until she'd downed a few swallows of good, rich, hot Arabica.)

Sitting up in bed with their backs against the headboard, swathed in terry cloth Rock Hotel robes, they sipped away and talked some more about the vertebrae, but couldn't come any closer to a plausible explanation for the attempted theft, or even for the very existence of that mystifying T10, than they had the previous night.

"Why don't we join the others at breakfast and ask them about it?" Julie suggested as he was refilling their cups. (By her second cup she was not only able to speak intelligibly, but to make a certain amount of sense.) "You can show them the vertebrae, tell them you know they're from Gibraltar Woman, and see what they come up with."

He frowned. "What would be the point of that? One of them damn well knows how it figures in, but he's not about to elucidate. Or she."

"There are several points. First, maybe one of the others can cast some light. Second, it gives us a chance to watch how they react, which might be helpful. Third, it will make me happier because you'll be safer."

"Come again? How will I be safer?"

"Well, think about it a minute. Whoever was after the vertebrae must have been after them to keep you from figuring out what they are."

"For which he's too late."

"But *he* doesn't know that. Well, after *everybody* knows what they are, there wouldn't be any point to throwing you off another cliff or zapping you to keep *you* from finding out."

He sipped and nodded, sipped and nodded. "I like it," he said.

"ANYBODY else happen to recognize what these are?" Gideon asked, nonchalantly placing the vertebrae in the middle of the table just as the plates were removed and the diners were settling down with their third or fourth cups of coffee or tea. "Because I sure do. And it's pretty interesting."

They were all there, Adrian, Corbin, Pru, Buck, and Audrey. Everybody but Rowley. While their eyes were on the bones, he took the opportunity to do what Julie had suggested and watch their reactions. She was doing the same thing, he could tell. Alas, nobody's eyes bugged out, nobody's jaw dropped, nobody appeared to swoon with apprehension. They just looked at the glued-together bones with mild, scholarly curiosity.

"It's those neck bones that were in the bag," said Buck.

"Actually, they would appear to be thoracic," Adrian corrected. "Lower thoracic, if I'm not mistaken."

"Correct, as always, Adrian," Gideon said. "T9 and T10."

"And they would appear to have that pathology, what was it, that you found on Gibraltar Woman," observed Audrey. "Ankylitis spondylosis . . ."

"It's ankylosing spondylitis, Audrey, dear," Adrian said with a tolerant chuckle.

"Right again," said Gideon. "Anybody notice anything else significant about them?"

"Wait just a minute . . ." Corbin said. He picked them up, turned them around, fingered them. "This one's a cast. But this other one is real."

"Right again."

"But they go together perfectly, see?" Corbin said, demonstrating, and then setting them back down on the table, one atop the other. "They have to be from the same person. You know, they almost look . . . I don't understand . . . they almost look . . ."

"Holy cow!" Pru blurted. "Hey, let me see those things!" Her muscular arm shot forth for it. Corbin flinched away and gave it up without a fight. It was the T9 she was interested in. "You know what this is a cast of?" she exclaimed when she had it in hand. "You know what this is?"

"I know what it is," Gideon said quietly.

"This is a cast of Gibraltar Woman's ninth thoracic vertebra!" She brandished it for everyone to see. "I should know, I spent all day digging it out with a couple of chopsticks and a damn toothbrush. But . . . this is incredible . . . this tenth . . . this tenth . . ."

"Did she even have a tenth?" Audrey asked with a scowl. "As I recall—"

"No!" Pru practically shouted. "That's what I'm trying to say! She didn't! She doesn't!" She turned incredulous eyes in Gideon's direction. "Where did you get this, Gideon?"

"A friend wanted to know if it was human."

"Your friend, the policeman?" Adrian inquired after a short pause.

"Yes, Chief Inspector Sotomayor."

"And where did *he* get it?"

"He got it from Sheila Chan's room at the Eliott Hotel."

This time there was plenty of eye bugging and jaw dropping, but, with the exception of Buck, who, as a nonarchaeologist wouldn't be aware of the bone's scientific importance, it was universal, so it provided no useful information. It did, however, produce an excited flurry of observations.

"My God," Adrian whispered, "she found another piece."

"Sure," Pru said angrily, "remember how she was always down there, prowling around the site, even though she wasn't supposed to? Now we know why. She had no right to keep this to herself. For all we know, she turned up more than this. There may be other bones."

"I'm sorry, I refuse to believe there was anything left to find," said Corbin with a distinct edge to his voice. "As Adrian will confirm, we were *extremely* thorough. We left no stone un—"

"I bet that's what her paper was going to be on!" Pru said. "She wanted all the credit for herself."

"No, I think not," Corbin replied. "The topics for the papers had to be in two months before the conference, so a bone that she found a day or two earlier couldn't possibly have been the subject."

Gideon took advantage of the calming, damping effect of Corbin's sensible, put-you-to-sleep delivery to raise a question. "What exactly was the topic of her paper, does anybody remember? Pru, you were the program chair."

"Yes, I was," she said, thinking. "But you know, as I recall, it wasn't anything that grabbed you. *Europa Point Reevaluated*, something along those lines. Nothing about a new find."

"*The First Family: A Reevaluation*, actually," Audrey corrected. "I remember being quite curious about it."

Adrian was peering hard at Gideon. "I have the impression you know more about this than you're saying. I suggest you let the rest of us in on it."

"No, I don't, Adrian. You've come to the same conclusions I have. You have the same facts I do, and the same questions." Which was pretty much the truth, if you didn't count the fact that no one but Gideon (and Julie) was aware that Sheila's death was now the subject of a murder investigation.

"Why exactly would the police have had it?" Adrian asked, scowling at Gideon. "Perhaps you can tell us that."

Corbin answered for him. "From when she disappeared—when nobody knew what happened to her— the police were looking into it, remember? They would have searched her room. And afterward, inasmuch as she didn't have any next of kin, there would have been nobody to send—"

"Yes, yes," an impatient Adrian said. "I understand all that. But why is it of interest to them now?" He turned again to Gideon. "Why should they care if she had some vertebrae in her room? She was an archaeologist. And why exactly would they care *now*? She's been dead for two years."

"That's a good question," Pru said, also looking at

Gideon. "Have they reopened her case? Do they think there was something suspicious about it?"

"Well, um—" Gideon began.

He was saved by a hearty *knock-knock* coming from the entrance to the dining room—Rowley's cheerful greeting. "Your opulent transportation to the Society meetings awaits outside. All aboard that's coming aboard." His eyes did some bugging of their own. "I say, what are *those*?"

While everybody tried to tell him at once, Gideon snared the vertebrae, which had been making their way around the table—under his extremely attentive scrutiny— and popped them safely back into the sack.

"What are you going to do with them?" Corbin asked as his eyes greedily followed their progression.

It was just the question Gideon wanted. "I have to return them to the police, of course. I'm off to do that right now." This much was true. Just before coming down he'd received a call from police headquarters asking him to be in Fausto's office at ten.

"But will they return that tenth thoracic to us?" Corbin asked. "The cast doesn't matter, but that tenth is a new find. It belongs in the British Museum with the rest of her."

"Oh, I'm sure it'll get back to the museum eventually," Gideon said.

But for the moment, at least, two important points in regard to his safety had been established. Everyone at that table understood that (a) the T10's provenance was now common knowledge, and (b) it would no longer be in Gideon's keeping.

Very good, Julie's satisfied nod told him. *Mission accomplished.*

WHILE Julie went off to make a prearranged courtesy call on the head naturalist of the Upper Rock Nature

Preserve, Gideon walked down to police headquarters at New Mole House. He found the DCI waiting for him, seated behind his desk in his usual office uniform—an immaculate silk dress shirt (plum colored this time) with the cuffs neatly folded over his forearms, and a tie (blue-gray) that must have been carefully chosen to match. A few forms were spread out before him.

"You know an archaeologist named de la Garza?" he asked without looking up.

"Good morning to you too," Gideon said, sitting down across the desk. "Estéban de la Garza? Yes, I do. A prof at the University of Cádiz."

"Correct. Well, he's not up there at the Cádiz campus, though. They've got a branch down here at Algeciras, right across the bay—la Escuela Politécnica Superior—which is where their archaeology department is."

"Is that so? That's very interesting. And why are you telling me all this?"

Fausto slid one of the forms across the desk to him. "Check out the last two lines."

The form was from the Eliott Hotel, a list of Sheila Chan's outgoing phone calls. Gideon scanned down to the bottom of the page.

21/08/05	08:37 AM	34 95 663 05 72	Algcrs Sp	01 minutes
21/08/05	09:50 AM	34 95 663 05 72	Algcrs Sp	11 minutes

"Uh-huh. And this tells me . . . ?"

"This tells you that what we believe were the last two phone calls Chan ever made were to your pal de la Garza. I was hoping you might have some idea why."

"Nope, not a clue."

"Do you know what his connection to Chan was? Was she ever a student of his or something?"

"Not that I know of. She was at Cal. But maybe she was, I don't know. Look, why ask me about it? Why don't you just give him a call?"

"Ooh, hey, what a great idea. Duh. I *did* call him, but it's his office number, and the school wouldn't give us his home number, and he doesn't get in today till eleven thirty. He's supposed to call then. I just thought it'd be helpful if there was something you knew about it."

"Sorry, there isn't. Well, I do know her dissertation was on Iberian Paleolithic skeletal anomalies. I was helping her. Maybe he was working on it with her too."

"Yeah, maybe." He took the sheet back and stared at it for a moment, receding into his own thoughts, then yawned and looked back up at Gideon. "So what are you doing here, anyway?"

"We had a meeting at ten. One of your people called."

"A meeting about what?"

"Good question. He said be here, and here I am. I always do what the police tell me."

"Yeah, right," Fausto said. "Well, it beats me." He clasped his hands behind his neck and leaned back with another yawn, his swivel chair creaking. "What the hell, what's new?"

"Actually, there's been another development you probably ought to know about. Somebody broke into my room last night."

Fausto's hands unclasped. The chair snapped forward. "I *probably* ought to know about?" He raised his eyes heavenward. "Jesus Christ, I don't believe this. Somebody breaks into your room and you don't run for the phone and call the cops first thing? After all that's been happening?"

"Well, it was almost two in the morning by the time we found out, and nothing was taken, and everybody's fingerprints were already in the room, and their DNA for that matter, so—"

"Okay." He sighed. "Save it, tell me later. What were they after, do you know?"

"Oh, yes, this." He placed the bag on Fausto's desk. "The little vase that Rosie made out of those 'plaster' vertebrae. She dropped it off at the hotel last night."

"Why would anyone be interested enough in a couple of plaster—"

"Turns out they weren't plaster, Fausto. The top one was, but the bottom one was real."

Fausto stared at him. "The bottom one was . . . ?"

Fifteen minutes later, as Gideon was winding up his explanation, the phone buzzed. Fausto picked it up and listened. "Okay, tell him I'm on my way. Now I remember why I wanted you to be here," he said to Gideon as he hung up. "It's Orton, the dynamite guy. He said he'd have something for us by ten, and I figured you'd want to hear it from the horse's mouth. He was supposed to come here, but now he says he wants us out at the Point. He wants to show us something."

"Whoa, whoa, whoa, what are we talking about here? What dynamite guy?"

"Didn't I mention it?" Fausto was inserting his cuff links. "Ted Orton is from FSS—the Forensic Service Lab in London. He's checking over the Europa Point site for signs of dynamiting."

"And he's already here? He already has a report to make?"

"Yeah, sure, I called him yesterday, right after you told me about the maggots."

"Did you, really? I wasn't sure how seriously you took me. I wasn't sure if you believed me."

"Hey, man, you wound me. I always believe what you say. Anyway, he was here by four o'clock; it's less than a three-hour flight. He spent maybe two hours at the Point yesterday, till it started getting dark, and eight o'clock this morning he calls to say he got some interesting results." He shrugged into his jacket and shot his cuffs. "So? You coming or not?"

"I'm coming," Gideon said.

TED Orton was a gangling, horse-faced man in his late forties, wearing crisply ironed jeans, blindingly white tennis shoes, and a new "Rock of Gibraltar" sweatshirt with a picture of a Barbary ape mother and infant on it. Having led them down to a sunlit, windy spot atop the ridge of earth that had buried the Europa Point Cave—in fact, no more than a dozen feet directly above the hole from which Sheila's body had been dug out—he knelt down and yanked on a foot-long length of thin, orange tubing, made of plastic or rubber, that disappeared into the earth at his feet. "Anybody have any idea what it is?"

Fausto and Gideon, hunkered down beside him, shook their heads. "Nope," Fausto said. "What is it?"

"It's just what I've been hunting for," Orton told them. "If it's proof of an explosion you're looking for, you couldn't ask for anything better than this." He was practically bursting with pride at having discovered something important, a feeling Gideon understood very well.

"So you're saying somebody *did* trigger the landslide?" Gideon asked. "You're positive?"

"Completely."

Fausto fingered the tubing doubtfully. "What's it supposed to be, some kind of fuse? No, wait, it can't be a fuse. If it was a fuse, it'd be burned away. It wouldn't be there anymore."

"Correct, Chief Inspector, it would not. But the fact of the matter is, fuses are not much in use nowadays. Too unpredictable, too inconsistent. This—" He gave it another tug. "—is a piece of what is called a 'shock tube.' Made of plastic. It serves the same function as a fuse, but is far more reliable and infinitely faster. The inside of it, you see, is generally coated with a thin layer of HMX explosive mixed with something along the order of ten percent powdered aluminum. This makes a highly sensitive but low-power detonating medium. It would likely have been set off with some small, handheld device—a percussion primer, an electric match—by a person standing somewhere nearby, but well out of danger—unless of course, he was somewhat lacking in intellect. Once it was set off, the detonation would have raced along this tubing for a hundred, two hundred feet, perhaps even more, at the end of which it would have detonated a blasting cap, which would in turn have set off the terminal high-explosive charge—oh, dynamite, gelignite, ammonium nitrate, something along those lines—the result being—"

"So if it acted like a fuse, how come it didn't burn up?" Fausto interrupted. "Like a fuse."

"Oh, the layer of powder on the inside is extremely thin, and the detonation, as I said, literally *races* along the inside of the tube—at over a mile a second—so the powder is consumed, while the tube is unharmed."

"Uh-huh. So where's the rest of it supposed to be?"

"Down there," Ted said, gesturing at the dirt, "however much was left of it after the explosion. I hope you didn't expect *me* to dig it out. That's not part of my contract. I just do the brain work, not the muscle work."

"No, I mean where's the rest of it up here? What, the bomber took it with him? That's what you're assuming?"

"That would be my assumption, yes," Orton said. If his feelings were hurt because he'd expected congratulations from Fausto, not skepticism, he wasn't showing it. But then, maybe he already knew Fausto.

Gideon, now down on his knees, had been peering at the end of the tube while they'd been talking. "Ted, it looks to me as if the end here has been cleanly cut, not torn apart by an explosion. Why would that be?"

"Yes, you're quite right. Would you like to hear my scenario?"

"We'd love to hear your scenario," Fausto said.

The three men stood up, to the accompaniment of a creaking of middle-aged knees. A gust of wind off the Strait brought an unexpected whiff of fragrance—a spice of some kind, coriander, caraway—perhaps from the freighter off in the distance, perhaps all the way from Morocco.

"I envision your bomber in a safe place—up there somewhere, or maybe a little off to the side," said Orton a little dreamily, "setting off his bomb from his end of the shock tube. He assumes that after the explosion, it'll be a simple matter for him to reel it in and take the evidence away with him. But ten or twenty feet at *this* end get caught in the huge mud slide he's created and he's unable to pull it out. So, in something of an understandable hurry, he cuts the tube at the point where it enters the mud, thinks no one will ever find the rest of it in any case, and makes good his escape. Two years go by, during which a certain amount of erosion takes place, revealing a foot or two of the tubing lying on the newly exposed surface, at which point I enter the picture and discover it. End of scenario. How does that strike you?"

"Pretty good," Fausto allowed. "Not bad."

"One thing bothers me," Gideon said. "This 'thinks no one will ever find the rest of it' part. Ted, all of our suspects are pretty bright people. They'd take something like erosion into account. It's hard to imagine they'd just assume nobody would ever find it, and let it go at that. *You* found it, after all."

"That's so, but only because suspicions had already been raised. I was searching for it, and I knew what I was looking for. But finding it is very different from merely seeing it. Let's take you, for example. You're an intelligent person, a famous paleontologist, as I understand it—"

Gideon was used to this and let it pass.

"—and let's say you were prowling around the slide area hunting for some old bones or whatever, and you came upon this, sticking out of the ground. What would you make of it?"

Gideon looked at the dirty orange tube. "I'd think it was a piece of old plastic tubing, just some miscellaneous trash."

"And there you have it," Orton said.

"Wait a minute, Ted," Fausto said, doubtful again. "Didn't you say the powder inside it would have been consumed?"

"I did. Totally."

"And the tubing itself wouldn't have been affected?"

"Not a bit."

"So how do you know it's a shock tube? How do you know it *isn't* just a piece of miscellaneous trash?"

"I know because my experience of a dozen years tells me that it is not," Orton said stiffly.

"Oh," said Fausto.

Oh, thought Gideon.

"That," Orton said with his first smile of the morning, "and a subtle but telling clue on the exterior of the tubing itself."

He produced a folding, rectangular magnifying glass from somewhere and offered it to Fausto, who knelt and studied the tubing through it.

"Huh," said Fausto, handing the lens to Gideon. "That's subtle, all right."

Gideon took his turn. "Let's see . . . there's some kind of tiny lettering . . ."

With the aid of the glass, it jumped into focus.

VOLOX LOW DENSITY POLYETHYLENE SHOCK TUBING.

TWENTY-TWO

AT eleven thirty they got back to Fausto's office. At 11:31 the phone buzzed. Fausto snatched up the receiver, and listened. "Okay, thanks." He reached for another button, then paused. "It's de la Garza. How well do you know this guy?"

"A little. We run into each other at meetings."

He remembered Estéban de la Garza as a courtly, elderly archaeologist with a lean, pockmarked, deeply lined face. Like Ivan Gunderson, he struck Gideon as a throwback, but Gunderson had been late nineteenth century; de la Garza was more early eighteenth. He would have looked right at home in a wig and knee breeches, serving as royal schoolmaster to the court of Philip VI. His patrician manner put off some of the freer spirits who attended the anthropology conferences, but Gideon had always liked him. (But then, Gideon liked just about everybody, a personality flaw that he couldn't seem to overcome, despite its having backfired on him many times more than once.)

"How's his English?"

"Fine, perfect, better than mine. Prettier, anyway." It was true. Estéban spoke English as if he were translating directly from the Spanish. He eschewed such rude English shortcuts as contractions and apostrophized possessives. For him there were no *it's*, or *wouldn't*s, or *don't*s; and *the fossil's bones* and *Dr. X's hypothesis* came out as *the bones of the fossil* and *the hypothesis of Dr. X*. His ornate, measured speech was a pleasure to listen to, Gideon thought, always assuming one had the time to spare.

"Good, you talk to him, then." He held out the telephone.

"Me? What do you want me to say?"

"You know, see if he knows what Sheila Chan was calling about. He'll be more open with you. Besides, it might get too technical for me. I'll listen in. Go *ahead*," he said impatiently, shaking the phone in front of Gideon's face when he hesitated. "Come on, come on."

Gideon shrugged and took it. Fausto punched the button. He kept a second cordless receiver to his ear.

"Estéban?" Gideon said.

Estéban's deep, sober voice sounded in his ear. *"Sí, señor, dígame."* Cautious, wary. But then, he was returning a totally unexpected call from police headquarters; why wouldn't he be?

"Estéban, this is Gideon Oliver. It's nice to talk to you."

This took a few seconds to sink in. More than a few seconds. De la Garza's quickness of mind did not quite match his impressive gravitas. Then at last: "You are in Gibraltar?"

"Right, I'm here for the Paleo Society meetings."

"Yes, but . . . is this not . . . I was under the impression that I was calling the police station."

"You are. I'm sitting here with Detective Chief Inspector

Sotomayor—he's on the line too—and we're trying to get some information on a woman named Sheila Chan."

"Sheila Chan." He considered. "This is the young woman who was working on a dissertation about bone disease in early modern *Homo sapiens*, is it not?"

"Yes, you do know her, then?"

"I do. For some time I have not heard from her. Is she all right? Is there something wrong?"

"Well, yes. She's dead. She's been dead since 2005."

"Aahh, that would explain why I have not heard from her."

From anyone else it would have been a somewhat lame attempt at humor, but from de la Garza, who knew?

"On the other side of the table, Fausto rolled his eyes and mouthed a single syllable: *Duh*.

"Yes, she was killed in a landslide here in Gibraltar—"

"I regret extremely to hear it."

"—but there are some questions about her death."

"Questions? Do you mean in the sense that there are suspicious circumstances? This is why the police are involved?"

"That's right. She may have been murdered."

Estéban digested this. "How can that be? Did you not say she died in a landslide?"

"Well, that's what we're trying to figure out. One of the questions has to do with a couple of phone calls she placed from her hotel the day she died. Apparently they were to you."

"To me? Two calls? Are you certain of this?"

"Well, to your office. She called twice, an hour or so apart. This would have been in 2005."

"Ah, wait, yes, I remember that, but it was only once that we spoke. I was not in the office when first she called. Thus, she left a message with my secretary."

Fausto nodded at Gideon across the table. That sounded

right. The first call had lasted only one minute. The second was eleven minutes long.

"Those were probably the last two calls she ever made, Estéban, so you can see why they'd be of interest."

"Uh, yes, certainly, I do see. And the police inspector would like to know the nature of her call."

"Exactly."

De la Garza meditated for a while. "Well, my friend, the fact is that I cannot tell you in honesty that I recollect the content, but I would have to assume it had to do with some assistance I was providing on her dissertation. I can think of no other reason. We had no other, er, relationship."

So de la Garza had been helping her too. That seemed strange. Sheila had been researching skeletal disease among late Pleistocene humans. It had made sense that she would turn to Gideon, a physical anthropologist, for help, but why would she have gone to an archaeologist?

"How exactly were you helping her, Estéban?" He held his breath. He had an inkling of what the answer was going to be.

"In only the most minor way. I had earlier let her borrow a late Pleistocene bone that exhibited one of the diseases that were the subject of her investigations."

Ah, he was right! In one of Sheila's e-mails to Gideon, she had mentioned coming across such a find in Spain. This, the mysterious T10, had to be it! His fingers found the vertebra, which he'd brought to Fausto's office and now lay on the desk. "And did you ever get it back?"

"Back? Why, I believe not, now that you mention it."

"Was it a vertebra by any chance?"

"Why, yes, it was. Why do you ask? How do you know this?"

"Because I'm pretty sure I have it in my hand right now. Estéban, this vertebra—where was it from?"

"It was part of our teaching collection here in Algeciras. We retain a small collection of bones and artifacts for didactic purposes. They come from some of the sites—the ones of little significance—that our department has excavated over the years. This particular vertebra . . . Gideon, may I be permitted to know why this is of concern to the police? I do not understand the connection to Sheila's death."

"Bear with me a little longer, Estéban. Do you remember where it came from originally? I mean, where it was found?"

"It was from a site in the province of Sevilla, about two hundred kilometers north of us. AN-34. It is known by no other name. A small excavation, of no significance, that I conducted as a summer field exercise for my students. The land was given to the university for that purpose expressly. You would not be familiar with it. There was little reason to include it in the archaeological literature."

He was sounding a little defensive now. "I understand," Gideon said. "The literature is plenty cluttered up as it is. Go ahead, please. Can you tell me anything else?"

"There is little more to tell. AN-34 was not even a 'site' in the usual sense. That is, it was not a habitation, or campsite, or burial site, although of course at first we had hopes that it might be. But no, it was merely a place where a woman, a lone woman, had once died, nothing more. A few pitiful bones, mostly fragmentary, embedded in the wall of an arroyo. Our work consisted of little more than digging them out and gathering them up. They had been water-disturbed, you see, and somewhat scattered by animals, and there had been some earlier, rather amateurish attempts at excavation, so that more sophisticated advanced archaeological techniques would have been—"

"Estéban, *when* did you do this dig?"

"Hmm . . . I believe it would have been in the summer of . . . 2001. Yes, 2001. I remember because it took but one month, so I was able to spend half of July in Croatia, at a most interesting consortium. . . ."

Fausto was looking at Gideon with a questioning, perplexed frown, but Gideon was as baffled as he was. How could de la Garza have excavated part of Gibraltar Woman's skeleton in Spain in 2001, a full year before she was uncovered at the Europa Point excavation in Gibraltar?

"Estéban, let me ask you: Were you right there when those bones—this bone—was excavated? I mean, did you yourself see it come out of the dirt?"

"I did, indeed. The vertebrae, being more fragile than the long bones, were excavated under my direct supervision. But why do you ask me this question? These questions?" Understandably, he was becoming perturbed.

"Hold on a second, Estéban. Give me a minute."

Gideon put his hand over the mouthpiece. "Fausto, I have to see those bones. Algeciras is that town right across the bay, isn't it? How long would it take me to get there?"

"An hour or so if there's no holdup at the border. Hell, you want to go? I'll drive you myself. That'll take care of any border hassle."

"Great." Gideon put the telephone back to his ear.

"Estéban, I would really love to see the rest of those bones—the woman they came from. If I showed up there in an hour, could you show them to me?"

"Today, do you mean? I would be delighted, of course, but I fear it would be somewhat awkward. I'm scheduled to confer with—"

Fausto cut in. "Professor de la Garza? This is Detective Chief Inspector Sotomayor. This is a murder investigation. We'd appreciate your cooperation."

They heard him swallow. "Certainly, Chief Inspector," he said with his usual dignity after a few seconds. "One hour. Are you familiar with the location of the Escuela Politécnica Superior?"

"We'll find it," Fausto said.

"Come to the main building. I shall be in room 203."

"With the bones," Gideon said.

"With the bones," Estéban agreed. "Of course."

AS Fausto had promised, their progress through the border crossing was smooth. His known face earned them a wave-through to the express lane, along with a few extra-poisonous stares at the Lamborghini from the less fortunate, stalled in a quarter-mile-long line that extended all the way back to the airport runway.

"The Spanish love to screw with us coming through," he said without rancor as they picked up speed on the A-7, the Spanish highway that would take them around the Bay of Gibraltar (officially the *Bahia de Algeciras*, now that they had crossed the border) and into the city. "We do the same to them coming the other way. Been like that ever since Franco."

"Tradition," Gideon said. "I love it."

They drove for a while in silence, through flat, dry countryside punctuated by occasional riverine marshes, small industrial complexes, and nondescript little working-class villages. As they rounded the bay and drew closer to the sizable industrial port city of Algeciras itself, Gideon realized that the richly colored sunsets they'd seen over it from their hotel terrace had been the result of the tons of smog particles hanging in the air above it—like the glorious, smog-generated sunsets over Los Angeles. But in the daytime, Algeciras, like L.A., was shrouded in heavy brown haze; a depressing place into which to be headed.

As anticipated, Fausto drove like the sports car nut he was, at anywhere between ninety and a hundred and ten miles an hour, depending on what the traffic would allow. It took a while, but eventually Gideon stopped grinding his teeth and propping his arms against the dashboard every time they began to overtake another car. If they hadn't crashed or spun off the road yet, he figured, maybe Fausto knew what he was doing and they'd both get out of this alive.

"Listen," Fausto said, "let me try to get this straight. I'm confused."

"That makes two of us, believe me."

"Okay, let's start at the beginning. What we're dealing with is two vertebrae that were, what do you call them, next to each other, one on top of the other . . ."

"Adjacent. Right." Gideon had them in his hands now, probing them yet again with eyes and fingers, hunting for anything he might have missed, anything he might have gotten wrong.

"The top one is a cast, and the bottom one is a real vertebra."

Gideon nodded.

"And they fit perfectly into each other."

"Perfectly," Gideon agreed.

"Which means they had to have been from the same person."

"Right."

"Gibraltar Woman."

"Gibraltar Woman. I *know* the top one is, and therefore the bottom one—*God*!" He braced himself instinctively against the back of his seat as Fausto, traveling at ninety-five, happily threaded the frighteningly small opening between a heavy, smoke-belching truck with a load of asphalt shingles on the left, and a Fiat with a startled, petrified driver on the right. In a couple of seconds, truck and Fiat were left far behind, although, in the side mirror, Gideon could see the truck driver's arm out the window vigorously giving them the finger. He closed his eyes. That had been the closest one yet. He wondered vaguely if he might be able to come up with a way to take the bus back to Gibraltar when it was time to return.

"—therefore the bottom one is too," he finished when his breath returned.

"Okay," Fausto said. "So they're definitely from the same person. That's what I thought. But *he* says he dug up the skeleton that the bottom one came from six years ago, up north in Seville province, and it's been sitting in Algeciras ever since."

"Yes, he does."

"And *you* say the top one is a cast made from the skeleton of Gibraltar Woman, which was dug up *five* years ago, in Gibraltar."

"Yes. I do."

"Well, how much sense does that make?" Fausto demanded. "You can't both be right."

Gideon sighed. "No, it wouldn't seem so, would it?"

"What do you mean, *seem* so? She couldn't be—"

"Fausto, please," Gideon pleaded, "keep your eyes on the road, will you? You can talk without looking at me."

"She couldn't have been buried in both places, could she?" Fausto persisted.

"You wouldn't think so, no."

"Look, no offense, Gideon, but isn't it at least possible they're not from the same person? I mean, look, nobody's perfect. Admit it, you could be wrong about this, couldn't you?"

Gideon shrugged. "Sure, I suppose I could, Fausto."

Like hell he could.

TWENTY-THREE

THE University of Cádiz's Algeciras branch provided a welcome haven in the heart of a clanking, grubby, hard-working city. With its clean, white, two-story buildings, its neat lawns, and its concrete paths planted with young trees, it might have been a suburban community college campus in the United States. About the only difference, other than the signs in Spanish, were the students—clean-cut and conservatively dressed, with not a pierced nostril or a stud-transfixed tongue in sight.

To get to room 203 of the main building they walked the length of a long, gleaming corridor lined with faculty office doors and a few clusters of apprehensive-looking students waiting outside them, hatching their stories, or explanations, or excuses. Again, thought Gideon, just like home. Room 203 itself was a lecture hall smelling strongly of floor polish. There were five tiered rows of empty chairs with writing-desk armrests, and a long, laminate-topped lab table down in front for the instructor. On the table was a grocery-sized cardboard box, and in front of it, waving them in as gracefully as an orchestra conductor signaling a pianissimo passage, stood a somberly smiling Estéban de la Garza, balding a bit now, but otherwise much the same as the last time Gideon had seen him: erect and aristocratic in his usual three-button suit.

"I have them here in the carton," he said after the introductions. "I would have laid them out for you myself, but I thought you would prefer them thus, for you to do."

"That's good, Estéban," Gideon said, undoing the flaps of the carton. "Okay, let's have a look."

As soon as he reached in and removed the first few fragments—a partial rib, the proximal three-quarters of a left fibula, most of a sacrum—he was struck by the near certainty that they did indeed belong to the same female skeleton that he'd examined five years earlier. They were the right sex and the right age to begin with, but it was the bones themselves—their red-tinted gray-brown color, their texture, their weight, their size, and of course their various evidences of AS—ankylosing spondylitis—that all shouted "Gibraltar Woman" at him. But he wasn't ready to say anything aloud yet. Bones shouted at him a lot, and sometimes they turned out to be flimflamming him. There were more scientific ways to go about things. Unconsciously, he rubbed his hands together, removed the rest of the bones from the carton, and went to work. Fausto and Estéban watched silently.

The first thing a well-trained anthropologist such as Gideon Oliver does in such a situation is to lay out the remains in as close to correct anatomical position as their number and condition allow. Then he carefully examines them to ensure that they are not commingled—that is, that they do not come from more than one individual. This is done by careful sexing, ageing, evaluation of general condition, etc.—but most obviously and significantly, by checking to see that there are no duplications. (Two mandibles, for example, would be a good clue to there being more than one person represented.) Then, in this particular situation, would come a mental exercise: a similar analysis in which the anthropologist compares the bones that lie before him to the absent but well-remembered remains of Gibraltar Woman. Are there duplications between the sets? Are there differences in condition, age, sex? And so on. It is all a matter of proceeding in a logical, orderly fashion, systematically narrowing the field of possible alternatives until a single plausible conclusion can be reached.

Of these steps, so often demanded of his students, Gideon performed not a one. He proceeded instead like a six-year-old set loose in a candy shop and instructed to thoughtfully, prudently consider his choices before making a selection. That is to say, he immediately grabbed the most alluring, enthralling morsel of all: in this case, a columnar section of three solidly fused-together vertebrae, the upper two complete, the lowest one broken. The middle and lowest ones still had stubs of rib fused to them, another abnormality associated with AS.

"Ah!" he couldn't help yelling. It was better luck than he'd dared hope for. "This," he exclaimed excitedly, "will settle it for good."

"Settle what?" said Fausto. "What are we settling?"

"Watch," Gideon said magisterially, "and learn." He laid the three-part vertebral segment on the table. "What we have here are the eleventh and twelfth thoracic vertebrae, plus a chunk of the first lumbar. Now, then . . ."

"Okay, I'm watching," Fausto said after a few moments of silence and immobility. "What am I supposed to be seeing?"

"Where the heck is the other piece, the one we brought with us?" Gideon said irritably. "The one from Sheila's room—the T10?" He had scanned the table without success and was now searching perplexedly through his own pockets.

"You had it," Fausto said accusingly. "You must have left it in the car."

"Damn. Lend me the key, will you?"

"No, you stay here and keep doing whatever you're doing," Fausto said wearily, turning toward the door. "I'll get it."

"Okay, thanks, Fausto. Bring them both, will you? The cast too."

Fausto's response, a muttered "Absent-minded professors," hung in the air behind him as he left.

While he was gone Gideon filled in de la Garza on what had brought him: the T10 that had been discovered in Sheila Chan's room was a previously undocumented vertebra from Gibraltar Woman. There was no question about it. The only question was, where had it possibly come from? Now it appeared that it might have—

"Come from these?" de la Garza supplied, indicating the bones on the table. "From AN-34? In *Sevilla*?" He had been startled into emitting an extraordinary three fragmentary sentences in a row. "But how can such a thing be possible?"

Gideon spread his hands. He didn't have an answer he liked. He'd come up with a few vague possibilities that he *didn't* like, but they were too convoluted, too unlikely—and too unwelcome—to think about.

When Fausto returned with the now limp and wrinkled paper sack, Gideon offered the T10 to de la Garza to examine. "Can you tell if this is the one you lent her?"

De la Garza scrutinized it with scrupulous care. Fausto, impatient as ever, went striding around the room rapping the backs of the chairs and humming tunelessly to himself. He had circled the entire room and returned by the time de la Garza had his answer ready.

No, he couldn't be sure one way or the other, he said, handing it back. It certainly looked like the one he'd lent Sheila, yes, but, unfortunately, inasmuch as the bones were used for teaching purposes only, they had not been marked with identifying codes or abbreviations. Alas, he could not give an unqualified reply.

"Well, I think I can resolve it," Gideon said. Indeed, he *knew* he could resolve it. While de la Garza had been poring over the T10, Gideon had made some visual comparisons between the bones, and they had shouted at him again, louder than before. This time he trusted the shout.

"Now then, in my left hand I am holding Gibraltar Woman's tenth thoracic vertebrae, and in my right hand I have the segment of thoracic and lumbar spine from AN-34—eleventh thoracic through first lumbar."

"I think this is the watch-and-learn part again," Fausto said dourly.

"Cheer up," said Gideon. "It won't take long." He pressed the two segments gently together, and as he knew they would, they fit into each other as neatly and tightly as the T9 model had fit up against the T10 earlier. For good measure, he now put the T9 on top, forming a contiguous, reasonably firmly joined stack of five adjacent vertebrae—four thoracic, and a fragment of the uppermost of the lumbars.

De la Garza stared at the column for a few seconds before comprehending. "All are from the same individual," he said slowly.

"That's right," said Gideon. "And yet the top one is a cast from Europa Point, the middle one was found in Sheila Chan's room, and the bottom three are yours."

De la Garza's long, grave face grew longer and graver. "But this means," he said slowly, "this means . . ."

"It means," Gideon said, "that what you have on the table here—" He swept his hand over the bones. "—is actually part of Gibraltar Woman—the part they didn't find at Europa Point."

De la Garza struggled with this. Unsuccessfully. "Will I be expected to turn these over to the British Museum, then?" he asked, brightening a little, perhaps at the prospect of the renown that would come his way over it.

Gideon shook his head. "I don't think so." During the last few minutes, some of the unlikely possibilities that had been bouncing around his brain had resolved themselves into something a bit more likely—no less convoluted or unwelcome, but more likely; plausible, even. "My guess is that the British Museum will be turning over *their* material to *you.*"

"I do not understand," de la Garza said. "I do not understand any of this."

"He lost me a long time ago," Fausto said.

"Estéban," said Gideon, "when we were talking on the telephone, didn't you say the Seville site had been donated to the university for teaching purposes?"

"Yes, that was my understanding. As I said, it held nothing of archaeological or anthropological worth."

"Would you happen to know who gave it?"

"I do. It was the American, Ivan Gunderson."

Fausto's jaw dropped, but it was the answer Gideon had expected . . . but had hoped not to get.

He thought he knew the answer to his next question too. "And where, again, was the site located?"

"It lies in the province of Sevilla, in Andalucía, but near the border with Extremadura."

"I mean precisely."

"You would like geographic coordinates? I can provide them."

"No, but was it near a town of any sort?"

"Yes, it was at the edge of a small village of a few hundred inhabitants. You would not know of it."

"Maybe I would." Gideon's throat had become dry with anticipation. "What's it called?"

De la Garza opened his mouth to speak: "—"

"No, let me guess," Gideon said, heavy hearted. "Would it be Guadalcanal, by any chance?"

De la Garza blinked his surprise. "You know of it, then?"

T W E N T Y - F O U R

JULIE too blinked at the mention of the name. "There's a Guadalcanal in Spain?"

"Sure," Gideon said unhappily, "why wouldn't there be? There's a Guadalquivir, a Guadalupe, a Guadalajara . . . why wouldn't there be a Guadalcanal?" He shook his head. "It should have occurred to me before."

"And that's where Gibraltar Woman really came from? Or I guess I should say, 'Guadalcanal Woman.'"

"I guess you should. Ivan had it right that night, after all."

They were sharing a bench on the Line Wall Promenade, a parklike esplanade atop a portion of the old fortified town wall, where the ranks of gleaming, black cannons that had once defended the colony against flotillas of seaborne invaders now protected it against the cars in the landfill parking lot just below. In the distance, the impending sunset over smoggy Algeciras across the bay looked as beautiful as ever. Gideon, slouching uncharacteristically against the seat back, his legs extended, his hands in his pockets, had just given Julie the upshot of his visit there, as far as he and Fausto had worked it out on the drive back to Gibraltar.

In a nutshell, the First Family was a fake. The dig had been "salted." The trustworthy, decent, reliable Ivan Gunderson had pulled off the biggest anthropological scam since—well, yes, since Piltdown Man. Oh, the dig at Gibraltar Point had been honestly and efficiently administered by Adrian and Corbin, no reason to doubt that, and Gibraltar Boy was (probably) an authentic member—a Neanderthal child—of the group that had lived there. That much still held up. But the fly, the very large fly, in the ointment was Gibraltar Woman, who didn't belong there at all. And without Gibraltar Woman, Europa Point was just one more moderately interesting Neanderthal site; the whole wonderful edifice of theory, hypothesis, and feel-goodness that had been constructed around the First Family came crumbling down.

In retrospect, it wasn't that hard to see how Ivan had pulled it off. He had, after all, been working both the Guadalcanal and Europa Point sites at the same time, back in 2000. At that time, as he usually did, he was working with crews of local laborers, not trained archaeologists or even students (since he didn't have any), so there was no one at either dig with the experience or knowledge—or interest— to note any funny business on his part. Apparently, he had found the remains of Gibraltar Boy at Europa Point and been struck by their somewhat ambiguous appearance, which could conceivably be taken as a mixture of human and Neanderthal traits. Prompted by whatever compulsion or momentary impulse—and no one was ever likely to know for sure what it was—he decided to give his beloved admixture theory a colossal shot in the arm. From the Guadalcanal site he took what he needed—parts of the cranium, shoulder girdle, arms, and upper vertebral column of the female remains he'd found there, brought them to his other excavation at Europa Point, carefully tucked them into the soon-to-be-famous "hanging crevice" with Gibraltar Boy, and covered them over.

"But why would he have left *any* of her up at Guadalcanal?" Julie asked. "Wouldn't it have been better—safer—to take the whole skeleton?"

Gideon shrugged. "Who knows? Maybe people already knew that there was a partial skeleton there, so he couldn't take it all. Or perhaps someone came along and interrupted him. Or, most likely, it's simply that the upper part was all he needed for the hoax. So that's what he took, along with a few fragments of the lower body so it didn't look too remarkable. Why risk fooling around trying to find and dig up the rest?"

Whatever the reason, once that was accomplished, Gunderson donated the Guadalcanal dig to the University of Cádiz, and the Gibraltar Point site to the Horizon Foundation. After that, it was merely a matter of sitting back and waiting for the world-shaking discovery of the First Family. It must have been a long, devilishly impatient wait, because, bureaucracy being what it is, it wasn't until March 2002, two years later, that the Horizon Foundation got through the usual red tape and legalese and began excavation. And then another six months, now under Adrian's methodical direction, before they got to the hanging crevice and news of the First Family burst upon the world. In the meantime, up in Guadalcanal, where the red tape was pretty loose, to say the least, the lower portion of the female's remains had long ago been excavated by de la Garza's students and had gone onto their unheralded postmortem career as teaching tools in the polytechnic institute in Algeciras.

"I'm having a hard time with that part of it," Julie said with a frown. "These people—Adrian, Corbin, Pru—they're all professionals, they know what they're doing, isn't that true?"

"Sure, pretty much. Pru maybe isn't quite as experienced in fieldwork as the others, but what's your point?"

"My point is: How could they all have been fooled? How could Ivan have gotten away with it? Aren't there signs when a dig had been messed with like that? Doesn't it disturb the sediments, or strata, or whatever you call them? Can't a competent archaeologist recognize a, a . . . what do you call it, an inserted burial?"

"An intrusive burial. And yes, sure there are signs, because when you do what Ivan did—insert bones or anything else at a level they don't belong, you necessarily disturb the beds—the layers—of sediment above it. It's not that hard to spot."

"Well, that's my question. Why didn't they spot it?"

"They did spot it, as a matter of fact. On the way back, I stopped by the conference downtown to ask Pru about it, and she said right out that there was no question about it. The burial itself was in bed IV, down at the bottom, so ordinarily, you'd expect the more recent layers—beds I, II, and III—to be intact above it."

"But . . . ?"

"But when a farmer with his bulldozer has been there before you, doing his damndest to turn the place into a mushroom farm, all bets are off."

"Okay, I see that," she said, nodding, "but I would have thought there were some kind of geological tests that could confirm it, one way or the other."

"There are: soil tests, skeletal tests, tests on associated flora and fauna. And I have no doubt they are now going to be performed. But they're expensive and they take time. You don't do them unless you have some specific reason."

"And the possibility of a hoax wasn't a good enough reason?"

"Julie, the possibility never arose! Gunderson wasn't the greatest excavator in the world, but he *was*—we thought he was—a reputable archaeologist. Of long standing. The possibility of, of—" He could hardly bring himself to say it. "—of *fraud* would never have crossed anybody's mind."

"Uh-huh. Because the science of archaeology relies on the integrity of its practitioners."

He sighed. "That's about it," he said miserably. "Let's get a bite. I forgot all about lunch."

They walked the few blocks to Main Street more or less mentally chewing their cuds and found a palm-shaded patio table at Latino's Classic American Diner, which, despite its name, featured an eclectic menu of European, Chinese, Tex-Mex, and Moroccan foods. Another cruise ship was in port and the streets were again mobbed, but, at four o'clock in the afternoon, the restaurant was relatively uncrowded. Julie, who wasn't hungry, asked for an iced tea. Gideon ordered a chicken BLT on ciabatta bread and a Coke.

"So," Julie said, "why was Ivan killed? Why was anybody killed? Why were you attacked?"

"Well, there, all we've got is surmise, but the most probable scenario is—"

"—That someone else besides Ivan knew the find was faked, and was desperate to keep anyone *else* from finding out."

"Yes, that's the way I see it. If you start with the first person killed, Sheila, the fact that she had those two matching vertebrae from the two different sites makes it clear that she'd found out about it. And she was going to expose it at the conference. I mean, why would she have brought them with her to Gibraltar except to use them as Exhibit A?"

"But if that's the case, why wouldn't the killer have gotten rid of them? Apparently he got rid of the paper she was going to present and any notes she might have had. Why leave the vertebrae? They were her proof positive. Wouldn't he have taken them too?"

Gideon spread his hands. "My guess is that he didn't know about them. Remember, Sheila played things pretty close to the vest, according to everyone. She was probably saving them to make a big splash at her talk. Which they would have; a huge splash."

"But obviously she told *someone*, or she'd still be alive."

"Well, yes; told, or implied, or insinuated—anyway, enough to scare him into killing her."

"Or her," Julie amended. "So the question is, who would Sheila have told?"

"For which I don't have an answer, do you?"

"No, it could have been any of them." She paused while the waiter set down their orders. "And what about what happened to you? Was that on account of that newspaper article? Someone was afraid you'd found out too? That you really *had* something that was going to leave Piltdown in the dust?"

"Looks like it."

"Which it would have, I gather."

"And still will, when it gets out."

"And poor Ivan himself was murdered because *he* was going to give a speech the next day."

"Uh-huh," Gideon managed around a heavenly mouthful of bread, chicken, bacon, tomato, and mayonnaise.

She paused to sugar her iced tea and have a first sip. "But wait a minute," she said thoughtfully, "we talked about this before. Ivan must have given plenty of other speeches over the years. Why would someone think he would choose to reveal it now?"

"I doubt if anyone thought he would *choose* to reveal it, but now—"

She finished the sentence for him. "Now someone was

afraid he was might reveal it inadvertently—because of that Guadalcanal slip."

"I think so." He put down the sandwich. "If only I'd realized what it was about at the time, I might have been able to prevent—"

"No, you couldn't have. There was no conceivable way you could have known what that 'Guadalcanal' meant. How could anyone?"

"You're right, I know," he said with a sigh. "Still, I can't help thinking that if I'd been a little quicker on the uptake—"

"Now you stop that right now," she said firmly. "Eat your sandwich. Don't be so hard on yourself. If somebody had told you then—what was it, four days ago?—what you've just finished telling me, would you have believed it?"

"Not in a million years."

"You know," she said, while he returned to chewing away, "this pretty much settles it. It *has* to be one of our people, someone who was right there in the dining room that night—someone who heard Ivan get confused over Gibraltar and Guadalcanal."

"That's right. Rowley, Audrey, Buck, Adrian, Corbin, Pru—the very same people, by the way, who were around last night, when George brought those two vertebrae to the table. One of them obviously recognized what they were, what they represented, and rifled our room hunting for it. Which," he added with a smile, "we still wouldn't know about if old eagle-eye here hadn't spotted a jacket hung backward."

"Rowley, Audrey, Buck, Adrian, Corbin, Pru," she recited. "So who had the motive? Which of them would benefit most from keeping the fake a secret?"

"Hey, you're thinking like a cop now—that's exactly what Fausto asked me."

"And what did you say?"

"I said it was a pretty good motive for all of them, every last one." He dabbed mayonnaise from the corner of his mouth and explained.

For each of them, the fact that there was no Gibraltar Woman, no First Family, would be a hideous blow to their reputations and even to their livelihoods. Adrian and Corbin probably had the most to lose. They had written the standard academic books on the First Family, and they had supervised the dig itself; there was no way they could come out of this without looking like bunglers and—worse than bunglers in the minds of fellow scientists—dupes. Or maybe it was Rowley that had the most to lose; he hadn't been involved in the dig *per se*, but his precious museum was founded on its supposed findings, and his new book, the book he'd been working on for three years, was now worse than meaningless. Audrey—

"That does look good," she said, indicating his sandwich. "How about cutting me off some?"

"It is good. Want one of your own?"

"No, I'd rather have a piece of yours."

He sliced off a quarter for her and went back to his rundown.

Audrey, heretofore esteemed for her expertise and acumen, would be ridiculed as another dupe, and, considering her long record of caustic remarks about others, there were plenty of colleagues just waiting for the chance to do it. Buck had had nothing whatever to do with Gibraltar Point, but his devotion to Audrey couldn't be missed, and who knew what lengths he might go to in order to protect her? Pru probably had the least to worry about. True, she was the person who had actually dug up the remains, but in her case there were extenuating factors; namely, the depredations of a rampant bulldozer before she ever got there. On the other hand, extenuating factors were probably not going to entirely get her off the hook. There was no getting around the fact that she had personally excavated the sham "First Family" and had never had a clue that there was anything wrong. She would go down as one more dupe. Maybe not a world-class dupe like the others, but a dupe all the same.

Between them, they had finished the sandwich. Gideon ordered coffee and Julie got a refill on her iced tea. She pulled slowly at the straw with a contemplative scowl.

"What?" Gideon said.

"Well, I was just thinking . . . what about *your* reputation? You were the senior author of the paper that started the whole thing, after all—I mean, the thing about Gibraltar Boy being a hybrid, and all."

He put down his cup. This was something that hadn't occurred to him. "I think I'll come out of it all right," he said, not as confidently as he might have liked. "Remember, we went out of our way *not* to call him a hybrid. Other people did that. We just described him as accurately as we could. What *does* bother me a little is that we didn't spot the fact that the two sets of remains came from two different sites over a hundred miles apart—different soils, different weathering patterns. We did say—I hope we said—something about them differing more than one would anticipate for bodies that had been buried together—in their color, in their preservation, and so on—but when you're dealing with bones twenty-five millennia old, you expect that kind of variation, so I don't think anybody's going to fault us for not making something of it."

"Uh-huh, I see," Julie said. "Extenuating factors, is that it?"

He laughed. "Hmm, you think maybe you're looking at one more dupe, after all?"

"Oh, I doubt it, but I wouldn't worry about it anyway. If they frog march you out of anthropology, you've got your other career all ready and waiting for you."

"I do? What career would that be?"

"Writing 'stunning exposés' for Lester Rizzo and Javelin Press, of course. Which reminds me—" She drained her tea. "The Javelin reception starts at five. We'd better get started if you want to go."

"I don't."

"But you have to. Lester is your editor, and you're one of their star authors; he's going to want to show you off. You have to make an appearance. Besides, Rowley would be crushed if you weren't there."

"You're right, as always," Gideon said, getting up reluctantly. "Let's go, then. Oh, by the way, we're not supposed to mention any of this to any of the others—orders from Fausto."

Julie responded with a snappy salute. "Yes, sir. Will do . . . *sir*!"

TWENTY-FIVE

THE Paleoanthropological Society cocktail reception-*cum*-book-launch party had gotten off to an early start. The Eliott Hotel's rooftop terrace, bathed in mellow, late afternoon sunshine, was hopping by the time they got there, with knots of attendees chattering away on the wide patio surrounding the outdoor swimming pool. Most had a drink in one hand and a plastic plate piled with food in the other. Those that didn't were either in line at one of the two portable bars, or gathered around food tables near each end of the pool. At one, a blonde woman in a tall white chef's toque carved slices off a giant hunk of roast beef. At the other, an ice swan, dripping wings outstretched, hung over dozens of plates of quintessential ye olde English appetizers: sausage rolls, Scotch eggs, potted cheese toast triangles, miniature Cornish pasties. Waistcoated, bowtied waiters threaded their way smoothly through the crowd with trays of champagne and hors d'oeuvres. And in an out-of-the-way corner of the terrace a tuxedoed quartet, sans amplification, was unobtrusively, almost apologetically, tinkling out Boccherini's Minuet in C.

"You do have to hand it to Lester," Julie said as they came through the doors from the elevator. "He throws a heck of a party."

"Seems a bit understated for Lester," said Gideon. "I mean, Boccherini? I was expecting a fully staged *Phantom of the Opera*. Or if he wanted classical music, a symphony orchestra and full chorus doing Beethoven's Ninth at the least."

"Well, you know Lester. *Understated* is his middle name."

"Right. Get you something to drink?"

"A white wine would be nice."

On the way to the nearest of the bars, Gideon almost bumped into a Prada-Gucci-Ferragamo-clad Fausto smoothly gliding among the fashion-clueless academics like a sleek shark in a school of flounders. He was one of the few without a glass in his hand.

"Wow," Gideon said. "I didn't know you were a dignitary. I'm impressed."

"Commish gave it a pass," Fausto said with a shrug. "Officially, I'm here representing him. Personally, I wanted to come, kind of look around, check on the people." With a hand on Gideon's arm, he steered him to the fringe of the crowd, near a giant poster of Rowley's bright blue book cover with its long-winded title: *Uneasy Relations: Humans and Neanderthals at the Dawn of History: Implications for Today's World*. Under it was a table laden with copies to be given to the attendees as gifts.

"Listen, Gideon, remember when we were talking about licenses for explosives? Well, I did a little poking around and came up with something pretty interesting."

As Fausto had told him earlier, there were only two construction companies in Gibraltar that had explosives licenses. He had spoken with the owners of both and one of them, the owner of G. Barrows & Sons Demolition and Excavation, had admitted reluctantly that they were missing—they were pretty sure they were missing—they thought they *might* be missing—twenty-two sticks of gelignite from their stores. In any case, their records couldn't account for them. They hadn't reported the disappearance as the law required, because at first they were sure they'd just misplaced them. Then, as time passed and they didn't find them, they'd been worried about having waited so long to report the loss—there would be fines involved—so that they had just let it go and hoped it would never come back to bite them. And after all, it had been two years, hadn't it, and nobody had blown anything up yet, at least not in Gibraltar.

"Two years?" Gideon said. "So this would have been in . . . ?"

"The fall of 2005, from an excavation job they were doing out at Catalan Bay, on the other side of the Rock."

"And Sheila was killed in September of 2005," Gideon said, nodding. "So it fits. Now the question is—"

"Here," said Julie, thrusting a Scotch and soda into his hand. "Since you weren't going to get me one, I did it myself. And I got one for you. Hi, Fausto."

"Sorry about that, Julie," Gideon said, taking the drink. "Fausto and I were just—"

"Gideon! Hey, my man, glad to see you here!"

And there was Lester Rizzo in the flesh, all six feet four of him, energetically pumping Gideon's right hand and looking his normal ebullient, slightly insane, and painfully overstuffed self. It wasn't simply that he was overweight (which he was), but that he seemed positively overinflated, as if, if you stuck him with a pin, there'd be this *whoosh*, and off he'd go, careening crazily through the air, banging into walls and furniture.

"Lester, a wonderful reception," Gideon said, wrenching his crushed hand back. "You know Julie, and this is Detective Chief Inspector Sotomayor."

"Detective Chief Inspector. Whoa! I love those great old names. Like Inspector Morse. He was a detective chief inspector too, am I right?"

"I wouldn't know," Fausto said, wincing as he got the hand-mangling treatment.

"Yeah, I'm pretty sure he was. Hey, I think you all know our guest of honor here . . ." He glanced around. "Where'd he go? Hey, guest of honor!"

"I haven't gone anywhere, I'm right here." From behind Lester, where he'd been completely hidden by his bulk, an abashed but beaming Rowley Boyd emerged, basking in the glow of his newfound celebrity. "Er . . . thank you all for coming."

"It's our pleasure, Rowley," Julie said. "Congratulations."

The others joined in with congratulations of their own, which the new author accepted with blushing self-deprecation, teeth clamped happily on his unlit pipe.

"Lester, are you doing some promotion for the book?" Gideon asked. "As you so kindly did for mine? Although I really don't see how you can beat, 'It's going to stand the scientific world on its ear.' "

Lester threw back his head and trumpeted with laughter. "Hey, complain to me after we see the numbers." He looked fondly down at Rowley. "I'll come up with something, don't worry. I know, maybe we'll submit it for the Nobel Prize in archaeology, how's that sound? You never know what could happen. I got some influential friends in Stockholm. Or is it Oslo? What the hell, I got friends there too."

"But there is no Nobel Prize for archaeology," Rowley said.

Lester looked at him as if he'd just discovered that the latest addition to his prestigious stable of Frontiers of Science authors was a simpleton. "Well, the peace prize, the literature prize. Whatever."

"Lester . . ." Rowley hesitated, embarrassed. "I appreciate the gesture—and your confidence in me—but . . . well, I really don't think it's the kind of book . . . I mean, it's just a popular treatment, it's not as if it contributes anything new. I'd feel, well, a bit awkward about . . ."

"I think Lester was joking," Gideon said gently. "He does that."

Now Rowley was really embarrassed. "Oh . . . well, of course, ha-ha." He chewed furiously on the pipe, shifting it from one corner of his mouth to the other with his teeth alone. "Yes, that's funny, really. I didn't get it at first. . . ."

"Well, great talking to you guys," Lester said, his burly arm coming down around Rowley's slight and shrinking shoulders. But now there are plenty of other people eager to meet our famous author."

"Oh, I don't know about 'eager' . . ." Rowley was murmuring as he was hauled away.

"Did he really think Lester was going to try to get a Nobel Prize for him?" Julie asked. "You told me he was literal-minded, but that's amazing."

Gideon smiled. "That's Rowley for you. He's—hey . . ." His observation, whatever it was, petered out. He stood without speaking, staring intently into the middle distance.

"What?" Fausto asked, puzzled. And then again: "What?"

"Don't bother," Julie told him. "When he gets like that, he's inaccessible; you just have to wait him out. He's hatching something."

So he was. He had just that second, out of the blue, experienced that minute, barely perceptible *click* he was coming to know; the sense that a few small parts of a difficult, intricate puzzle had separated themselves from the jumble of pieces and snapped neatly into place, with the rest now poised to follow.

Or maybe not. Getting a couple of pieces fitted together didn't necessarily mean you were on the way to solving the puzzle. More data was needed.

"Have you seen Buck?" he asked, surfacing.

Julie pointed. Buck was coming from one of the bars, carefully balancing the brimful glasses of wine he held in each hand. Gideon put down his own glass and intercepted him.

"Buck, can I ask you a quick question?"

Buck came to a careful halt, sipping a little from each glass to keep it from slopping over. "Sure, what?"

"Well, remember when you went on that tour of St. Michael's Cave before my talk? With Rowley and the others? Did you happen to mention what we talked about in the van on the way up there?"

Buck frowned mightily. "What we talked about on the way up?"

"You know, the problems that go along with erect posture—what my talk was going to be about."

"Oh . . . well, yeah, I guess maybe I did mention it." He looked like a kid whose secret history of cookie stealing had finally caught up with him, even going so far as to scuff his feet. "I'm sorry, Gideon, I know I promised not to, but it was just so damn *interesting*. It blew my mind. And I thought . . . I mean, I figured it was just some of us, just, you know, Rowley and Audrey and Corbin, so—"

Another *click*; another piece in place.

"—Anyway, I'm sorry if I spoiled anything for you."

"No, don't worry about it. You didn't spoil anything. Far from it."

Far from it, indeed. If what he was thinking was right, Buck had saved his life.

The cloud lifted from Buck's meaty, friendly face. "That's good to hear. You had me scared there for a minute."

"What was that about?" Julie asked as Buck headed off. "What *are* you hatching?"

"Maybe nothing at all," Gideon said slowly, "but on the other hand, I just might be on to something. I need one more piece." He scanned the terrace and found what he was looking for. "Let's go, Fausto. If this amounts to anything, I think you'll want to be in on it."

"I want to be in on it too," Julie declared.

"Then come on along."

Fausto's mouth formed to say, "In on what?" but Gideon wasn't waiting for them. He was striding after Buck. Fausto and Julie looked at each other, shrugged, and hurried after him. "What the hell," Fausto sighed to himself.

Buck's destination—and Gideon's—was a gaggle of people clustered near one end of the pool, next to the roast beef buffet. There Audrey, Corbin, Adrian, and Pru, drinks in hand, were bunched around Lester and a frazzled if happy-looking Rowley, who was accepting their compliments and congratulations.

Gideon waited until there was an opening in the conversation, at which point his silent, waiting presence was sensed. They turned expectantly.

"Rowley," Gideon said as casually as he could manage, "didn't I hear you saying something the other night about doing an archaeological site survey on the west side?"

"It's quite possible," Rowley said. "I do them with some frequency. It goes with my job. Why do you ask?"

"This would have been, oh, a year or two ago—2005, I

think. It was during that Europa Point retrospective that they had here."

Rowley removed his pipe and tapped his lower lip with it. "Mmm . . . you know, I think you're correct. I believe I was evaluating a potential sewer construction site near Casemates Square. Nothing came of it, though. They went right ahead and installed the sewer."

"No," said Gideon, "it couldn't have been Casemates Square. You said it was on the west side of the Rock."

"Did I? Hmm, well, I do a lot of them, you know." He was beginning to get edgy. "What's the difference? Why do you ask?"

"It was Catalan Bay, wasn't it?" Pru said. "I'm sure that's what you told us."

Fausto and Gideon exchanged a quick, extremely meaningful look. Gideon could almost hear the *click* in Fausto's head. *Catalan Bay.*

"Catalan Bay?" Rowley coughed softly. "Yes, by George, I believe you're right. Now that I think of it, it was—"

"Mr. Boyd," Fausto said, "I think you and I should have a little talk."

"A talk," Rowley repeated dully. A muscle below his eye twitched erratically. He brushed at it as if he could sweep it from his skin. "Of course, if you like, but this is hardly the time. What is this about, Chief Inspector?"

The others had become quiet as well, and intent, sensing something in the air.

"I think it'd be better if we talked privately," Fausto said.

"You mean it can't wait? We're right in the middle of a party."

"Probably best to take care of it now."

Scared as he was, Rowley stood his ground. "No, sir, I demand to know what it's about."

"Yeah, I demand to know," put in Lester, who could have had no possible idea of what was going on, but wasn't one to pass up an opportunity for a little theater.

Patience had never been Fausto's long suit. His lips tightened. "Okay, then, I got a couple of questions about some sticks of gelignite missing from a construction project at Catalan Bay."

"And what is that supposed to have to do with me? Exactly what are you implying?" Despite the brave words, his voice was choked. He could hardly be heard. He had grown perceptibly paler, perceptibly more still. *He knows it's over*, Gideon thought. *He's dying by inches.*

Fausto, finished with cajoling, moved toward Rowley to reach for his arm, bringing Rowley suddenly to life. Twisting just out of Fausto's grasp, he grabbed a shocked Audrey by the bun at the nape of her neck, quickly getting his arm around her spindly throat and jerking her up against him.

"Hey!" Buck cried, starting forward, but Fausto stopped him with an arm across his chest.

"Rowley, damn you, don't be ridiculous," Audrey snapped. "You know you're not going to hurt me." She tried to pull away his arm but couldn't. Rowley wasn't a big man, no more than five-eight, and not powerfully built, but Audrey, for all her lean sinewiness, was little more than five feet tall and weighed perhaps a hundred pounds soaking wet. It was hard for her to get any meaningful leverage.

"This isn't going to do you any good," Fausto said. "You gotta know that, Rowley."

"If you come any nearer," Rowley said in a choked voice, "I'll kill her, I will." He spat the pipe out onto the terrace.

It seemed too incredible, too histrionic, to be real. Some of the onlookers began to laugh, under the impression they'd been roped into one of those interactive murder mystery plays. But that impression was quickly dashed when Rowley snatched up a barbecue fork from the roast beef table and quickly pressed it against the side of Audrey's neck, creating two little dents that immediately filled with blobs of blood. There was a collective gasp, a whispered chorus of "Oh, my *God*!" Audrey instantly stopped struggling and stood stone-still, her eyes open very wide, as if she were straining to listen for some faint and distant sound.

"Rowley, if you hurt her, I swear to God I'll kill you," Buck snarled, his voice husky and trembling with rage. There was little doubt he meant it.

"Rowley, come on, don't you see you're making it worse for yourself?" Fausto said reasonably. "Think about it a minute. Look, you haven't hurt her yet. We can still sit down like reasonable people, you can call your solicitor—"

"Shut up!" Rowley said, or rather screamed. With that, even the people at the other end of the terrace became aware of what was happening. Conversation ceased. The musicians stopped playing. Many of the women had their hands to their mouths. All eyes were on Rowley and Audrey.

Rowley looked quickly behind him. A few people were standing between him and the double doors that led out to the elevators. "I don't want anybody behind me," he yelled. "Move out of the way!"

They quickly grasped the situation and retreated toward the walls, except for one wide-shouldered man who looked as if he intended to bar the way, but Fausto motioned him aside. "Do as he says, please. I'm a police officer."

With reluctance, the man complied. Rowley began to move slowly backward with Audrey, keeping the fork pressed against her throat. Audrey moved with him, rigid and unresisting. The blood had begun to dribble down her neck in two streams. Gideon, along with everyone else, watched helplessly.

"Rowley," Fausto began. "Mr. Boyd—"

"Shut *up*!" Rowley shrieked. "Just . . . shut . . . up!"

He looked quickly behind him again to make sure the way was clear, then continued backing toward the doors some thirty feet away.

Julie grasped Gideon's forearm. "He doesn't see the tub," she whispered excitedly. "I don't think he sees the tub!"

"The what?" Gideon asked, but even as he said it he saw what she was talking about. Not far behind Audrey and Rowley, between them and the elevators, there was a circular, ten-foot-wide hot tub sunk into the terrace floor. It was obvious that Rowley wasn't aware of it; he was dragging Audrey directly toward it.

There were more whispers as the watchers pointed it out to one another. An electric ripple seemed to flow among them. They watched, transfixed, many holding their breath. Now they were eight feet away . . . now six . . . now four . . . two more steps and . . .

With his foot almost on the rim, Rowley sensed the crowd's restiveness and twisted around to glance nervously behind him. As he did so, the points of the fork came a few inches away from Audrey's neck, and she responded instantaneously. A hard whack in the ribs from her right elbow, an almost simultaneous one from the left, and then a scrape down his shin with the heel of her shoe, ending in a full-bodied stomp on his instep, all of it in the space of a second.

"Ow! Ai—!" Rowley teetering on the rim of the tub, one arm still around Audrey's neck, flailed with the other one, struggling for balance, but a last, sharp elbow in the gut ("Whoof!") sent the fork flying and tipped him over backward. In the two of them plunged with a huge *sploosh*, the barbecue fork plopping in a moment later with its own modest *splish*.

AND so what might have culminated in high tragedy ended instead as low comedy, in a fooraraw of spluttering, splashing, and thrashing of arms and legs. Buck dived gallantly but unnecessarily in (the tub was only four feet deep) to "rescue" Audrey, hit his head on the sitting ledge, and wobbled dazedly to his feet, from where he had to be led unsteadily up the three steps by Audrey. Eager hands reached out to help them, but she batted them away like pesky mosquitoes. Audrey didn't like being rescued any more than she liked being abducted.

Rowley too hit his head, stood up, and sank dizzily back onto the ledge, from which he was unceremoniously fished out by the wrists by Gideon and Fausto. Passive and unresisting, he was then led away by Fausto and another police official who was there as a guest. Dripping, drooping, and utterly wilted, leaving a snail-like trail of moisture in his wake, he looked like an old sneaker that had been put through the wringer one time too many.

The barbecue fork, resting quietly on the bottom of the tub, was left for the pool attendant to retrieve.

TWENTY-SIX

GIDEON spent the next several hours at New Mole House, getting his statement recorded and transcribed—a long, fatiguing process—and then, over coffee in the break room, sharing notes with Fausto (who had been busy interrogating Rowley). Then he was driven back to the hotel, where, hoping to go up to the room and call it a night, he was spotted by Pru as he crossed the lobby and hauled off, protesting, to the Barbary Bar. There he found everyone, including Julie, congregated and awaiting him and his explanation of the evening's bizarre events.

Happily Julie had already filled them in on the faking of the First Family by Ivan, and the fact that Sheila Chan had not been the victim of a natural landslide but of murder, so he was spared going through all that. She had also enlightened them on why the mere mention of Catalan Bay had precipitated the extraordinary episode that had followed. Beyond that much, of course, she was as much in the dark as they were, so the rest was up to him. He considered begging off till morning, but on reflection he decided he owed them more consideration than that. After all, he had come close—sometimes extremely close—to believing each of them, his friends and colleagues, a multiple murderer.

He ordered a Scotch and water, settled back in his chair beneath a wall of photographs, and, under the disinterested black-and-white gazes of Michael Palin and John and Yoko, gratefully swallowed down half the drink and wearily began.

It was a combination of things, he told them, none of them really conclusive in itself, that brought it all to its extraordinary conclusion. What had first gotten him started on the right track was Rowley's reaction to Lester's joking comment about the Nobel Prize. That had made him think of Rowley's earlier response to a comment of Pru's during the group visit to the Rock. ("Yeah, but you could have done a better job with the weather," she had said, provoking smiles from everybody but Rowley, who had replied, in all earnestness, "But what could I possibly have done about the weather?") And that, in turn, had reminded him of how Rowley had swallowed *Discover* magazine's April Fool's story about the Neanderthal tuba, hook, line, and sinker.

"I fail to see where you're going with this," Audrey said crankily. She and Buck, having returned from police headquarters themselves not long before, were still wearing the clumsy, collarless suicide-watch paper uniforms given to them by the police to replace their sopping clothes. On Audrey's neck were two flesh-colored Band-Aids. "If there's a point, I wish you'd get to it. I'd like to go to bed before morning."

"Easy, honey," Buck gentled. "The man's doing his best." His big hand was steadily, gently massaging the nape of her neck.

The point, Gideon said, was that, of all the people who

might have been behind the killings, Rowley Boyd was the only one who could possibly have taken seriously the newspaper story about how Gideon's presentation at St. Michael's Cave was going to be "the most sensational exposé of a scientific scam in history." And given the commemorative nature of the meetings, the fifth anniversary of the Europa Point dig, and their location, here in Gibraltar, what else could the scam in question be but the faking of Gibraltar Woman and the First Family?

"And that's why he tried to electrocute you?" a skeptical Adrian demanded. "To prevent your revelation of the hoax?"

"Yes."

"I fail to see how that makes sense," Corbin said bluntly. "It was Rowley who *saved* you from being electrocuted. I was right there. He was the one that called your attention to the absence of a rubber mat."

"No, it was Buck who saved me from being electrocuted."

"Me?" Buck exclaimed, looking pleased. "What did I do? I never even noticed it."

"No, but on that little tour just before, you told Rowley what I was going to be talking about—erect posture, varicose veins, birth problems—so it finally got through to him that I had no big hoax to reveal. There was no point in killing me; it would only be another complication, another risk. So he told me about the mat—which he was perfectly aware of, since he's the one who set the whole electrocution thing up in the first place."

"But you can't *know* that," Audrey said. "Or has Rowley confessed?"

"Not as of the time I left New Mole House. Fausto says he's not saying anything until he sees a solicitor in the morning. And you're right, at this point I can't *know* he set it up, or that he's the one who tried to shove me off the

Rock—who *did* shove me off the Rock. I told you, there really isn't any one piece of incontrovertible evidence at this point; there's a combination of a lot of things that all point in one direction: that it was Rowley who killed Sheila, it was Rowley who killed Ivan, and it was Rowley who was trying to kill me."

"Now there's another thing right there," Adrian declared truculently, pouring some Tullamore Dew—rather more than his usual few drops—into his coffee. "If it was Ivan who perpetrated the hoax, as you *claim*, then why in the world would *Rowley* be the one going around killing anybody and everybody to keep it a secret? Are you telling us he was involved in it originally? With Ivan?"

"Well, as far as anyone knows," Gideon said, "Rowley didn't even know Ivan at the time of the Guadalcanal dig, so I'm assuming—"

"Assuming," Adrian sniffed.

"—assuming that he wasn't, but at some point later on, Ivan must have told him about it, or accidentally let it slip. After all, Rowley was probably closer to him than anyone else, especially these last few years, as Ivan was declining."

"But then why would Rowley want to kill him?" Buck asked.

"Because—"

"More assumptions?" Adrian said.

"Look, Adrian, if you—" he began heatedly, but stopped himself. As far as anger went—real, teeth-gnashing anger—Gideon had a pretty high boiling point. It was an emotion that didn't come naturally to him; he'd felt it only once or twice in his life. But temper was another story. It wasn't that hard to get under his skin, and the belligerent, confrontational, openly skeptical nature of their questioning had done just that. They were acting as if the whole mess was his fault. Still, he understood their feelings and he did sympathize. *Put a lid on it, Oliver,* he told himself. *This is all coming as an extremely unpleasant shock to them.*

"It is an assumption, yes, but a reasonable one," he said more quietly, "one that Chief Inspector Sotomayor goes along with. It was that Guadalcanal slip at the testimonial dinner that did it for Ivan. When Rowley realized that he could make that kind of gaffe in public—and remember, he was going to give a speech at Europa Point the next day—Ivan had to go. Rowley was worried sick he might do it again and the whole scam would come tumbling down."

"No, no, no," Corbin said. "If it was Ivan who perpetrated the fraud, what in the world did Rowley have to be so worried about? It simply doesn't make sense. No." His head rotated slowly, decisively, back and forth. "No, no, no. Sorry."

That did it. The hell with their feelings. "What he was so worried about is what you're all so worried about," he shot back. "And I don't think I have to tell you what that is."

"Oh?" said Audrey coldly. "And just what would that be?"

Out of the corner of his eye he saw Julie pleadingly lift her hands a few inches off the table, palms outward, as if holding him back. *Take it easy, now.* Nevertheless, he was about to get himself in deeper when Pru intervened, coming valiantly to his defense. "What Rowley was so worried about, and what we're all so worried about right now—including me—is that, when it gets out that the First Family was a sham, that Gibraltar Woman was a complete, unadulterated hoax—or rather, an adulterated one—we're all going to look like a bunch of bumbling, gullible idiots—complete chumps. And it's scaring the socks off us."

"Well, now, I'd hardly say—" Corbin huffed.

"No, you wouldn't say it," Pru interrupted, "but that

doesn't make it any less true. We've all been dining off Europa Point for five years—books, lectures, cushy appointments—and the whole thing was nothing but a hoax, right from day one." A tinge of bitterness had put a metallic edge on her voice. "We were clueless, that's the whole truth of it. Ivan—the great, the generous Ivan—suckered us all, and we never knew what hit us." She folded her arms and sat back, head down, glowering at the table.

"She's right," Audrey said softly into the silence that followed. "Ivan hoodwinked us. He made fools of us, and we let it happen because we wanted it to be true. And taking it out on Gideon," she muttered, "isn't going to help any. I think we owe him an apology." She looked sharply around the table. "Or would you rather that he *hadn't* discovered it?"

There were embarrassed murmurs of demurral and apology, and then a thoughtful, more receptive mood seemed to take hold. The tension evaporated.

"It has been the bane of science since time immemorial," Adrian said sadly. "It has happened before, and it will happen again, because fidelity to truth is implicit in the scientist's creed. And that makes us gullible, because there will always be charlatans, but in the end, archaeology, like any science, must rely on the integrity of its practitioners."

Gideon and Julie couldn't help exchanging a small, private smile at that, and then Audrey said, "Please continue, Gideon. Is there more?"

"Not much. When it turned out that Rowley had been at the right place at exactly the right time to steal the missing gelignite, Fausto had heard enough. And of course, when Rowley grabbed Audrey—and by the way, Audrey, if I haven't said it before, you were magnificent . . ."

"Hear, hear," said Adrian, and Audrey modestly bowed

her head while Buck grinned proudly and rubbed her neck a little harder.

"Well, that sealed Rowley's fate, and . . . I guess that's it."

There was a round of nodding and a few dejected sighs, after which Audrey and Buck were the first to rise, their paper clothes rustling. "Thank you, Gideon," she said civilly in leaving, and within a few minutes the rest followed suit. Gideon and Julie were left alone at the table.

"That was tough," Julie said. "You want another drink?"

"No. Yes." He signaled the bartender, who brought him another Scotch and water, and a second glass of Riesling for Julie, although she hadn't meant to order it.

"So I was right after all," she mused with some satisfaction.

"About what?"

"About Rowley. Don't you remember? I pointed out that he would have had the easiest time setting up the electrical stuff in the cave. But you maintained it couldn't have been him because he was the one who warned you about it."

"Well, yes, that's all true, but at that point there was no way to know . . . I mean, it was only what we found out later . . . I mean, there was no way you could have . . ."

"Yes?" She was looking at him with her eyes wide and her chin resting on her clasped hands. "There was no way I could have . . . ?"

"Okay," he said, laughing. "I admit it, you were right after all. If only I'd listened."

Along with the drinks came the total bar tab. Gideon looked at it. "Seventy-two pounds," he said with a wince. "Ah, well, I guess I owe it to them. I sure spoiled their day." He took a moody sip from his glass. "I didn't do anything for mine either."

"Oh, well," Julie said, "look on the bright side."

"You're sure good at that," he said with a smile. "Looking on the bright side. So tell me, what is it?"

"Well," she said, her eyes twinkling, "looks to me as if you've gone and come up with the biggest scam since Piltdown Man after all."

THIS aspect was not lost on Lester Rizzo, whom they ran into at the airport snack bar the next morning, waiting for their flight to London.

Lester wedged his ham and cheese sandwich and paper cup of coffee into one big hand so he could churn Gideon's with the other. "Gideon, my man—"

"Lester, I'm really sorry I spoiled your party last night."

Lester stared at him. "Are you kidding me? That was the best book launch in history. Outstanding! It'll get picked up all over the world. It'll put Javelin on the map. I mean, we'll have to eat his stupid book, but what the hey, that's life."

"Well, you know, I do plan to put in a chapter on the whole affair in *Bones to Pick*, so that should—"

"Chapter? Screw 'chapter.' We're gonna do a whole book on the thing. I already came up with the title. Ready?" He cleared his throat. "*Shame!*—that's *shame* with an exclamation point—*Shame! Murder, Lies, and Skuldiggery in Gibraltar*. And then under that: *Bad to the Bone*. Well, I'm not sure of that last part. It might be *Science Gone Wrong* instead. So what do you think?" He bit off a corner of the sandwich with an audible snap of his teeth and looked happily, expectantly, at them.

Julie spoke first. "I believe that's 'skull*dug*gery,' isn't it?"

"It's a *pun*," Lester explained. "Dig . . . archaeology . . . see?"

"Oh. Yes, I see."

Lester was not pleased. "Well, what do you think, Gideon?"

"Umm . . ."

"And I already know who's going to write it."

"Oh? Who?" Gideon asked in all innocence.

"You, of course!" Lester said with a honk of a laugh. "The only thing is, we need to come out fast with this because there's gonna be lots of competition, so I need the manuscript in three months. That's not gonna be a problem, is it? I mean, you know more about it than anybody. Interested?"

"Uh, well, to tell the truth, Lester—"

Lester circled in closer. "I was figuring on doubling your last advance," he said conspiratorially.

"No, it's not that. It's just not something I—"

"Oh, gosh," Julie said, "they just announced our flight for the second time. We'd better get going, Gideon."

"Whew. Thanks, kid," Gideon said once they'd made their quick good-byes and were headed for the gate.

"Maybe I could triple it!" Lester was bellowing exultantly after them, the words muffled by a mouthful of ham and cheese. "I'll be in touch, buddy!"

TWENTY-SEVEN

THEY had been assigned the same seats, 17A and 17B, for the British Airways return flight to Heathrow, so as the plane banked on its ascent, they were once again treated to a panoramic view of the Rock and the clustered settlement at its base.

"There's the Moorish Castle," Julie said thoughtfully. "The prison. Is that where Rowley is now?"

"I imagine he's still in a holding cell at New Mole House," Gideon said, "but that's probably where he'll spend the rest of his life. It's their one and only prison."

"How awful. Can you imagine what it must be like inside? What the cells must be like? No windows, no daylight, just cold, damp, six-hundred-year-old stone walls . . ." She shuddered and turned away. "Not that he doesn't deserve it," she finished.

"Mmm," Gideon agreed just as he caught a whiff of Irish whiskey and sensed someone leaning forward from the row behind. *Oh, boy*, he thought.

"Actually," the plummy familiar voice from seat 18B intoned, "it's closer to seven hundred years than six. It was constructed in 1335, on the site of a still older Moorish structure. And the term *Moorish Castle*, although in common use, has no basis in fact. More properly, it's the Tower of Homage, which was part of an extensive, intricate complex of walls and courtyards—"

"Oh, dear," Julie whispered.

"—presumably with some defensive capabilities, but primarily—and this aspect is quite interesting . . ."

Gideon sank back in his seat and closed his eyes. It was going to be a long three hours.

COMING SOON

From Edgar® Award–winning author

Aaron Elkins

SKULL DUGGERY

Gideon Oliver and his wife are on vacation in Mexico when a local police chief requests his assistance on a case. Starting with a mummified corpse and a skeletal examination, Gideon soon discovers that two bodies have been misidentified, and their deaths could be related. Finding the connection between them will prove more dangerous than he could possibly imagine—and place him into the crosshairs of the killer he's hunting.

Also from the Edgar® Award–winning author

Aaron Elkins

LITTLE TINY TEETH

Sailing the Amazon with a group of botanists, "Skeleton Detective" Gideon Oliver is on his dream vacation. But it turns nightmarish when fierce headhunters narrowly miss killing the group leader, and then a deranged passenger kills a botanist and flees. Long-past enmities and resentments—and new ones as well—might explain things. When a fresh skeleton turns up in the river, Gideon is sure that, in this jungle full of predators, humans may be the deadliest of all.

M434T0309

Don't miss any of the
Professor Gideon Oliver novels, with
"a likable, down-to-earth, cerebral sleuth"
(*Chicago Tribune*).

From Edgar® Award–winning author
Aaron Elkins

"Aaron Elkins is a gifted storyteller."
—*Midwest Book Review*

"Elkins has established himself
as a master craftsman."
—*Booklist*

UNEASY RELATIONS

LITTLE TINY TEETH

UNNATURAL SELECTION

WHERE THERE'S A WILL

GOOD BLOOD

M432AS0309